# A Matter of Assassination

# A MATTER OF ASSASSINATION

## Patrick Raymond

CASSELL

LONDON

FOR LELLA

**CASSELL & COMPANY LIMITED**
35 Red Lion Square, London WC1R 4SG
and at Sydney, Auckland, Toronto, Johannesburg,
an affiliate of
Macmillan Publishing Co., Inc.,
New York

First published 1977

ISBN 0 304 29794 1

Typesetting by Malvern Typesetting Ltd.
Printed in Great Britain by
Fletcher & Son Ltd,
Norwich

F1276

# 1

The land I came to know as 'Jason's Country' lay south of Cancer but north of the slaving coast. It was called the Saharan Republic when I first saw it; it has another name now. Jason had led me to expect a desert country of no great interest, but in fact the Atlantic seaboard was luxuriant with date gardens and thirty miles back the escarpments of the Southern Atlas made a fine display. For three centuries the English had kept a trading post at Mogalor but they were all gone now. The Spanish had come, building castles and a reputation for cruelty, but they had been impoverished by the power of the bandits, both Arab and Nebanese, and they had withdrawn to the north with their horses and slaves. The French had been here too, leaving their mark in the waterside architecture and in the laxity of the administration; and French remained the language of the cultivated. More recently the country had worn the trappings of an Arab kingdom, independent of Europe but sending its officers to British military institutions for their training in loyalty. I liked the look of Jason's country with its mountains and sea. I was glad that I had come. It seemed possible that we might make something of Jason's opportunity.

§

Jason and his brother officer Solly Yusoff had been students of mine at the Imperial Staff College at Eastleigh — that home of the military virtues where commanders were shaped for our own defence and that of our friends. The college was founded on the principle that the traditions of the British peace could be maintained by the infant states freed from British tutelage, or from British influence, if their officers received a training in the methods of restraint. If these states had to go to war it was clearly better they did so effectively and within decent limits; it was better their commanders behaved predictably, with regard for the principles of war and the rights of the defeated. Many lasting friendships had their beginnings at Eastleigh, but such were the accidents of alignment that graduates found themselves sometimes on opposing sides, and then they signalled each other a greeting phrased in the astringent language of the college. I cannot say how well the lesson of Eastleigh was learnt by the soldier-students. Some graduates I heard of behaved with a savagery clearly learnt elsewhere; but I am certain the relaxed good humour of the place, the traditions of sanity and decorum, made an appeal to every officer no matter where his origin lay.

For many years the college had resided in a Jacobean mansion of old red brick that had been Lord Eastleigh's country home in Oxfordshire. The students took their volumes of strategy into the rose garden, where their uniforms rivalled the blooms, or they drank boisterously in the drawing room. My memories of Jason and Solly during the twelve-month course are not clear. I remember that I helped Jason with his thesis and that he had been grateful, but Solly I recall only as a tall disdainful figure who did not seek help or companionship. As an Arabic speaker I had tried sometimes to tempt his confidence, but I got nowhere with that. I learnt later that Solly was descended from a royal house of the Maghreb while Jason was the son of a slave.

My clearest memory of Eastleigh is of the final Guest Night, when the officers were clothed in their gold and scarlet and the band played all the national and regimental airs. Lord Eastleigh's great hall was bathed in candlelight; the log fire spread a glow across the hearth; the mess servants kept the glasses filled. The officers toasted every sovereign and head of state who had his representative at Eastleigh, including two rulers who were locked in conflict and another whose present whereabouts was a matter for conjecture. Later in the night the officers marched on the tables holding the candlesticks high in the air. Jason and Solly together sang a marching song of the Maghreb, the revolutionary sentiment of which was at odds with the occasion, but Eastleigh

2

could tolerate even the most bizarre opinions and at the end of the piece the applause was unstinted.

After dinner the officers drank in the library until very late. They would disperse in the morning. I walked in the garden because a problem of my own was intruding even into the gaiety of this unique place. Perhaps I was there for half an hour; I cannot now remember. I was disturbed by a mess steward, an old white-haired man whom I knew; he asked me to come back to the library and together we walked up the steps to the terrace and through the French doors. I did not know why he called me. Still I don't, though the following minutes remain clear in my memory and mark for me the beginning of Jason's strange progress. Perhaps it was Jason himself who sent for me.

Jason and Solly were at the far end of the library, alone. I think they had quarrelled. At any rate they were not speaking and it was a moment before Jason looked up. 'Ah, my dear Colonel! It is a memorable evening, is it not?'

I nodded, waiting for him to continue.

'Solly and I will drink with you. It is an occasion of some importance, not simply of military nostalgia. The steward is bringing you a port.' He threw the words away while his mind was elsewhere. He was smaller than Solly, neatly made and immaculate in white mess kit. His origins were as plainly African as Solly's were of the Arabic north. His next words showed a wilful deference. 'Of course, our country is small and you will not know where to find it on the map, but we have our traditions, our comradeship, notwithstanding our recent independence. You understand, my dear Colonel, we too can be moved by loyalty!'

'Good,' I said. I thought he might be joking.

The steward brought glasses on a tray which Jason handed to Solly and me. 'I desire to propose a toast,' Jason said. 'Solly and I will drink it in lemonade because we are Moslems of the strictest sort, but that does not make it the less heartfelt. Colonel, you will not object to drinking with brother officers from a far-away country? Very well; you are indulgent. I give you President Moulay Khalid of the Saharan Republic.'

We drank to this gentleman, standing at the far end of the library at Eastleigh. Solly put down his glass abruptly.

3

'It is an abuse,' he said.

'May God increase his power. May the state live peacefully in his shadow.'

'It is an abuse, an impiety.'

I could not think why Jason's remarks should be taken as blasphemy, even in the mind of an Arab of princely caste. I said, using the formal Arabic I had learnt on the Canal, 'Pledges are in order, Solly. I see no harm in drinking to the President.'

'You do not understand, Colonel Warfield. Your mastery of Arabic does not mean you understand our country nor the direction it has chosen. Jason's words are a sacrilege.'

'I give you the President,' Jason said recklessly.

In Egypt I had learnt caution with the Arab temper and I did not again contradict Solly. 'I suggest we join the party,' I said.

In the ante-room the officers were playing the spirited games traditional on these occasions.

'To make a false pledge is dishonourable,' Solly said.

This was getting serious; such disputes were contrary to the spirit of Eastleigh. I still did not know why Jason's toast should be seen as a profanity by his fellow Saharan. As I remembered him, President Khalid, the 'Father of the Nation', was a lazy but not particularly despotic ruler who some years earlier had deposed the Sultanate to widespread satisfaction. He was a benevolent, mildly corrupt potentate given to a policy of reform and inter-racial harmony. His brilliant smile had been caught by the cameras at Lake Success and the Cannes Film Festival. He was clearly no worse than some of the murderous sovereigns and heads of state to whose continued life and activity we had raised our glasses that evening.

'Peter, you are dismayed!' Jason said, giving no weight to Solly's indignation. 'You take me too seriously. After all, I am only a poor major from a far-away country whose value to Britain declined with the slave trade. Why should you bother with our divided loyalties?'

Solly said, 'You should not say such things.'

'We have no secrets from Colonel Warfield.'

'It does not become you. This is a time for restraint and dedication.'

4

'Come on, Solly! We are at Eastleigh; we take nothing seriously here.'

'What has happened?' I asked.

'A matter of small consequence,' Jason said.

His composure had not broken. He looked more African than I had seen him, his brow drawn, his lips turned outward, but he was master of himself while Solly was not. Jason was not wholly black; I doubted if the African part of him measured more than half; but I had noticed that his features fell into the African mould when a challenge was offered him.

In a furious whisper, Solly said, 'I deplore all that Jason has told you. I do not respond to his pledge. He should be giving himself to reflection and a chastening of the spirit. Instead, he makes a jest out of our country's brave decision. I do not care for such mockeries.' Which was the last we heard from Major Solly Yusoff that evening. He went abruptly into the garden, where the air was less foul, leaving Jason and me in silence.

I said, 'I think you'd better tell me what's going on.'

Jason giggled. I knew him to be a man of swift intelligence but I didn't know how far his judgment was rooted in commonsense. As a student, I had found him adept at detail but sometimes forgetful of the underlying principles. I judged that he would be a good commander at battalion level but that he lacked the vision for the higher staff. Solly I did not trust at all.

'Well?' I said.

'My dear Colonel, you must forgive us our differences. Solly has the Arab romantic temperament which turns every issue into a matter of unbreakable commitment. He would stake his life upon a worthless argument. He would go to his death for every item of the morning's agenda. He's really very silly.'

This was my own judgment of Solly but I saw no need to agree with his fellow student when it was my job to keep the peace of the college. 'None the less, Solly is angry with you on what's supposed to be a pleasant occasion. Did you do it on purpose?'

His smile was brief, guilty, vanishing the moment I looked at him. He stiffened in offence. 'You suggest I would torment a fellow officer out of devilry?'

'Yes.'

5

'Late in the evening? Upon consecrated ground?'

'It looked like that.'

'You do me an injustice. I am a soldier, bound to discipline; I have respect for the tradition of the mess. I would not provoke a fellow soldier for my amusement, not even a prig like Solly.'

Clearly the rift was deep, perhaps as deep as the rift dividing Africa; I was touching an old wound which the years had not healed.

'Perhaps he will kill me,' said Jason complacently. 'In anger, in contempt.'

This was Jason at his worst. I had to suppress the notion before it developed in his mind.

'Forget it. There's nothing to be gained by having a row with Solly. No doubt he had good reason for losing his temper.'

He smiled and drew himself up to his modest height, as if in accomplishment.

'He *had,* hadn't he?' I continued. 'Your toast affronted him.'

'Who am I, dear sir, to say what moves the heart of royalty?' He took my arm and steered me into a corner to protect his confidence. 'It is an unusual situation. You will find it droll. Of course, Solly was justly indignant because my behaviour was inexcusable. I drank to a man who is dead! Yes, dead, destroyed by the forces of progress. The Father of the Nation was assassinated in El Desmara this afternoon, after which the mob tore his body to pieces.'

I may have shown disbelief, but Jason did not repeat his story.

'You will see it in the newspaper tomorrow, at the foot of the page given to the African nether regions. I do not suppose it will feature largely.'

'This is the truth, Jason? You have heard it officially?'

He nodded. 'It was the soldiers, of course. It is always the soldiers.'

'And they will govern the country?'

'Naturally. In the interests of security. In the name of fair practice. They will denounce President Khalid as a corrupt and squalid mountebank. They will cleanse the country of his influence. They will appoint a new leader.'

'And he will be a soldier?'

6

'O yes, a soldier. A man of strength. A man of temperate behaviour. In a country such as ours he must be neither wholly Arab nor African but a fusion of the elements, a foul expedient. He must hold the country in his iron hand until it reaches maturity, which is to say, for ever! He must withstand the scorn and abuse of the world outside where he will be called usurper and Fascist. He must abandon every impulse that does not match the image of saviour.'

I began to understand. I faced him squarely. 'I see. They have chosen you.'

He said simply, 'Yes, they have chosen me.'

§

From the day he left Eastleigh Jason's progress became a matter of public record. The more attentive of the national papers noted the assassination of Moulay Khalid and the appointment of a young soldier, Major Jeso Khymer, to head the military government. Correspondents claimed that the choice of an 'African' would reassure the black Nebanese in the south and demonstrate that the Arab ruling caste had no fixed ambitions. Under such leadership the odds against a holocaust were lengthened. It was possibly so. I wished him well. He was setting out on a dangerous path where most had come to grief and none that I knew of had reached a worthwhile end. Jason had some of the marks of the leader upon him. I believed him to be honest, he commanded sympathy and his mind was supple if not creative. Time might give him the strength to succeed.

My own progress in the weeks following the last Guest Night at Eastleigh has no bearing upon Jason's story: let me say only that the trend was sharply downward. It was a time when every weakness, every cruelty of which I had been guilty in the last twenty years came back in hideous array to compel a decision. My wife and I separated and a divorce was planned. Our friends retreated into an embarrassed silence. I was posted to a staff job in the Ministry of Defence which bored me. My career in the Army was plainly in suspense and this did not surprise me because my mind was dull. My old ambition of becoming a writer could not succeed when imagination had died and I had not the strength to

7

labour. I needed a change of scene. And it was at this time, like a star swinging back into vision, that Jason made his second entry into my life.

His letter surprised me; I had not expected to hear from him again. It was typewritten but I could recognise Jason's style. He wrote: 'By now you are a General. If you are not, it is their fault. As a very important person you do not have to pay attention to this letter which comes from your African friend. You do not even have to answer it. But maybe life has not treated you so kindly. There was trouble in your eyes at Eastleigh'—he was more perceptive than I had thought—'and now perhaps you will need my help. At present I lead a country of two and a half million people as President and Commander-in-Chief. All power is mine. All do as I say. And for you, dear Peter, it is time for a change! You come here. You make our struggle your own. You earn the gratitude of our people. My agent in London is instructed to offer you employment on the most favourable terms . . .'

To consider such an offer was madness as I had no reason to suppose that Jason's position was secure, but I was stale and the prospect of a new job, no matter how chancy, made a strong appeal. I got out the large-scale maps and had a look at Jason's country, which lay in the eye of the sun between the sea and the desert. It was about three hundred miles deep as half as broad. I noticed that the eastern boundary, which ran through the Fahdia Waste, was indicated by a dotted line, showing that the cartographer had been unable to say quite which direction it took, but these lands were of interest only to the nomadic Tuareg and once to the merchants who carried gold and slaves northward from Timbuctoo. I saw the agent and learnt the terms of my appointment which was described as Military Adviser to the President.

I couldn't make up my mind. I took a plane in the opposite direction, to the north of Europe, as if this would diminish the problem, and I spent a week in stupid indecision alongside a Finnish lake. I spun a coin and it rejected the offer; I spun it ten times and again Jason lost by the greater number of falls. When I had tossed the coin twenty times I realized I was trying to make it come out in Jason's favour, and that decided me. I resigned from the Army and took my retired pay. At forty-five I felt young enough to fail once more, and to recover, if that was the way it went; I was prepared to follow where the trail led and to accept the consequences. I booked myself on a flight to Mogalor.

# 2

When the aircraft left Gibraltar on the second leg of the flight and broke into clear Atlantic sunlight my doubts returned in double strength. What on earth was I doing? I had known Jason only as his instructor in strategy and military philosophy in the relaxed society of Eastleigh. There we were held in check by an ancient courtesy and by the starch in our uniforms. I had no means of knowing how he would behave in a position of supreme authority. I knew he had imposed a soldier's peace in the country and that the Army remained loyal, but it would be absurd to suppose him other than vulnerable. I understood that Solly Yusoff had been appointed Chief of Staff, no doubt to give the Arab community a sense of participation at the top; but in my opinion Solly's support would not bear much weight, nor would Jason have chosen such a prop if the choice had been his.

We flew south for an hour; then I judged the aircraft to have crossed the northern frontier of Jason's country. An Arab boy sitting next to me — a boy with fine features — told me the red landscape was indeed the Saharan Republic, his own country, but he would say nothing more. I could see the white mountains of the Southern Atlas which here pointed like a finger to the Equator. A city of domes and towers and with an investing wall lay in a seaward fold of the mountains: this I knew to be the old holy city of Kezzan, where the Arabs had founded a university in the twelfth century. Southwards lay El Desmara, Jason's capital, but it was dissolved by the haze into a dull red stain and I could see nothing of it. Still further to the south and beyond my sight was, I knew, the vast featureless landscape of the Neban, the place where Jason came from: it lay beyond the Skar River, a black country where the Arabs had never gone but to raid and plunder. The aircraft began a long descent into Mogalor, the third city and only seaport in Jason's country. At the coast the Atlantic rollers made an inscription of white along the yellow sands.

Islam, which I had known on and off for twenty years, which had given me the best and the worst of my life, met me squarely at the airport: the staff were off duty, the lavatories did not work, the restaurant had closed a year ago. I fretted in the passenger lounge, where the African sunlight burst through the windows, waiting for my baggage.

A fellow passenger, a restless man in a purple suit, charged me like a bull. 'Brother, this won't do! There should be liquor, there should be knick-knacks. The public address should speak a welcome. But there's sand on the floor and no one in sight but a beggar without legs. . . . Have you seen my daughter, who was here a minute ago?'

I could do nothing to ease his frustrations. The tourist industry hadn't yet spread this far south, bringing a blind efficiency, though I noticed the runway was being extended and a large terminal building was already one storey high.

'I mean, it's a military government, isn't it? There should be somebody here?'

'I don't know that it follows,' I said.

'They killed Khalid. They kicked his head down the street like a football. In the stadium they shot three hundred people and left their bodies for the crows.'

I didn't see the connection, and I had declined to believe the story of the murders, supposing them to be the invention of the defeated.

'I mean, that should have waked the place up!' He walked round the lounge like a dog following a confused scent; then he came back to me in a rush. I recognized the overspill of power that obliged him to vent his distaste upon a stranger. 'I can't come here if it's like that. Now can I?'

I had learned fatalism in Egypt; it was the gift they made me. I said, 'Somebody will come soon.'

He dropped into a chair. He was a heavy man with shoulders built for labour, but I noticed that the purple suit had been cut by a good tailor and that his jewellery was expensive. A moment later he was on his feet again and blocking me into a corner.

'Now look,' he said, as if he were naming his final price: 'the place either meets my specifications or it doesn't. It's true I want the country. Never said I didn't. I want it for reasons of my own that are nothing to do with you. But if it's not right the French or the Germans can have it. Get me?'

I did not; but in recent years I had seen enough of commercial dictatorship to know that a man in a vulgar suit might have the means to buy a country.

From the window I watched a Negro porter, the one man alive in Mogalor, as he unloaded the aircraft on to an ox cart. Other passengers had found their way into the lounge. I was aware of a tall woman with shoulder-length gold hair who stood by the immigration desk. She carried an instrument case. I knew that her gaze rested upon me, but the smile was too large for my taste; it had a dimension that could only be American. Clearly she was not the business man's daughter. She was waiting for me to speak to her but I wouldn't answer the summons—I would not be drawn by so blatant an imperative no matter that we shared a problem. The young Arab who had travelled with me from Gibraltar stood by the exit. I went up to him; I had to talk to somebody.

'I had thought there would be someone here to meet me. I must learn not to be self-important.'

He brightened. 'But I am here to meet you! Hatim Haud ben Yusoff, brother to the Chief of Staff. Your aide.'

'But you flew with me from Gibraltar!'

'Exactly so. I met you in Gibraltar.'

'Then why didn't you say something?'

A cloud passed over his face. 'You were engaged in thought. It would have been a discourtesy.'

I could not be critical of this amiable youth, and I laughed, laughter in which he shared as a good aide should. He gave me his credentials. He was the youngest of the many sons of the old Sultan and he was a captain in the Republican Guard. I knew the office of Sultan to be extinct but that the trappings of the Sultanate survived; the Republican Guard was the name given to the old Royal Guard. His Sharifian Majesty the Sultan lived on in

Kezzan at a great age.

'I attend the Army Academy for three years between other engagements. I receive the sword of honour for my labours. Also I hunt gazelle in the mountains.' In other words, his style of life was the same as any other fashionable cadet, in any country, and I had to content myself with the thought that Arabs of good family were soldiers by instinct. I tried him in the role of aide. 'I wonder if you can find my cases, Hatim, and the customs officer. No doubt there are formalities.'

'Your cases are in the presidential car. The customs officer has been attended to and all other formalities are waived. The President sends his greeting.'

He glowed with achievement. As an aide Hatim certainly had good points.

'Then what are we waiting for?' I asked.

'Upon your desire to leave the airport.'

I recognized the courtesy and the dream-like regard for the rights of the stranger belonging to a people I had held in petulant affection since I first knew them. I felt a responsibility for my fellow passengers who were not served so well as I, and who had now come to rest, apparently for ever, in the lounge. I asked Hatim if it was possible to help them. He stared; it was not in his nature to question the lassitude of the public services.

'They are quite comfortable. It is early in the day . . .'

Through the window I could see that the Negro porter had gone off duty, his task incomplete. The man in the purple suit lay horizontally in a chair, waiting upon death or some other oblivion. The woman at the desk still watched me.

'Hatim, I will be grateful if you will do something to help these people. After all, they are visitors to the country.'

'Ah so! They are our guests. They shall have every service if that is your wish.'

My aide leapt the desk and vanished into the office behind. I do not know what method of persuasion he used, backed by what royal temper, but a while later I saw the Negro porter run out of the building as if for his life, and an official appeared at the counter.

The man in the purple suit woke up suddenly, moved by this

13

activity. 'Thirty-seven minutes,' he said. 'Four would have been too much. I can't accept it. Really I can't.'

The woman at the desk inclined her head towards me in acknowledgement of a service. I saw her better then: the face was oval, the eyes large and blue, the nose prominent; she had the composed beauty of one who has looked too often into a camera. Her gesture would have pleased me if it had not been so carefully managed. I bowed, too deeply, allowing the exaggeration to speak my mind, and she raised her head in offence, a tiny symbol of displeasure that no one but me could have noticed but none the less marked a break in composure. Clearly this lady had a measure of pride.

Hatim came back a moment later, saving me from making a bigger fool of myself. At this time in my life, with a dead heart, I had no wish to enter into a contest of this sort.

I thanked Hatim for setting the airport to rights but he raised the flat of his hand towards me. 'A small matter. The airport manager had a stiffness in his motions and had sealed himself in the executive suite. It was necessary to force the door.' He flicked dust from his robe, as he might have wiped clean his sword. 'Now we will drive to the Capital. The car is supplied with refreshment. Sir, you will follow me!'

I waved to my companion in the purple suit and made a gesture of reconciliation to the tall fair lady, wondering what either could be doing in Mogalor, and together with Hatim I went out into the blinding light of the forecourt.

§

The presidential car dated from Khalid and was all that Hatim had claimed—a black Mercedes with a spacious interior. A soldier drove and he was accompanied by an armed guard, so clearly there were hazards under Jason's military government. A large pennant flew at the bonnet which would not have disappointed a commander-in-chief. Hatim told me it was mine, specially introduced by order of the President, and I felt some misgiving because an adviser should not wear plumes of this sort.

The airport lay between Mogalor and the new resort of Sidi-bel-Said. As we drove toward the hills, gaining a little height, I could

14

see both the old town, a squalid mess like every city at this latitude, and the new white concrete of the resort. Khalid had brought in foreign capital to build a tourist centre at Sidi-bel-Said, but the plan had lapsed when his presidency ended in the street at El Desmara, and most of the hotels were incomplete. No doubt investors were waiting to see what form of 'peace' was established by the new government. A military quietude, supported by a few regiments of armour, did much to restore the affections of international capital and Jason might get things going again.

Behind the towns lay the vineyards. I did not know what type of wine grew here as it had not found its way to Europe. Further from the sea, where the land broke into stone and the sun hammered the road, the olives grew left and right as far as I could see. I don't know how far we travelled through the olive groves; perhaps it was thirty miles; but finally they thinned as the ground worsened and we climbed the lower escarpment of the Southern Atlas towards El Desmara, the old slaving capital which was now the seat of government.

I had no reason to feel hope for the future. I was following the star of a man I hardly knew, of a race different from my own, in a country of fast-changing loyalties; I could expect nothing but whatever failure the wind might blow. But I told myself that Jason was in with a chance. True he was a soldier, but soldiers I understood, and I saw no reason why a military man should govern with greater cruelty than anyone else. For the first time in months I felt a lift in my jaded spirit, as if the miseries of the past were dispersing in clean mountain air, and I looked forward to renewing my friendship with the President of the Saharan Republic.

§

Jason had his office at the Tamran Palace which the military government had made into a headquarters. The old palace, where the Sultan had once spent his winters, dated from the eighteen hundreds, but the main extensions had been made at the turn of the present century. The sovereign of the time had built with a spirited vulgarity matched only by the other bandit

15

dynasties of the Maghreb. Today the lower windows were sandbagged and soldiers in camouflaged overalls guarded the main entrances. Machine-gun positions had been established in the gardens and on the roof. I could not tell if these were the clichés of revolution or if Jason indeed felt himself insecure.

The President kept me waiting nearly half an hour in his outer office, no doubt to discourage too great a familiarity, but he rose affably when I was shown in. His office was a large room on the ground floor which seemed once to have been a room of state; pillars of green marble supported a roof fluted in white. Jason wore his uniform which now bore the insignia of a full general. He was smart, cool and apparently at ease.

'My dear Warfield, you are welcome! It is—let me see—seven months since we met. A time of great activity and change. Eastleigh seems a long way in the past.'

The hint was obvious but he need not have worried; I had already decided not to presume upon our relationship as instructor and pupil. I said, 'There have been many changes, Mr President, not least in our personal fortunes. I congratulate you on your promotion.'

'A chance, an accident. The ball fell at my feet and I simply played it.' He could afford the magnanimity; he was an autocrat with five brigades at his shoulder. 'I did not desire the appointment but someone had to serve the people.'

'Of course. You have done well to gain their confidence so quickly.'

'We gave them food, we swept the gutters, we cleared away certain obstructions——'

I didn't like the sound of that but I was in no position to be critical. He noticed my concern, smiled wickedly and developed his theme.

'—certain elements in opposition to progress. Come, Colonel, you must not look so shocked! This was not a paper exercise at Eastleigh but an actual conflict in which the loser could not expect to be treated other than severely. In Britain you do not understand a revolutionary situation.'

I let that pass; he might have been right. 'I believe you did only what was necessary, sir.'

16

'There were factions in the officer corps, some cliques in the administration, some professors, some priests. . . .' (God, how many nameless people had died?) 'They were taken out in their tens, in their hundreds——'

'I suspect you exaggerate, Mr President. In London I was allowed to see the report prepared by the International Commission. In fact the Army behaved with restraint.'

He rocked his head from side to side as if restraint were something that could not be quantified. He raised the pitch of his voice. 'I was your student. You have to think well of me! Yes, Colonel, restraint is an admirable thing; the British army should place the pacification of India high among its battle honours. The restraint of the mighty! But you will excuse me if I tell you that restraint is a luxury that a small nation may not be able to enjoy. Here we have been engaged in the reconciliation of forces violently opposed, in cooling savage tempers; we have not been discharging an imperial responsibility in a country far from home where the virtues of Eastleigh can be properly applied.' It was a prepared speech, but he was entitled to make it; I simply waited for him to continue. 'You should know from the beginning what sort of country, and in particular what sort of regime you have pledged yourself to support.'

I had then to speak with equal candour. 'Mr President, I would not have come here if I thought you a bloodthirsty tyrant. I believe you had no choice but to take power when you did and I think you have tried to run the country honestly since then. Like you, I am a professional soldier. I am not concerned with theoretical politics nor with making moral judgements about the actions of other people in a violent situation. I don't even condemn violence if there is no other means of establishing some sort of order. But I won't give my support to needless cruelty.'

'Of course not. But if I told you I was a party to the murder of Khalid, that I suppress all liberal opinion, that you have joined a brutal dictatorship——'

'Then I would need to see the evidence before I believed you.'

He laughed, but the laugh was cut short. He rose from the desk and walked the length of the room with a brisk step. Though small and slight Jason was one of the smartest soldiers I had ever

17

known, his uniform fitting exactly, his movements precise and within the range permitted to a military man. His features were neat, only slightly negroid and without line or blemish of any sort. I knew him to be about thirty-eight years old. I watched him now, the complete soldier, without race or nationality.

'I am not a dictator; I don't believe in military government; I would rather rejoin my regiment.'

Well, it had been said before, and doubtless it would be said again, but perhaps this time it was true. I simply nodded.

'However, you have a right to know the sort of man you are serving.'

He told me then he had been born in the village of Rif el Tiba in the heart of the Neban. His father was a Nebanese slave who was freed by the Jesuit fathers at San Georgio; his mother was a Berber of the lowest class. His childhood had been spent in the desert where his father earned a few fils trading in salt. It was not possible for me to conceive the austerity in which they lived; such degrees of poverty did not exist in Europe. Sun, wind, salt — that was his childhood in the deserts of the Neban! Jason came to a halt in front of my chair, feet together, knuckles at the trouser seam. He addressed me frontally. 'Understand, Colonel, that you have entered the service of a waif, a beggar, an outcast.'

He continued his parade of the tiles. When he was six years old his parents sold him for the price of a hunting rifle to a merchant in Mogalor. He served in the kitchen as scullion, as servant to the servants; he slept on the stone floor. I could not know to what vile uses a boy might be put in a Mohammedan household. When I was at my public school he was scraping the grease from the cooking pots with handfuls of sand. That was his education, his training for the Presidency! He could remember no kind word spoken to him while he was in the house of the merchant. Fortunately — or was it good fortune? he couldn't say — the merchant failed in business and Jason was offered in recognition of a debt to a neighbouring ironsmith, a Negro from Rabat, a man with the principles of a jackal. Now his occupation was the feeding of charcoal into the furnace where the iron was softened. 'I worked in a black pit where the daylight did not penetrate; I worked from darkness to darkness. I do not know how many years

18

I served the ironsmith.'

Jason turned abruptly towards me, challenging my disbelief, but I said nothing. I tried to fit the immaculate soldier to this history of misfortune and saw no obvious connection. He read my mind exactly.

'It's not true, you tell me. A fairy story! Come, I am not the only head of state to have risen from the abyss. Look around you. There are presidents and protectors who have sprung from the dung heap in every continent. They gain their education in the streets or in prison.' He smiled mysteriously, leaving me to guess which school sharpened his intelligence, gave him a command of language, taught his mind to move swiftly and accurately through the problems of state management. He relented ever so slightly. 'There was a man, a nobleman of El Desmara, who recognized the wit of a poor boy and gave him an education. It does not matter now.'

I had to be satisfied with that. Now I needed to know his plans for the future. 'Mr President, you have employed me as an adviser, you have supplied me with an aide and a handsome pennant. I speak Arabic and a little French and I am used to a full job. Just what would you like me to do now that I am here?'

The question embarrassed him. His lips rolled in and out as if he were trying to find words to please me, and for the moment we had returned to our relationship at Eastleigh. Now the Negro in his make-up was uppermost; his voice softened, his limbs were loosened from the military habit.

'Why did you send for me, sir?'

He returned to his desk, seated himself and recovered his authority with a struggle. He straightened his uniform as if this would put his mind in order. He said indistinctly, 'The country is divided between Arab and Nebanese, which is to say between the rich and the poor. Seventy years ago the division was between slaver and slave. The present government is pledged to racial integration and universal social progress, but there is still difficulty in making appointments if one side seems to gain an advantage. The Chief of Staff is Arab; I am Nebanese. I accordingly thought it best if the principal military adviser was drawn from neither side. Of course you are already known to the

19

Chief of Staff.'

I was indeed; I had marked his essays, which were very poorly constructed, taking care not to offend the dignity of that princely figure.

Jason allowed his innermost thought to escape. 'Yes, His Excellency Suleiman ben Yusoff, prince, kalifa and nitwit. He is unchanged.'

'And he approved my appointment?'

'Well, not exactly. He recommended a member of the Sharifian family which of course I could not accept. We compromised by appointing his younger brother your aide.'

'I see.'

Now I could understand better Jason's purpose in sending for me. At first I had supposed it to be bravado, to show his old instructor how far his star had risen, but now I could see that he needed someone to stand between himself and the Chief of Staff. He knew I didn't like Solly. He knew I had a low opinion of his intelligence. In any division of opinion he had reason to believe I would take the President's part.

I said carefully, 'It will be a pleasure to meet the Chief of Staff again. I feel sure I can work with you both without upsetting the racial balance.'

Jason became suddenly awake. 'Of course, of course. You will have an office in the palace, a car and a driver, and the assistance of Hatim. I would like you first of all to make the acquaintance of the senior commanders and to study our dispositions and contingency plans. Later there are studies of re-equipment and reorganisation I will wish you to undertake. Rooms in the palace have been set aside for your private use and personal servants have been appointed.'

I was impressed by this efficiency and hoped that the body of the Republic was as well managed. I thanked the President for his consideration.

Jason looked at me closely. 'My dear Peter, your eyes are sad, your cheek is drawn. The months have not been kind to you, I think.'

No matter what our present relationship might be I was not going to be patronized by Jason. I said firmly, 'You need feel no concern, sir. My wife and I have now separated and sometime there will be a divorce. I have no plans for re-marriage. Now if you have no further instructions for me, I will introduce myself to the Chief of Staff. You have already given me too much of your time.'

I could not tell if he was offended; he had put on his soldier's manner. He gave me a stiff bow from the desk and I left the room without waiting for the aide.

# 3

The Chief of Staff could not see me until four o'clock. Hatim told me he was 'inspecting establishments', which seemed to describe some form of truancy. Instead I introduced myself to the three other members of the Officers' Committee, men who had no military appointments but who met with the President to decide issues of policy: they were of course the original conspirators who had found Khalid too great a danger to the state and planned his dismissal. They were drawn from different ranks, presumably to give the Committee the widest appeal to the officer corps. The senior of them, General Salam, was a kindly old man brought out of retirement and probably harmless. The middle ranks were represented by Colonel Aziz, a regimental soldier with the lazy incompetence of a landed gentleman. Captain Ismael, the voice of the junior officers, was an unsmiling young man who used the vocabulary of the New Left and looked uncomfortable in his uniform. They did not fill me with confidence. Still, they made me welcome and assured me of their help.

As I had an hour to waste before I could present myself to Solly, I asked Hatim to take me to the market where I could buy clothes of a better weight for the climate. We drove down to the great open market under the old walls where such things could be had. I suppose there were a thousand people between the booths or watching the dancers. Here, for a few fils, you could employ any magic or remedy that might improve the human condition. Fifty years ago slaves from the south were bartered here, but today the booths mostly offered cheap Japanese goods sent in bulk from Mogalor. The cries of the vendors merged with the beating of the Berber drums. I watched a juggler who kept six knives in the air and a troupe of acrobats whose antics stirred the dust until they were almost hidden.

I left Hatim with the car and passed along the booths selling tropical clothing, dodging the outstretched hands of the stallkeepers. At a distance from me but holding my attention a girl in emerald made a bold stroke of colour as she moved away from me. I could not see her face. I willed her to turn towards me, but she did not. I could not think what a white girl was doing in the great market. In a moment the crowd had covered her, then it divided again so that I could see her still further away and behind a veil of dust. The appeal she made to me added something to my loneliness even here among the press of people and voices.

Voices. Voices raised in banter, in argument. Voices speaking all the languages of the Maghreb. Then I was startled into complete stillness. One voice — I could not tell where it came from — was speaking my name, addressing me in formal Arabic.

'She did not see you, Colonel Warfield. There is nothing for you here.'

I turned quickly and saw nothing but robed figures and, further off, a water carrier following me in the hope of a sale; but it was not him who spoke.

'Who are you? What do you want?'

'Your help, perhaps. I cannot tell.'

'In what design?'

'To punish the guilty.'

'Then show yourself. I do not speak to shadows.'

No one came forward. It might have been any one of a dozen hooded figures who had spoken to me. I was not inclined to leave it there, so I lunged at the man nearest and spun him towards me. I found myself looking into an expressionless Negro face marked with tribal scars across the cheeks. I let him go, certain this was not the man who spoke. Then the crowd pushed me this way and that and I lost the direction from which the words came.

A moment later I was again accosted, and this time I stood still and did not try to identify the speaker; more than anything I wanted to hear his message.

'You are listening, Colonel? You can hear me?'

'What is it you would tell me?'

23

'Of a killing.'

'Who was killed?'

'An old man, a holy man, a long way from here. I am telling you of an Arab killed in the Neban. It is a matter of importance.'

'Tell me, stranger, who did this thing? Was it the soldiers?'

My informant laughed softly. 'They will tell you so. When a man is killed they will always blame a soldier.'

'What can I do?'

'Tell the President to pursue the guilty.'

'Why don't you tell him?'

'I did, friend, but he paid no heed. Now follow the girl if that is your will. She is the daughter of a rich man. I would not hamper such pleasures.'

That was all. The speaker left me then to lose himself in the shifting crowd. I waited a minute, then moved on. The girl was still within my sight over by the southern gate but I did not go near her. I was too old, too disappointed. I chose the things I needed, agreed a price with the trader, and rejoined Hatim at the car.

'Hatim, can you tell me of a holy man who was murdered, perhaps recently, somewhere in the Neban?'

But my aide was not interested. 'A holy man? The country is full of holy men. Sometimes they are murdered. Sometimes not. You have now to meet the Chief of Staff.'

§

The wing of the palace occupied by the Staff carried all the signs of a military government hastily introduced. Telephone cables lay across the hallways and temporary notices had been pinned to the walls. Hatim showed me the way to Solly's office, losing his direction no more than twice. In what must have been an ante-room of the old palace, where now visitors to the military court waited for an audience, the man in the purple suit lay prone in a wicker chair in some further cessation from progress. I waved to him, but he simply turned a sour eye towards me, raised his shoulders in hopelessness, and sank back into whatever dreams he had.

In my long service I had waited on the Chief of Staff in every

24

climate and in most states of fortune, but I had never entered an office quite like Solly's. The Chief of Staff wore the uniform of a major-general in the Republican Army but I saw nothing else to confirm his appointment. Fleeces covered the floor, cushions were spread in no sort of arrangement, the remains of a hearty meal still lay where the guests had left them. Men of the Republican Guard in djellaba and headcloth squatted in one corner, their weapons within a hand's reach, deep in some unspecified task; perhaps they were flaying an ox. For some reason of his own Solly invited Hatim to stay with us. His greeting was sombre, without warmth.

'Warfield, I am happy to see you. I hope my brother is serving you properly. You will take coffee, fruit? I should tell you that I opposed your appointment.'

He had never been one to put a guest at ease. We sat on rolled blankets in the centre of the room. Solly had taken little trouble with his appearance and his khaki drill was stained and out of shape. His hands and feet were large and clumsy. His eyes I had noticed at Eastleigh; they were black, commanding and touched with a deep fatalism. I don't think Solly had even the beginnings of a sense of humour. Hatim, his duty accomplished, composed himself for sleep.

I said, 'Naturally you were concerned at the appointment of a foreigner; I would not have expected it otherwise. However, now that I am here I hope that I can do a practical job of value to the military government.'

Perhaps he had not heard me. His mind followed a pattern of ancient grievance. 'The Europeans have interfered in the life of this region for three hundred years. The Spanish, the French, the English. Each has left behind his own peculiar stain; in their train there was decadence and disease. You are very welcome, sir.'

'I am comforted,' I said.

'The country must find its Islamic identity. We cannot adopt the manners of the West.'

'Of course not.'

'Khalid, the mountebank, aligned himself too closely with Western culture. He attended the Cannes Film Festival. He was struck down——'.

I was surprised. 'Was that his only offence?'

'—his head was used as a plaything by the children of El Desmara. His torso lay on a pile of refuse. Even if that had been his only offence, the punishment was apt.'

Hatim laughed strangely; perhaps he shared his brother's dislike for the finer flowerings of western civilization. He said simply, 'Khalid, Khalid, they buried you in an unmarked grave!'

Of course, these were not the first conspirators to be obsessed by the leader they had killed.

I said, with the best strength I could manage, 'Nevertheless you now have the opportunity of building a new country free from outside influence. I am sure it will take its natural shape as a multi-racial society.'

Solly shook his head. 'We have changed little of consequence. The stains were not wiped out. Even now the influence of Europe is creeping back under the military government.' His next words were in Arabic, which in translation would have meant, 'The robbers, the prostitutes, the evil-doers are returning.'

I replied in his language. 'What evil-doers?'

'The Atheist, the Christian, the Jew.'

'What do they want?'

'Our testicles, our heritage.'

'In particular, who do you mean?'

'Langley. The man Langley.'

'Who is he?'

Hatim, on his back, gazed at the ceiling. He spoke in English. 'He wears purple clothing. He wishes to meet the President.'

I asked, 'But what can Langley do against the will of a united people? He is simply a businessman.'

Solly continued in the royal Arabic of the Maghreb. 'He will sap our strength. He will introduce infections. He will change the nature of our people. He will build a holiday camp for Christians.'

I had to admire Solly for the quality of his disdain, which I had not seen bettered anywhere in Islam. His long dark face swung towards me in emphasis of his loathing: in such a way had sultan and sheikh conferred a sentence of death in the years before the French brought their justice to the wastes of Barbary.

'But that need not be fatal to the Saharan people,' I said. 'The

26

tourists will not go outside Sidi-bel-Said.'

'They will spread their vulgarity throughout the country. This has already happened in Tunisia, in Morocco. They will wear obscene knickers. Already the harlots are converging on a country notable for its innocence. This morning a female singer of songs, an American, came here from Gibraltar.'

I noted the speed and accuracy of his intelligence service.

'Miss Iris Mason,' said Hatim. 'Her songs are politically biased. She favours peace and brotherhood.'

'In Sidi-bel-Said there are groups of young people given to intolerable visions,' Solly continued. 'They plan a Socialist state. They are school-children against whom the lash should be used as argument. The President must stand firm against all these impurities.'

Solly paused, his mind sunk in bitterness. Then he said, 'I remember the Sultanate. It was different in those days.' In reflection his face put on a dull melancholy which showed how powerfully he regretted the past. He told me then that he was the son of the Sultan's favourite wife and had lived in the palace at Kezzan when a child. He had many brothers and sisters because the Sultan had ten wives and unnumbered concubines. The palace had twelve courtyards contained within a high white wall. A thousand servants worked there. The gardens were very beautiful; fountains and streams played between banks of flowers. As a child he rode upon the shoulders of a giant African slave called Hero whose duty it was to protect him from all dangers. He dug his heels into Hero's sides to make him gallop, and together they ran round the upper walls of the palace until Hero could run no more, Solly beating the guards with a cane. At the feast of Aid el Kabir twenty oxen were brought into the palace forecourt where they were slaughtered, the tiles running with their blood, and the carcasses taken whole to the ovens and braziers; then the Sultan's family, and his servants and slaves, had eaten until they collapsed, and they had slept in the garden under the cypresses, Sultan and slave together.

Now he allowed his innermost thoughts to escape. 'The Sultanate was the best government we had. It accorded exactly with the wishes of the people.'

I reminded the Chief of Staff of my appointment as adviser. I had expected a brief on military policy, not the reflections of nostalgic royalty. His shoulders rose as if to deny a need for a briefing or indeed for my advice.

'The Army is in effective control of the country,' he said shortly. 'We have the undivided support of the people of all races and I see no reason why the regime should not be sustained indefinitely.'

This was dangerous thinking in a chief of staff who must be watchful for a breach in his defences. The strength of the palace guard told a different story. I remembered the dictum of Eastleigh, the wisdom of a nation that had used the Army in support of governments in every part of the world: *there is no military solution, the soldiers can only buy time . . .'*

With failing confidence I asked him the question that would have troubled the mind of even the most casual observer. 'Excellency, the country contains two cultures, it lies across the line that divides the Arab from the African. You have killed the President and seized power by violent means. You maintain the government by using the Army to shield it from opposition. You have done these things, let me say, in a country that is not racially cohesive and which has a history of Nebanese unrest. I must therefore ask you what chance you have of keeping control of the people for the indefinite period that you foresee.'

This was risky; he could regard the question as deeply provocative; but in fact he only swung a sallow, mournful face towards me as if he had expected no better from an infidel stranger. 'Khalid was a notorious criminal——' he began.

'Khalid, Khalid,' said Hatim.

'—who paid the price of his iniquity.'

'He had no dignity, even at the end!'

I said, 'I dare say; but the villainy of the former ruler is not a justification for military dictatorship, nor does it guarantee its safety. Tell me about the Nebanese. How are they distributed in the Army?'

'There is one brigade serving in the Neban,' Solly said. 'It is wholly Nebanese. The other brigades are Arab.'

'Who is in command?'

'Colonel Nathan, an African.'

'Why is he not a brigadier?'

'We thought it best to limit his rank. The brigade is not, after all, very important; the headquarters is a long way off at Dharat.'

'And he does not serve on the Officers' Committee?'

'He does not.'

I no longer cared how far I angered the Chief of Staff. 'I would not say that the brigade was unimportant, sir. It would seem to be of the highest importance. Under a military government the Nebanese can only find expression through the commander.'

'I do not expect trouble in the Neban.'

'Forgive me, but I suspect there is trouble in the Neban already.'

'What do you mean? You have no experience of the province.'

'Someone has died there. Someone of importance. Someone who cannot be forgotten.'

'I do not know what you mean! Well, not exactly. There have been some disturbances, some vendettas. The Nebanese are a savage people.'

'Was the brigade involved? Can you tell me if the brigade has acted in any way against the Moslem hierarchy? For instance, if they had taken the life of a religious teacher as an expression of tribal indignation it would obviously matter.'

'I cannot say what happens in the Neban. It is a vast, primitive area where the people practise strange rituals. We do not go there. The brigade keeps order and that is enough.'

I was getting nowhere with Solly. I rose to leave.

Solly said angrily, 'You are making difficulties where none exist. You are a soldier who must invent dangers to justify your own employment. I have seen such things before.'

So had I, but I was pretty certain I was not guilty of this fault at present. I made a last attempt at breaking his mistrust.

'General, I cannot share your optimism, but differences of opinion need not prevent us from working together provided I have your confidence.'

Solly grunted; it was hardly an affirmation of trust.

'Tell me this, sir — may I expect your co-operation, and that of the Army commanders, in doing a worthwhile job? Needless to say, I will not be prepared to stay here without that assurance.'

Solly had not thought things out this far; I fancied that his mind spent its strength in pursuit of dark ambitions and did not make decisions easily. He actually smiled. 'My dear Warfield, we are old comrades. Our Agent in London has offered you a contract of employment and it is my job to assist you.'

'But do you intend to do so?'

'It is the President's wish.'

'Well?'

'I will do my best for the country as a whole.'

I had to be content with that. It was a sadness to me that so little of Eastleigh had rubbed off on His Excellency Suleiman ben Yusoff. Where was the tolerance of diverse opinion, the gaiety of command? Jason bore the mark of Eastleigh far more noticeably than did his Chief of Staff. I asked him one last question. It was out of order by a long way but I had to know where I stood.

'I may take it, I suppose, that the President has your undivided support?'

He did not reply at once, and I had to admire the effrontery which led him to believe that more than one answer was possible. 'He was the unanimous choice of the Officers' Committee,' he said at last.

'I need a firm answer, General.'

The Chief of Staff rose from the floor and turned his back to me, as he might have turned it on the President. 'There was thought to be an advantage in appointing an officer who was not an Arab. The Committee had in mind our relationship with the black population. I did not necessarily share this view.'

'But naturally you will support him in his role as Commander-in-Chief.' I tried not to make it sound like a question.

'I am a soldier. I respond to the needs of the situation. You may be sure that I will do my duty.'

But who could say what that duty might be?

As I left the office of the Chief of Staff, aware that I had earned his bad opinion, he called after me, 'There is game in the hills. You should hunt the gazelle, the wild boar. You should not concern yourself with politics.'

Well, such was my briefing, such the weather in Jason's country. I was not encouraged. I asked Hatim to show me where I was quartered but just then I was doubtful if I would unpack.

§

Hatim led me back through the main hall, from where Langley had disappeared, to a staircase of marble and gilt spoiled only by the hessian overlay, which went up at a gentle gradient to the old state apartments on the first floor. An elderly Nebanese bearer of gigantic stature carried my bags; two other servants, said to be a cook and houseboy, fell in at the rear of the procession. I had expected to find myself in an officer's bunk, but the rooms set aside for me stretched the length of the eastern wing and seemed once to have been occupied by a courtesan of extravagant fancy; the Moorish baroque would have shamed even the Bey of Tunis, whose lamentable premises I had once inspected.

Hatim saw nothing amiss in this accommodation. 'Here you will find comfort. The servants will attend to your needs . . .'

I said nothing. I was too far gone in disillusion to argue the toss with Hatim. I simply thanked him for his help and let him go. I wanted to rid myself of the black giant as well, but he spoke no Arabic — or admitted to none — and he sat himself inside the door waiting for my instructions: he sat without movement, wrapped in a stillness forgotten in Europe and very soon I lost sight of him. I unpacked the things I would need for a few nights, but I left unopened the case of books, pictures, the things I loved and which were all that I had of a home, as I could feel no comfort in these vast rooms.

I opened the shutters and looked across the garden and the old palace wall to the mountains beyond. Their beauty took me by surprise. I had not expected the splendour of the Southern Atlas with the evening sun lying across the snows. But nothing could lift my spirit from the place where it had fallen, and as I stood by the window I played with the idea of telling the President I couldn't help him and taking the next plane out.

I turned at a step behind me. It was Jason, whom I had not heard come in. 'My friend, you are tired, distressed; the problem of adjustment is a severe one. You must not let Solly upset you. He has no gift for polite conversation.'

I said, 'Mr President, I am doubtful if I can work within my present terms of reference. I do not seem to have the confidence of the Chief of Staff. It would be better perhaps for me to go.'

He did not take this up. He made a swift inspection of the room, the wall hangings, the ornate ceiling. 'These are the best apartments in the palace. The decoration is very fine. Even in the currency of the nineteenth century the palace must have cost a million dinars. Your servants are of the highest quality.'

I hadn't the strength to argue. I sat on the bench seat under the window and watched Jason quartering the room.

'Shall I tell you something? Would you care to hear? I have designed you a uniform, a bush jacket with brass appurtenances, on the British pattern. I am sure you will find it comfortable.'

'I'm doubtful if I should wear a uniform. I'm doubtful if I should stay.'

He came to rest in front of me, silent. I suppose I should have risen, but I didn't; I just waited for him to speak.

'Peter, I want you to stay . . .'

I was moved a little by this entreaty. I had always liked Jason, and I wanted to help him in his colossal task, but the lines drawn for me to follow were too indistinct, the hostility to my appointment too powerful. 'I do not see how I can help you, sir.'

'There is so much work to do. We have a shortage of senior officers.'

'But my presence will compromise you with the Army, with the Chief of Staff.'

'Oh, Solly is already opposed to my Presidency. The Sultan's family have always seen themselves as the natural leaders of the country. I beg you to stay.'

I got up and went out on to the wide balcony, the President following at my elbow. I stood at the rail listening to the distant cries of the market. I had to make a decision.

'Look, my help may prove less than a blessing, but I'll give it a month. After that time I will go if it hasn't worked out. There are things I must change, however.'

His anxiety gone, Jason was filled with excitement. 'Of course you will stay! We are both of Eastleigh; we have an obligation to work together, a common spirit, a common objective . . .'

'I must move out of the Palace. For the time being I will wear civilian clothes. I must employ fewer servants.'

'Servants? Why bother about the servants? The Chief of Staff arranged them personally.'

'My employment must be covered by a written directive to the staff.'

'Write it yourself, my dear Peter!'

'And—listen to me, sir—I must have access to all confidential papers relating to the senior appointments. In particular I wish to see the dossier on Colonal Nathan.'

'The files, the archives are open to you. All, all is yours.'

'We'll give it a try,' I said. 'I wouldn't be too hopeful of success.'

'Oh, we shall succeed . . .'

He left me then, the black giant rising to open the door, and I heard his eager voice on the stairway. I felt a little better. My doubts were legion but I'd said my say, and it was possible I could do some useful chores in the Saharan Republic.

I sat by the window and watched the quick spreading of the African night. The last of the sunlight went off the Atlas, the shadows deepened in the palace garden. A minute later the long demented cry of the muezzin, calling the Believers to prayer, asserting the fierce will of Allah, bringing the long past into the living present, diminished my problems with its power and dignity.

I loved Africa and all its moods. I tried not to think of Solly but I could not rid myself of his sombre presence. An idea broke into my mind and would not leave it. After a time I got up and went across to the bearer.

'What is your name?' I asked him in Arabic.

He made no answer, no movement.

'Speak, man! I think you understand me.'

'Hero,' he said.

Hero, Solly's giant slave. I had guessed it. And my aide was related to Solly by blood, just as the Nebanese was by bondage. How like Solly to suppose I wouldn't notice it!

'Go away, Hero,' I said. 'I do not want you here.'

Now it was dark and I heard them changing the guard on the palace roof. What enemies of fact or the President's fancy laid siege to the palace I did not know but I was pretty sure his principal enemy was inside the walls. I was frightened of the royal house of Kezzan and their ambitions in the Republic. For better or worse I was on Jason's side, his enemies were mine, and now it was clear that one at least was a force to be reckoned with.

# 4

In the following days I made the acquaintance of Jason's Army. The commanders treated me with more consideration than I had thought likely which encouraged me to think that Jason's authority was respected. Of the five infantry brigades, two were quartered in the capital together with a regiment of light armour. A third brigade was at Mogalor with instructions to join the force in El Desmara in emergency. This was too great a concentration and evidence perhaps of a dictator's insecurity. The other two brigades were those at Kezzan and Dharat. The Kezzan brigade contained the old Royal Guard, the regiment of which Solly was Colonel-in-Chief, and it was officered largely by members of the Sultan's family. The Brigadier was Rustum ben Yusoff, half-brother to the Chief of Staff, said to be a young officer with a taste for exotic pleasures. The Dharat brigade was a force of black soldiers far away in the Neban.

Meanwhile I dismissed all my servants except Hatim and moved out of the palace, keeping only my office there. If Solly took offence at this flourish of disapproval I couldn't help it. Jason found me a bungalow outside the old city walls. It was shabby and full of beetles and lizards when I first saw it, but I liked the low Spanish roof, the small courtyard and the date garden in which it stood: if I stayed in the country I could be happy here. I unpacked my books, promised myself I would do some writing, and adopted the local cat. My instinct told me to employ servants from outside the country, those less open to manipulation; so I engaged a Hindu couple from the Indian community, Ravi and Tansha, who seemed quiet and kind, and they occupied the rear part of the house. Later I found that the rest of their family, the generations both preceding and following, had moved in as well, but I had known India and its obligations and made no complaint. Together we set to work to repair and paint the old bungalow and to clear the overgrowth from the courtyard.

At this time I began a written account of my friendship with Jason, and his Presidency, using the most direct language I could find. I don't know why I did this when the story was incomplete; but a writer's instinct cannot be suppressed; and now that his Presidency is in the past I am glad to have an account of the military government to help me tell the truth about it. None of the other records I have seen is fair to Jason; one American narrative, which I believe to have been maliciously inspired, is a cruel assault upon a man whose name is nowhere honoured but who none the less deserves a better fate.

§

A week after I moved into the bungalow I was disturbed by a visitor I had not expected. It was late in the evening. I was seated in the courtyard watching the movement of the stars, which from the hills of Africa is a wonder unimpaired, paralysed by my own laziness, when a figure entered the courtyard gate and stood in the light from the open door. I paid no attention at first: Africa is full of silent white figures, benign but curious, whom it is polite to ignore, and I waited for my visitor to speak or go away. Then my eyes were drawn by the bold gaze in which I was held and the carefully composed languor of the tall figure, and I remembered the passenger lounge at Mogalor and my unspoken dialogue with an American lady I had been unable to like. I knew her name and occupation now: Iris Mason, a singer of folk songs. I should have risen but I was angered by the contrived stillness with which she meant to beckon my attention, and I spoke from the comfort of my chair, letting my voice carry my indignation.

'Miss Iris Mason, abroad in El Desmara, ignoring the bandits and bag-snatchers, makes a late call upon Colonel Warfield at his disreputable establishment.'

This was cheap, but she simply bowed her head as if she expected nothing better, kept her smile unbroken and came more fully into the light. She was certainly a striking figure to come out

36

of the turbulent dark of a Maghrebi city—her robe white, her fair hair hanging to her waist. Her voice, which I had not heard before, was deep, slow and intimate.

'Please forgive the intrusion, Colonel. I called at the Tamran Palace, and they told me you were here.'

'I moved,' I said. I owed her no explanation.

'You will help me, I am sure.'

I had to relent then. I found her a chair and called for Ravi. Now that I could see her clearly I noticed the prominent features, the hands as large as a man's. The white robe and sandals laced to the knee I took to be a tribute to the Mohammedan establishment.

'I do not see how I can help you, Miss Mason.'

'To tell you the truth, Colonel, I am no longer called Mason. The name didn't fit. You see, I intend to make my home here and do what I can to help these poor people. You may call me Osmani.'

It took me a moment to relate the Arabic-sounding Osmani to Iris Mason; it was an anagram of the surname and initial.

'Very well, Miss Osmani.'

'Just Osmani. I don't like titles derived from one's sex. There can be no place for them in a rational society.'

She could have it any way she liked, but I doubted if I could call her Osmani.

She said, 'They tell me you are acquainted with the Dictator.' This was accompanied by a radiant smile of forgiveness.

'If you mean the President, General Khymer, I am his principal military aide. You would like a drink, Miss Mason?'

She did not drink, she would take fruit juice; this obedience to the disciplines of the country sat well with the robe and sandals. She would not come to her point too hastily; I needed to be softened, changed. 'The President has such a pleasant smile, don't you think? It's surprising to see him leading the country. He does not seem to be a man of violence and hatred.'

I said nothing.

'Of course, the seizure of power was a terrible thing. I don't know what guided him to take so much innocent life. He eliminated all liberal opinion and most of the faculty at the

37

University. I have information that the General personally took the lives of the President Khalid's wife and two eldest children.'

I said, 'Madam, the General was in England at the time. He played no part in the revolution. And as far as I am aware the wife and family of the former President are living in Casablanca.'

'I am sure you believe that. I am very sure that is what they have told you. But I have other information.'

I let it go, she could believe what slanders best suited her; and I did not want to be stung into defending the Officers' Committee or the violence they used that day in August.

Her next words had the ring of quotation. 'A military government can only pursue military ends. Inevitably there will be further bloodshed and the destruction of innocent lives. Under a dictatorship there can be no enlargement of sanity, tolerance or love.'

Of course, anyone who supports a dictatorship has sooner or later to face an outraged liberal conscience and I had only myself to blame. I had my own doubts about Jason's government and his power to reach decent ends, but I did not want them given the form of words. Not yet. Not until I knew what was happening in the darkest corners of the country. I said, 'I have no reason to suppose the aims of the government are other than they are said to be—namely, peace, security and social justice. What advantage could they gain from a bloodbath?'

She nodded. Her charity was boundless. 'Now that's an interesting point. A very interesting point. But a repressive government can only advance in the direction of greater cruelty.'

'I'm not good at theories, Miss Mason. Military men tend to think practically, not politically. As I see it, General Khymer is a reasonable man doing a difficult job and I'm trying to help him as best I can.'

'I see. I know. But you would not wish to be part of a brutal dictatorship.'

'I've seen no evidence that it is one.'

'Come now! The dissenters were eliminated, the press has no freedom; I know of other repressions.'

'There have been distortions in the accounts published abroad. True, there have been some cruelties, but in this country there

38

always were. It's easy to dress it up as a Fascist dictatorship but that's begging the question. The present government is no worse and perhaps a little better than its predecessors.'

I didn't know if I was trying to convice Osmani or myself, but in truth I could see no signs of brutality in Jason. She drew her breath in mild astonishment, her head tilted in wonder; but she had patience enough to deal with the most conservative intelligence.

She said, 'You have heard of Colonel Nathan — ?'

'He's commanding in the Neban.'

' — and of the crimes he has committed there?'

I had not for certain, and I wondered what stale abuse from the dissenter's kitbag was coming next. Perhaps he was raping nuns. 'Tell me about them, but let me know the source of your information. Nathan has the right to be protected from invention.'

'As it happens, my sources are confidential.'

'They always are.'

'You must not close your mind to the truth.'

'Miss Mason, I'll hear what evidence you have, but I'm not going to listen to unsupported gossip.' She was touching an old wound, one borne by any soldier who had contained violence in the shabby parts of the earth. I had been stoned and shot at, I had listened to the shriek of the mob, and I had been called pig and bully. The spreading of fiction when the mob had dispersed, leaving only crazy footprints in the dust, was no less a violence than mine had been. 'Well?' I asked. 'What has Nathan done?'

'There have been executions.'

'Who has reported them?'

'Men of truth and courage.'

'But what were their politics, their ambition, their prejudice?'

'None, of course. They were men of fearless objectivity.'

'I don't know that there is such a thing. The truth gets beaten out of shape as soon as the incident has passed. Violence is always exaggerated.'

'In Sidi-bel-Said, where I have made my home, there is a group of young people who are working for the betterment of the poor and oppressed. Fearless, beautiful people. Some months ago a

39

party working in the Neban was arrested, tortured and put to death by Colonel Nathan. Without trial, without reason; their only offence was their opposition to tyranny. I can give you their names. More recently . . .'

'Yes?'

'The matter is too appalling. You may not believe me. There was an old man who spent his days in teaching, in prayer; a man of great sanctity . . .'

'Tell me what you have heard.'

'He was killed brutally, with a soldier's weapon.'

'And you believe it was Nathan who killed him?'

'Of course. Like many evil people he could not bear the spectacle of goodness. Believe me, there is a reign of terror in the Neban which the government has done nothing to suppress. I want you to intervene. I want you to go there. I want you to examine the evidence and to make a report to the appropriate body of the United Nations.'

I had seen this coming. She had forced me into a corner where I must examine my own conscience, but I was too far gone in dislike for this glib American, whose mind was coloured by the slogans of the New Left, to give her an undertaking. I would act in my own way, in my own time. I said now, too roughly, 'Madam, I am an official of the military government with a duty to the President. It is not my job to make reports to an outside agency. I'm sorry, but your request is impossible.'

We sat in silence, each with his own indignation. For all I knew Nathan might be the murderer she claimed and the Neban a place of unrelieved darkness. I knew very little about the Saharan Republic and its government of military men. And it was the weakness of my own position which put a match to my temper when I was challenged by a woman I did not care for and who came unbidden out of the night.

Osmani said, 'So you won't help me.'

'No, I won't.'

'I can't believe that you would condone brutality.'

'Don't be too sure of anything.'

'I had another request, but you will plainly refuse to help me.'

It seemed likely, but I asked her to continue.

40

She raised her eyes to a level above my head and spoke with unassailable detachment. 'There are means, methods other than the practical. I cannot hope that you will agree with me, Colonel Warfield. I do not suppose you have much sympathy with art.'

She was wrong in this; books had been the whole of my consolation for years and my heroes were writers; but I said nothing about that.

'It may be that I can help. It may be that I can disperse the hatred. One cannot tell; these things are beyond measuring. Were I to give a recital for the members of the Junta with songs dedicated to peace and the unities—you understand me, my work takes in world rapprochement—the effect might be a good one. You will help me in that?'

I suppose my amazement showed in my face because Osmani gathered her robe in her hand and stood up, in disdain for me and my callous heart. I had no word to say to this woman who supposed the world's disharmony could be corrected by a song. She had not seen the demented faces, she had not listened to the howls of anguish; she did not know how deep was the insanity sweeping the continents like a hot wind.

'Say no more, Colonel. It's obvious you believe only in force. It's obvious you will not help me.'

She gave me her formal smile which she followed with a dismissive lift of the shoulders, a movement so small I nearly missed it but which was designed, I knew, to reject any claim I might have had to her favour: what indulgences could have been mine, she suggested, had I not been so boorish.

Ravi took her back to the road where I believe she had a car. I would not bring myself to offer this courtesy.

# 5

Before I went south to the Neban, I tackled the President about Colonel Nathan. I needed to rid myself of doubt. I found Jason alone in his office, but he did not lift his eyes from the paper before him. 'Nathan? He was a sergeant prior to Independence. He was our boxing champion. I don't know him well.'

'And his style of command?'

'Tough, I should think.'

'Does he hold a warrant for the punishment of civil, as well as military, offenders?'

'Technically the country is still under martial law which confers on commanders the right to hear charges against civilians, and to award punishments. We will re-establish the civil courts soon. Why do you ask me these questions?'

'One other point, if I may, sir. Do the sentences require confirmation by the Commander-in-Chief?'

He didn't like this question; his hands made darting movements of displeasure. 'Really, it is pointless to ask me! Our Army Act is founded upon yours. You know very well that all sentences require my confirmation.'

'And that would apply for civil as well as service offenders?'

'Of course. Naturally. What did you suppose?'

I left him at his desk, looking small and hurt, and went out into the dust and sunlight of the palace yard where Hatim waited with the car and escort. I had little doubt that I was on my way to a meeting with the third most important officer in the state.

With the escort leading in a Land Rover, we drove south out of the hills. I had not crossed this country before. The olives lasted as far as the plain and here, at the extremity of the Southern Atlas, the desert began and the road followed a course which might have been drawn with a ruler across a wilderness of stone. It bore exactly towards Dharat. This highway, metalled for the first fifty miles, was an accomplishment of the late President, who had intended to tie together the Mohammedan north and the pagan south; but the macadam ended as abruptly as his Presidency had done, and the last miles were little more than a track beaten by the feet of travellers for centuries past. In fact, this broken path was one of the great trade routes of the world, because along this trail the slave-masters had driven their luckless captives to the great market at El Desmara where they had been sold and then shipped from Mogalor. We bumped over the punishing surface, making no more than ten miles an hour.

We saw no traffic for a time; then, in a dry watercourse, in sand to the axles, we found an El Desmara taxi which plainly had been heading back to the capital when it left the road. The driver had gone to sleep in a fragment of shade. The passenger was pacing the road, moved by intolerable frustrations.

'They told me there were gazelles,' he shouted at me through the car window. 'They told me there were jackals and wild boar. An ideal place for a safari, they told me. The ibis rose in a white cloud. Well, there's nothing here but a stinking desert.'

'What can we do to help you, Mr Langley?' I asked.

'I mean, it's not as if there were any camels or bedouin.'

'We'll pull the taxi out. There's a winch on the Land Rover.'

'Can you believe it? A desert without any bedouin?'

'There are Tuareg in the eastern region but they won't let you near them. You are right to return to El Desmara.'

'And to cap it all, the officer in charge is a black-arsed nigger who poked me in the navel. Just like that! As though he were ringing a door-bell!'

We wakened the driver and pulled the taxi back on to firm ground. Langley didn't thank us, he had fallen into the silence of lost illusion; he didn't even wave as the taxi started back to the capital.

We continued into the Neban which lay beyond the Oued Skar, the only river in the south. This was the country of Jason's birth, but it was hard to believe a head of state could have his origin in

43

this poor place. The river, empty but for a thread of stagnant water, here followed a convoluted course across the plain. If the division between Arab and Negro could be traced anywhere at all in Africa it was here in the bed of the Skar. In spring the river flooded, bringing a weak growth along the banks which just sustained the tribal Nebanese, but now the plain was dun-coloured and the flat horizon broken only by argan and dwarf palm. The villages we passed were built in mud and reed and lacked even the dignity of names. A vulture hung in the sky.

Fifty minutes more on the dusty road and we entered Dharat, the centre of the Nebanese wilderness. There was little to tempt affection in this God-forgotten place. An old slave station built like a fortress; a dusty square inhabited only by dogs; perhaps a hundred houses, many in ruin; a litter of rags and paper and naked children. In the last century the Arabs had lived here behind a palisade and their agents had raked a small harvest of slaves from the territory; other caravans, journeying north from the Niger, had swelled the numbers available at Dharat and kept stocked the great market at El Desmara.

I shivered, even in the heat of the day. It would not surprise me if affairs in the Neban were developing strangely.

§

The brigade was quartered a mile down the road in a cantonment erected by the French fifty years earlier, but in fact there had been a strong-point here for a century before that. A wall of sun-dried mud, castellated and with embrasures at the corners, surrounded an old kasbah that rose to a proud height above the plain. Huts of wood and asbestos were grouped at the foot of the old fortification. I noticed that within the camp whitewash had been applied and the fire buckets were painted red; there was proof of a discipline lacking elsewhere in the Neban. The sentry at the gate 'presented' his rifle with a ferocity of movement that was almost a parody.

Colonel Nathan met me at his headquarters. I saw him first as he came to the car door extending his hand. He was a powerfully built Negro, his face so black the features had no definition; he moved casually but with great economy like a fighter saving his strength. As far as I could see he was totally confident, in command of himself and his unit — a soldier in the British pattern in one of the damnable places of the world. He wore combat dress and carried a cane.

'Well, this is Dharat, old boy, the arse-end of the nation. I hope you like it.'

We mounted his Land Rover and went on a tour of the Brigade. I had visited many camps in the eye of the sun and there was nothing exceptional about Dharat. Only the walls and battlements of the kasbah gave it distinction. I saw the lines of low-roofed huts, the dust roads receding into mirage, the efforts to compel the growth of grass and shrubs where none would grow. Salutes were flung at us from every direction.

'I make them run about,' Nathan said in his explosive voice. 'I make them scrub and clean. You'll find no litter under the huts or in the wire. A Nebanese soldier will live in his own filth if you let him.'

'How do you prevent it?'

'One up the backside, of course.'

It was all there, the strength, the simplicity, the rough good nature of the professional fighting man. He was like one of the young colonels in our own Parachute Regiment. A black Patton, perhaps.

We dismounted at the parade square where some units were at drill. The formations responded briskly to the cries of the NCOs and the patterns changed with a clean emphasis which was evidence of much disciplinary training. The movements were made in double time, and the men wore harness and pack and carried their arms; a punishing routine in the blaze of the sun; but I could see nothing out of place in a tough unit where there was a need to encourage fitness, to correct a natural indolence, and I doubted if even the most scrupulous commander would have objected. Nathan said, 'I can do it myself, of course. I can outrun, outbox any of these niggers. After training the Nebanese tribesman makes a good fighting man — brave, obedient and not too stupid. He's no bloody good with machinery, so you could never turn this into an armoured brigade, but you couldn't have better infantry in this terrain.'

45

I wondered for what purpose this army was training. Where was the binding sentiment to justify these antics? What love of place could there be in this sour country? What history had these men but that of enslavement?

'I am not frightened of casualties or of criticism,' the Colonel said. 'The brigade could go into action this afternoon.'

In defence of what object, what leadership, what god?

I said, 'I'm sure the President will be pleased with the high state of readiness.'

'The President?' For a space of time Nathan seemed to wonder who that was; his was an autocracy complete in itself. 'Ah, General Khymer. He sends me directives about clothing and ration scales.'

I could not have called this insubordinate; it was simply the judgment of an independent commander at the end of a difficult line of communication.

'I'll show you the rest,' Nathan said.

We drove to the hospital, which was empty. Sickness did not seem to play a part in Nathan's programme. The classrooms, the library were likewise deserted. We stopped next at the detention barracks which occupied a section of the old kasbah. These low rooms at the base of the citadel must always have been a prison, and though the walls had been whitened and tubs of geraniums stood on either side of the entrance it remained a sombre place. The inmates quartered here, perhaps twenty defaulting soldiers from a force of fifteen hundred, not too great a number in a unit of rigorous discipline, leapt to attention as we entered. I asked Nathan what forms of correction he employed.

'Exercise, menial duties, reduced rations, harsh words.'

I could raise no objection; it was the same in every army, a defaulter could expect to clean the latrines, carry the slops and suffer abuse. As we went out Nathan slapped a soldier across the cheek, but it was more in expansive affection than cruelty.

'You need a drink, old boy,' he said to me. 'I'll take you to the mess. Mint and lemon, that'll put you right.'

It would have taken more than mint and lemon to set my mind at rest but Nathan told me he never touched alcohol. I would have preferred it if he had. I was disturbed by austerity coupled with a strong ambition. The mess was bare of comfort; there were no pictures, no trophies, nothing to set this army between an heroic past and a predictable future.

The three battalion commanders were pleasant young Negroes, softly-spoken and with the gentle courtesy of their race; none had the force of the Brigade Commander. I asked Major Sekondi of the first battalion where he had been trained. (In this brigade, all the ranks were inferior by one to the rest of Jason's Army.) He seemed surprised.

'Why, here, of course. The other officers were also locally trained.'

'None of you has been to England?'

'No, sir.'

'Has the brigade served outside the Neban?'

He laughed softly. 'Why would it go outside the Neban?'

I did not like the notion of an army without foreign service, whose officers had been exposed to no outside influences; I could not guess what mis-shapen ideas might take life in such a unit. Major Belawa, to whom I was next introduced, was so shy he barely spoke. He commanded the second battalion. The narrow eyes and pointed chin, the tribal marks slashed into his cheeks like arrows with the heads turned inward, started an uneasy movement in my memory. Like Sekondi, he was very young.

'You come from this region, Major?' I had to say something.

His lips shaped the word 'yes', but he did not speak it.

'You were educated in Dharat?'

'Here in the kasbah.'

'The officers are identified early,' Nathan told me. 'There is no secondary education in Dharat; so we teach them here, where they can do their military training at the same time. They are soldiers from an early age.'

I cannot say what disquieted me. There are military schools in every country.

My next question, to which there could be only one answer in a society of this discipline, I put to Belawa. 'Are any of the officers married?'

Again it was Nathan who replied. 'No, we are not married. We are soldiers; nothing more.'

47

Dinner, served upon bare boards in the mess hall, was frugal enough to pass without comment in a monastery. There were no toasts, no speeches, no antics; we took water in plain glasses and we did not wish long life to the President. A dinner without dedication and almost without laughter did not accord with my idea of regimental life, but these officers found it usual enough.

§

They went quickly to bed after dinner and I was conducted to a bungalow in the officers' compound where I was to spend my nights in Dharat. The verandah opened upon the plain. I sat for an hour watching the light fail and thinking of Nathan's strange command. He was certainly a tough soldier, he compelled a standard of discipline most armies would not endure in peacetime, but I could not so far call him brutal. The brigade was obedient to his rule. They were a race of Mamelukes in an empty land. I knew that an army had to keep its eye upon a nearby star; I knew there had to be promise or romantic illusion that the soldiers might follow; but I could not say what prospect was visible to this Nebanese army. What did Nathan intend to do with his order of celibates?

I did not go to bed. I saw the sky darken until there was no division between the sky and the plain. I felt wretched and at odds with the job I was doing. I had no need to be here; I had no obligation to prop up a military dictator who might at any moment default in his humanity. I could only claim that I still liked Jason and that at present he was the only friend I had.

Plainly I slept, because time had passed and there was moisture in the air which came only after midnight. The bitter taste of the desert lay on my lips. My head was full of crooked dreams. A revolver lay at my feet pointing out into the darkened plain, and somewhere at a distance a man laughed. I was frightened. I had entered a world I did not understand, a place of savage impulse.

Nathan said, from somewhere to my front, 'It's a game we play. It's called Nigger in the Dark. Pick up the weapon and advance towards me.'

I don't know why I obeyed him. I was weakened by the night, and what was left of my strength was no match for Nathan's fierce will. I took up the revolver, applied the safety-catch and walked thirty paces into the desert. With no light showing I quickly lost my bearing and though I strained my eyes to see through the dark I did not catch sight of Nathan. Then I guessed that he was unclothed.

The devil had read my mind. 'No, you won't see me, old son. Who can see a black man in darkest Africa?'

Who indeed? He had merged into the continent until he seemed no more than a watchful intelligence.

'On the other hand, I can see you. A white man cannot vanish even on a starless night in the Neban. That's my advantage. Unfair, you will say? A shit's trick? Well, listen; the odds have been made even. I am unarmed.'

I said, 'Colonel, I'm not in the mood for this sort of thing. What do you want me to do?'

'Shoot the nigger.'

'Don't be idiotic.'

He laughed, the volume of sound making him almost visible. 'How much does it matter, Peter, when you cannot see me? If you hit me I won't make a sound. You won't know if I am alive or dead. To feel pity you must see the wound or hear the cry of pain. That's the beauty of it, soldier: there's darkness enough. So shoot the big nigger! There are six rounds in the weapon.'

'What if I miss with all of them?'

'The steward will bring you a lemon juice.'

I was getting the shape of it. He wanted to show me his strength. More than that, he wanted to test mine. To this strange man strength was a virtue prized above injury or remorse. I had no doubt that my trial was to be as great as his: if I shot wide he would count it as a weakness and I would lose what chance I had of knowing what lay in his mind.

I said, 'A dangerous game, Colonel. I have used a revolver before.'

'No point if you hadn't.'

'I may kill you.'

'So may the scorpions.'

Now I was fully awake, the night air cool upon my cheek, my ear alert for his footfall; I had left the weakness of sleep behind me and my soldier's instinct was in play as if I faced an enemy who wanted my life. And, more, I was angry because I had to obey him. I guessed him to be about twenty-five yards distant, well within the lethal range of the pistol, and moving around me in a circle. He moved silently which was strange in so heavy a man. I knew I was infected by his madness, but I took a rough sight into the darkness and fired. The flash showed me nothing. I had not intended to hit him.

'A wide shot, Peter, and too high. You can do better than that.' His voice had lost its sharpness; he spoke with the soft caressing inflection of the Negro, in the affectionate undertone of the true adversary which perhaps only a soldier can know.

'Damn you,' I said. 'This is madness.'

'The game has no purpose if you throw the shots away, Peter.'

'Why should I take your life?'

'Because you want to.'

'Why should I want to?'

'I do not have to tell you. You know as well as I.'

'Tell me, Nathan.'

'You think me a murderer. You think I take the lives of the innocent. You came here to find the proof of it.'

In this minute, when there was an accord between us as close as friendship, he would tell me some part of the truth. With my finger taking the first pressure, with the foresight moving across the quarter where he had spoken last, I said, 'Sam, how many people have you killed?'

'A number.'

'Why did you do it?'

'I am that kind. Press the trigger, boy; destroy the loathsome Nebanese.'

'There have been executions, haven't there, here in the Neban?'

'I have put people to death. I have asked permission of no one. The remedy is in your hand.'

I held the pistol steady upon the sound of his voice and fired. I do not know if I intended to kill him in punishment of the crimes he had committed. I can only hope I did not. But there was no impact and I heard the bullet striking rock in the far desert.

I said now, in anger, 'What warrant do you hold for the

execution of civilians?'

'The same as yours, old boy; the warrant you hold when you shoot at a naked black. The warrant of Africa. Go on, put an end to wickedness!'

I moved my position and dropped to one knee, so that I could rest my elbow upon it and steady the weapon. For a moment I shared Nathan's enthralment with the game and I listened for the slightest sound that would give me his direction. I had discarded my scruples to the point where I was wholly obedient to him.

'Here, Peter!' he said from a different place in the desert.

I swung in his direction and fired — too wildly, the bullet ripping into the earth ten yards from me, and Nathan laughed in contempt for the shot. My mind was closed upon the world outside this circle of desert.

'Listen, Nathan — listen to me! There was a man who spent his days in prayer. There was a holy man ——'

'Quite so! His name was Kemel al Marabout.'

'What became of him?'

'He was killed.'

'Who killed him?'

'Who do you think? He died from a bayonet thrust.'

I took careful aim at a swelling in the darkness that was surely the naked black man and fired again. The shot must have passed close because his voice came on the line of flight.

'You recognized Belawa, didn't you, Peter. You had seen him before.'

'In the market at El Desmara. Was it you who spoke to me?'

'It may have been.'

'No, it was you. You told me of the holy man. You told me to pursue the guilty.'

'Well, you have done so. And you have three shots left.'

'Three shots to revenge Kemel. Is that the way of it?'

'As you say, Peter.'

I was tiring of the game. My sanity was returning, not fast, but there was already a sickness in my stomach at the way I had been used. I stood up.

'I'm not convinced it was you, Colonel. Maybe you didn't kill Kemel. How can I tell?'

'The proof was there. Who uses a bayonet but a soldier?'

'I need better proof than that.' I fired the remaining shots into the air. 'A crazy game. I regret that I played.'

His voice, his presence was close to me, but I still could not see him.

'Forget it, Peter. Your shooting was near enough.'

§

Nathan met me the following morning wearing clean working dress. He was filled with restless energy. 'Come on! I'll answer your questions; I reckon you've earned that much. But first we'll take a look at the Neban.'

He took me to the kasbah, where we climbed from floor to floor towards the tower. The old fortified building was the work of a Berber family who had farmed here in the early nineteenth century, and the walls were of the same sun-dried brick that had been in use in Africa and Asia since the time of Babylon. We came finally on to the battlemented tower, a hundred feet above the plain. At a great distance to the north the Atlas showed pink and white through the mirage; southward there was nothing but the rough brown landscape of Nathan's homeland. He looked into this country with no affection that I could see.

'The Neban. The end of the world. Look at it, Peter. Not a road, not a telegraph post. It's virgin country filled with some of the most primitive people in Africa. Yes, I have punished the people when it seemed fit. I've set up my table in the villages of the Neban; I've listened to the pleas and delivered my sentence. Sometimes the defendant has got it in the neck, sometimes the plaintiff. As often as not it's been one up the backside for both of them. What would you expect in a place like this?'

I was not going to be won over with these blandishments. I had not liked Iris Mason, nor had I accepted her stories, but I had to make sure that she was wrong. 'I believe there have been other punishments. You told me so yourself. Even under martial law you may not order an execution.'

'Ah, the books! I have not read the books.'

'Colonel, you must know that a sentence of death requires confirmation by the President.'

52

He rolled his lips in and out as if he were tasting this information. 'It is, as you say, a requirement; but, brother, there has to be a President! I shot two people when as far as I know the President was lying on a pile of refuse in El Desmara. There were riots in Dharat. With Khalid gone, the nation went insane; agitators rose out of the ground in an attempt to form a Marxist enclave in the Neban by intimidation and chicanery. They called themselves 'Le Ciel Rouge' and they killed two policemen and the resident administrator. I found the ringleaders, two young Arabs from Sidi-bel-Said, and shot them in the square at Dharat. Some sort of order had to be established. The need to get authority from El Desmara, when the President had been dismembered and the telephone lines taken for fishing tackle, could not be met.'

Le Ciel Rouge I knew to be a Marxist group with pan-Arabist leanings; they had undertaken a few operations in Sidi-bel-Said marked by a sophisticated cruelty. To shoot the ringleaders in the conditions of riot might have been just acceptable; at any rate I did not feel able to argue the point.

Nathan punched me in the shoulder. 'That was it, Peter! Those were my murders. Now I'll show you what happened to the holy man and your inspection of the Neban will be complete. We'll take my car.'

We went down from the tower and drove a mile from the camp to the remains of a village. A signboard told me it was called Rif el Tiba. Six square houses, once white and crenellated, were now in ruin; a well, the remains of a sheep pen, nothing much more. A round stone such as a miller might have used for grinding lay under the branches of an argan tree. Nathan stopped here, his foot upon it.

He said, and his voice had not softened, 'Kemel sat on this stone. Don't ask me why or for how long. He was here in my childhood. The villagers would tell you he had been here a hundred years but fifty would be more likely. As far as I know he was an old Arab who spent his days in prayer. You'll find any number of marabouts sitting under trees and cliffs in the Maghreb. I've no use for holy men, whether Christian or Moslem, nor for the pagan superstitions that pervade the Neban; it's not my thing. But Kemel didn't steal and he talked less rubbish than they usually do.'

I had heard of the maraboutic legends of Morocco which extended south until extinguished by pagan idolatry. A marabout could be anything from a juggler selling magic trinkets to an old bearded sage with a vision of the unities. The place where a marabout once sat, or wept or tied his sandal, could become a place of prayer and pilgrimage.

Nathan's voice thickened. 'Iman or priest, conjuror or djinn, they're all the same to me. The mumbling of prayers is enough to make me sick. But I wished no harm to Kemel al Marabout.'

I looked at the stone, covered now by dust and broken sunlight. I still did not know what had happened to Kemel. Then Nathan answered my question.

'He's under this stone, Peter, six feet deep.'

'Who put him there?'

'A sergeant and two men, at my direction. It might have been better to have destroyed him in fire, in lime.'

'Colonel, I have to know the truth. Kemel is being talked about in El Desmara. Rumours can do no good to you or your command.'

He smiled in recognition of a platitude but the smile was directed away from me into the shadows under the tree. 'Yes, my friend, the rumour will do me harm, as it was intended it should. They'll blacken a man already black. I should have built a pyre and reduced Kemel to ashes and spread them for twenty miles across the desert.' He picked up a tin which had stood beside the millstone and showed it to me. 'See this: herbs, aromatic oils, charms and potions. Rumour with a vengeance! The villagers have not stayed here; they've destroyed their houses and gone rather than stay close to a powerful marabout who may have turned into a fury; they've brought these offerings to calm his temper. Bah! Further afield —'

'Further afield they say that you killed him.'

'Of course. That was inevitable. He was killed with a soldier's weapon.'

'Was it you?'

He did not reply at once; a weaker man would have been swift to deny it. 'I might as well have killed him,' he said at length. 'He

54

stood for the things I disbelieve, things which are the curse of the Neban, and I shall take the blame for it in the end. But in fact I did not kill him.'

'Then who did?'

'Take your pick. The bayonet was in his back.'

'What does that mean?'

'It was not a soldier. To hide yourself when you take a man's life is contemptible and a military man would not have done it.'

'Well?'

'He was killed by someone out of uniform, someone with a contempt for religion, someone who intended to throw the guilt upon me. It was not one of the villagers who revered him and are now terrified of his ghost.'

No, it was not one of the villagers, and I no longer thought it was Nathan. I had a glimpse of the real murderer: a young man, one who did not fear the terrible displeasure of Allah, one whose head was filled with the new brutality and who had a blinding hatred of Nathan and a need to discredit him.

'You are telling me it was Le Ciel Rouge,' I said. 'They wished to blacken you for the execution of their members.'

'Brother, you are right! And from what you tell me they seem to have been successful. Blame the man in uniform; that's always the best line to take. Well, that completes your inspection of the Dharat brigade, Colonel Warfield. I've nothing else to show you.'

§

I spent another night at Dharat but this time I was undisturbed save for the cries of the guard commander when the sentries were changed. Much later I heard the howling of a jackal. Nathan had satisfied himself of my courage but the purpose he had in mind for me he had so far kept to himself. In the morning Hatim came with the car to collect my bags, and I drove with him to Nathan's office where I stopped to say good-bye. I found Nathan with Sekondi but I saw no point in speaking other than frankly.

'Colonel, you have a job for me, I think. I can guess what it is. You instructed me once before.'

'You're bloody right.'

'You want me to intercede with the President. You want him to suppress Le Ciel Rouge.'

He didn't answer that directly. He said, 'You've seen now how things are. The brigade is the only thing worth preserving in the Neban; the rest is so much dust and ignorance. My rule is a tough one, my officers are expected to give their lives to the brigade, but tell me what else would they do? Take Sekondi here.' Nathan kicked him by way of identification, at which the Major came sharply to attention. 'Take Sekondi if you need an example. One generation out of the bush, three years in a mission school, seven years with the brigade; and what have you got?'

It seemed impolite to give an opinion. Sekondi said nothing himself. 'I think you'd better tell me,' I said.

'A good soldier who can obey orders but with the black pit of savagery still yawning beneath him. His culture is that of the Bronze Age.'

I laughed, Sekondi laughed; Nathan punched him in the ribs.

'If a soldier does not accept a challenge,' Nathan continued, facing me squarely, 'he might as well put a pistol to his head. Le Ciel Rouge has challenged the brigade and so far they have got away with it. Boy, I don't want the brigade to be the loser; it would weaken our discipline and the soldiers would slip back into the cess-pit they came from. We can maintain our strength only by showing no weakness. I went to the President and asked him to root out the Marxist shit but I got only vague promises. Then I tried my luck with you in the market. God knows why I should pick on a white expatriate but you had the look of a soldier.'

'What will you do if the President doesn't support you?'

He placed his great hands together and squeezed the air from between them as he might have strangled a moral delinquent. 'I'm looking for the killer and maybe I shall find him.'

'Do you know his name?'

'Not yet, but I shall.'

'I wouldn't act on your own.'

'I'll have to if the President does nothing. I will not see the brigade emasculated.'

Hatim appeared in the door, bored with waiting. We had a long way to travel and the road was poor. I got up to go.

'I've told you the truth,' Nathan said. 'I wouldn't have done so but you gave me proof of your spirit.' He turned back his sleeve and showed me a scarlet weal across the forearm. 'That was near enough, Peter. A straight shot. You were ready to destroy villainy. Now I think you will help me get the real black devil who killed Kemel and tried to blame the soldiers.'

# 6

After my experience of the Neban I was happy enough to return to my bungalow where Ravi had finished with the whitewash. I took a day off from duty and together we cleared the courtyard of weeds, cut back the hydrangeas and brought into control the giant bougainvillea that was covering the walls. The wide low roof supported by arches gave my house a charm and intimacy that was wholly of the sun-soaked regions where I had spent my working life. I hadn't reported to Jason on my return which was perhaps a discourtesy; I wanted a day on my own to rid myself of the taste of the Neban and of the race of soldiers they bred there. I did not think Nathan guilty of murder, but for all that I was disturbed by his rule and the uses to which he might put his army of spartans.

I was reading under the arches, catching the last of the daylight, when I heard a vehicle in the unmade road outside and one of Ravi's children came to tell me it was an important car carrying a soldier. It could only be Jason. I was annoyed at his intrusion and wondered what he could want. The President came into the courtyard looking left and right at the new paint.

'Such industry, my dear Peter! You have created something of beauty. Did you divert yourself in the Neban?'

He was angry, I could tell, that I had not called to see him on my return and he had come alone and unprotected to draw attention to my neglect of him. My own petulance would not let me apologize.

'Mr President, I must suggest you travel with an escort and allow the Army to patrol your route in advance. It would also be sensible if you drove in an unmarked car and didn't wear your uniform.'

58

'Ah, the note of concern! How gratifying. But really I have no fear for my life. The grenade, the bullet, the assassin's knife — it's all the same damnation in the end, and the world will be rid of another tyrant.'

'There is no alternative President, sir.'

'Come now, there are dozens of alternative Presidents. His Highness Suleiman ben Yusoff, the Iman, the sweeper, the lavatory attendant —'

'Your friends will not approve if you take chances.'

'I have no reason to suppose my friends have the smallest regard for me.'

He was pressing the point too far, but I had to apologize. 'I am sorry if I have angered you. I should have come to the Tamran when I got back from Dharat. Now I suggest we go inside where we will not be overlooked. Ravi will bring you a cordial.'

'Water, if you please. I am not accustomed to sweet things.'

He seated himself on the edge of a rattan chair in the living-room and accepted a mineral water. Now he put on the manner of President. 'Tell me how you found things in the Neban, Colonel.'

I said, 'The brigade is in a high state of training and efficiency, but their isolation disturbs me. They are in need of refreshment. I would like to see the brigades rotated.'

He said, in the mincing voice he used when he disagreed with me, 'The racial divisions of the country do not allow me to re-deploy the units. That is something I understand better than you, Colonel. Where would you have me put them? In Kezzan, perhaps?'

'You might try it. Is it impossible?'

His answer followed an oblique course. 'The Kezzan brigade is the oldest in the country. Many of the officers are of royal birth. They hunt in the mountains, they ride in the races. They would not like it in the Nebanese plain.'

'Sir, the Dharat brigade is becoming dangerously self-absorbed. Their loyalties are more to the brigade than to the State. Why not let them carry out the duties of the Kezzan brigade for a while, and send that brigade to get some battle training in the Neban?'

But his mind was adrift in a broad sea. 'The Neban, the Neban! It has the smell of poverty. I would send no one there. Of course, the Nebanese have never submitted to the will of Allah; they much prefer the arts of the witch-doctor.'

I thought of Kemel al Marabout sitting on his millstone under the argan tree and wondered if Jason knew the story of his end.

'There was a man called Kemel——' I began.

'Ah, the Marabout! I remember him from my earliest days. There, under his tree, Allah had authority. Shall I tell you something, Peter? It was from Kemel that I learned the fundamentals of Islam. He told me how the soul can only be cleansed by prayer, fasting and abstinence. I owe my faith to Kemel. A single flame in a dark world. Imagine it!'

'Mr President, I must tell you that Kemel is dead.'

'My friend, you do not understand the maraboutic tradition. The man is a saint; he can never die.'

If this was a device to disregard his murder I did not care for it. 'He was killed brutally,' I said, 'without the smallest mercy.'

'Ah yes! But you must see this with Mohammedan eyes, as part of a larger design. The power of the Marabout is increased by death.'

'That's not a good reason for ignoring his assassin.'

'He is unimportant. A vile agent in a sublime purpose. Perhaps Nathan killed him.'

'It wasn't Nathan, neither was it one of his soldiers. The killing was devised to implicate the Army and was plainly political. Only by finding the man responsible can we do justice to the brigade.'

'Such determination, my dear Colonel! You have been here only two weeks and already you are solving murders. The police, perhaps, have knowledge of the matter.'

'The police have done nothing. You should compel them to take action.'

'Against whom? A ghoul, a nightshade?'

'The group known as Le Ciel Rouge was probably responsible for the murder.'

'It may be so. It has their style. An outbreak of devilry.'

'Will you do this, sir? The brigade must be cleared of blame; they may act violently if the culprit is not found.'

But Jason had no interest in the case; his eyes were drawn closed. 'Peter, you are a soldier, you seek always the practical

60

answer. All, all will be sorted out at the Commanding Officer's orderly room! To every disorder there is a solution, for every sickness there is a medicine. And if a man is drunk or insane, then lock him up in the guard room until he gets better.'

He sank into some mystical reflection of his own. 'We shall never know who killed Kemel, only why. It was a part of his life's purpose, a stage in his development. One day you will understand.'

'I cannot agree that we should do nothing.'

Jason got up to go. He had forgotten Kemel. 'I will open your eyes, Peter. It is a duty of friendship. One day I will take you to Kezzan, which is the centre of our religion. There you will meet the Iman and listen to the voices in the Golden Mosque. And then you will ask yourself which discipline, which solution from the soldier's rule book best fits a country such as this. I shall do just that, my dear instructor! I will take you to Kezzan.'

§

I had not taken Jason seriously, neither I thought had he; he had spoken in a moment of reverie and I imagined he would forget it. But when I went to the palace next day I found that he had issued instructions for a visit to Kezzan, as an expedient linking them with the feast of Haraq Tedj, the saintly founder of the city, which fell in three days' time. He would make an address to the Sultan; he would pay his respects to the Iman; there would be a parade in the Medina. Jason told me he had foreseen this visit for some time, but the Secretariat knew nothing about it and neither did the planning staff. 'Naturally I shall mount a parade,' he said with some affront, when I asked him if the gesture was wise at present. 'You cannot expect the government not to mark Haraq Tedj. I shall attend with the Chief of Staff.'

Well, a decision had been made by the highest authority in the State and the staff must comply. Even Solly was not too disturbed at the suggestion; he asked only that time be set aside for prayers. I made my report on the Dharat brigade to the Officers' Committee, recommending the brigade be rotated for a temporary period with another unit I did not specify. The Committee 'took note', and thanked me.

61

Then I took the staff car down to the office of the Police Commissioner, which was in the old town, and had myself announced to that official. I was out of order by a mile but at this moment, when I did not know if I would continue to serve Jason, I simply didn't care. The murder of Kemel and Jason's high-minded indifference to the crime had dulled my sense of loyalty.

The Commissioner, Sadek Ali, was a shapeless Arab with a lugubrious eye who was said to be only partially corrupt. His uniform was stained with sweat at the armpits. The police had played no part in the re-alignment of power beyond a studied inattentiveness, and they had joined the soldiers only when their rule was established: now they suffered from an inferior moral stature which hampered their operations. The Commissioner showed no surprise at my sudden entrance and did not rise from his desk; his gaze played over me with a disdain for the military which became the more marked when I told him my errand.

Kemel? Yes, he knew of the case. The murder was unsolved. His buttocks sought greater comfort in the chair.

I said, 'I do not think it was a simple demonstration of godlessness. I believe the murder was meant to incriminate the Army.'

Sadek Ali cleared a passage in his throat, I hoped for a statement of opinion but I fancied it was simply because the phlegm was troubling him. 'I cannot tell you who devised the murder, or why. During the military coup there were any number of murders committed for a variety of political or personal reasons. There were soldiers killed, and there were people killed by soldiers.' He lapsed into silence and I controlled my patience as best I could.

'But the Marabout was not killed during the coup. He was killed recently. After the troubles were over in the Dharat region.'

'There is a pattern of killing. Assassination is followed by murder, murder by revenge, revenge by counter revenge. The violence is not yet over.'

'The organization known as Le Ciel Rouge——' I began.

'——is an extremist movement, Marxist in sympathy, which operates from Sidi-bel-Said.' He spoke as if he were quoting from a police memorandum. 'I cannot tell you if they killed Kemel.'

'I would have thought it likely.'

His head revolved slowly towards me until I was fixed in his dull gaze. The soldiers had preceded him in revolution and he did not want to relinquish the theory that they were imperfect. 'It might be so, or it might not. Why would Le Ciel Rouge kill him?'

'To discredit the Army, who had shot two revolutionaries on the first day of the coup.'

Sadek Ali swung his eyes away from me, towards images that pleased him better. 'Our enquiries will continue in Dharat,' he said.

I doubted if they would; I doubted if anyone in the capital was bothered by the killing of Kemel. Yet the sunlight which fell on El Desmara fell alike on the old millstone where the Marabout sat. I did not know why this particular death left so sour a taste in my mouth; these last years had seen worse cruelties; but I could not forget the old holy man who brought a tiny enlightenment to the Neban. I left the Commissioner without thanking him.

§

I returned to the Tamran Palace where Hatim met me in the hall. A man had called to see me. A Christian. He had left his card, which Hatim gave me. The card read ALBERT LANGLEY. LANGLEY'S TOURS. BRIGHTEST AND BEST. In a large impatient hand that seemed to lack practice, Langley had inscribed the name of his hotel and the words 'Grateful if you will assist, as I can't speak Wog and don't seem to be getting anywhere.' I could not resist this honest appeal; I recalled the staff car and drove up through the steep cobbled streets towards Mount Hemron, where Khalid had built a tourist hotel on the brow of the hill. By some oversight of the present administration it was still called the Hotel Khalid.

The fierce African sunlight and a lack of maintenance had already done damage to the old President's dream. The paint was falling, the woodwork had everywhere gone out of shape, the lift went down when I signalled up. Langley occupied a suite on the top floor which opened on the roof garden, and it was here that he met me. I didn't hear his first words; I was mesmerized by the landscape which fell from the snow-capped Atlas to the olive green coastal plain where the haze was in movement.

63

Langley's words forced themselves into my head. 'I called upon the President but he wouldn't see me. I called upon the Chief of Staff but he had a woman in there. I asked when it would be over and they said Wednesday. I mean, it's not as if I hadn't been before; I left my cards with the President the day I arrived.'

I said, 'The President is certainly busy, but I will ask him to see you if you like.'

'I mean to say, you'd think they didn't want intercontinental hotels.'

'Shall I do that, Mr Langley?'

'I'm not very happy about the ibis, mind you. There are supposed to be clouds of ibis. All I saw in the south was a shite-hawk and an African sparrow.'

We were not alone in the roof garden. Behind the vines a girl was moving away from me towards the edge of the roof; she was taking herself beyond earshot so that Langley and I could talk in private. I could see her only in outline but I knew beyond doubt that this was the girl I had seen in the great market and whose shape had stayed in my memory. Then, too, she had been moving away with her face concealed. I closed my eyes to rid myself of the image that in the past had led to disenchantment and misery, but when I opened them again and tried to keep my mind on Langley's frustrations she remained at the corner of my vision, a promise renewed, until I had to turn away from her and look instead across the parapet at the roofs of El Desmara.

Langley said, 'Seven months ago they shot the President and most of his followers and took over the government. I had nothing to do with it, see? I was in Isleworth, see? Khalid was not the squalid ape they said he was but he spent more money than he had. I've no objection to the Army taking over a country if they think they can do better. I know soldiers and I'm not frightened of them. In the Second World War I was a corporal in the Service Corps, right? But they must make the place run; they must treat businessmen properly; they must clear the streets of rubbish and all the hairy freaks who put people off. What's the good of a first-class hotel if there's a double-jointed fakir passing a motion in the portico? I mean, under a Junta or whatever it is, shouldn't there be some cleaning up, some bull? Isn't that what soldiers are for?'

As Langley had not offered me a chair, I sat on the parapet and faced him. He wore shorts and a scarlet shirt from which his stomach obtruded. His large face carried a look of decent outrage. The girl had reached the edge of the roof and turned. I didn't want her to come towards us; I was old, scarred, not in the game; but my eyes kept trying to disengage her shape from the foliage as if the last years had meant nothing at all. I said, 'Mr Langley, what can I do for you?'

Now he remembered that I was his guest. With a note of vexed authority he ran through every luxury a well-stocked hotel could provide: a John Collins, a daiquiri, the juice of the passion fruit. . . . I settled for lager and he spoke the order over the house telephone. Then he sat in front of me, silent, waiting for me to speak. The girl had drawn close to us, so close her shadow fell across the tiles between Langley and me, but I did not look at her, and Langley did not seem to know she was there.

'You were going to tell me, Mr Langley, just what I can do for you.'

It was as if I had touched a nerve which set him in violent motion. He jumped to his feet, crossed the roof to the further rail, and came back with his head lowered. 'You can tell me what's going to happen in this man's country. You can tell me if the left-wing shit are going to take over. I'm not prepared to put money into a tour operation if the country's not well managed. You can't tell me the Saharan Republic doesn't need the money, and the place is not without possibilities, but I have to be sure the Army has got things in hand.'

I searched in my mind for the answer but did not find it. I said carefully, 'The government seems to have reasonable aims but there are divisions in the Army which must weaken its authority. The police are not an effective force. I don't think there's much chance of a left-wing take-over because neither of the races would have the smallest regard for Marxist principles. The revolutionary element is confined to Sidi-bel-Said. Frankly I can't believe the country is less stable than a dozen others where you operate.'

'I see. It's like that. Well . . .' Despite his great commercial power, Langley had a humble side; he seemed to believe the things I had told him better than I did myself. 'And the President?

He is a real strong man, like they say?'

'He's the best man available at present.'

'And he'll sweep up the shit?'

I wasn't sure, and I couldn't quite lie. 'I hope so,' I said.

'I don't like the way things are going. In the south they told me a preacher was killed. Just like that. Ungodly. I was brought up a Unitarian.'

'The government is profoundly Mohammedan,' I said, as much to comfort myself as to reassure the travel operator. 'The Iman has great influence amongst the Arab people.'

'That's better than nothing,' Langley said.

I could no longer ignore the girl standing beside us and I turned towards her. I thought I knew what she would look like. I thought I knew the pitch and inflexion of her voice. It was as if I were to meet someone I had known before, someone tall and darkly beautiful and with whom it had all gone wrong. But in fact this girl smiled without bitterness and the voice when I heard it was the voice of someone else. There was trouble in the eyes, but I could make nothing of that.

'My name is Carol Langley,' she said, as Langley had forgotten to introduce her. She seemed used to this treatment. She spoke in a flat soft voice without class which I found attractive. I rose and took her hand while Langley gazed at the landscape as if the smoke of revolution were rising there.

Carol said, 'My father has been trying to see members of the government. It upsets him to get nowhere.'

'I understand. I will ask the President to see him.'

Langley sat beside us, his mind following a separate path, and for a moment we were alone. I would have said she was thirty. She was tall, dark, the hair pulled back sharply as if in some new determination. With the vision of experience I recognized the shock that lay in the eyes and that had scored the lower eyelids. She too was a casualty of mischance. There was a new sympathy here, an intelligence only lately awakened, a regret for the way she had used the past and a lack of faith in what the present might offer. I asked in my mind: How were you hurt? How did it go wrong? Perhaps the words were audible to her, because now she raised her eyes to the level of mine, as if to test my honesty of

66

purpose, and then dropped them again. She moved three paces away from her father, and I followed her. 'My father has been very good to me,' she said. 'I want him to succeed here. There are — well — reasons why this market is important to him.'

'It might be as well to let the government settle down first. There are problems of leadership. Does he have to start his operations now?'

'I think so — yes.'

'Why?'

'He has a reason. You are a friend of the President, Colonel Warfield?'

'I believe I am. I'm not very clear about anything at the moment. I accepted a job here after the coup, but I don't know if I shall stay.'

She nodded. She was too injured to be critical. I was drawn by the lines of sadness, which are the same as those of pity, which I could see in the corners of her mouth; I was old enough, bruised enough, to find most comfort in a face that was marked. This girl had once been pretty: an accident of chance had left her beautiful.

'Can you arrange a meeting with General Khymer?'

'We are going to Kezzan tomorrow and will be there three days. If you will come there I will find an opportunity of introducing you to the General.'

'To Kezzan? I would like to go to Kezzan.'

'The university dates from the twelfth century,' Langley said, but he wasn't speaking to us. 'The walls are the colour of honey.'

I knew well enough why I had invited them to the old northern city. I wanted to see the girl there, where her presence would give point to a fool's errand.

'The mosque has a dome of pure gold,' Langley continued. Then he looked at me with renewed attention, freed from the vision of lost investment. 'Colonel Warfield, let me introduce you to my daughter.'

'I will see you in Kezzan,' I told him. 'I feel sure the President will be happy to receive you.'

I went down from the roof garden soon afterwards and took the car back to the palace. For the first time I looked with some pleasure upon the old stones of El Desmara and upon the light that was breaking in the dust.

§

The following day we flew to Kezzan in the Presidential aircraft. The de Havilland jet, a part of the extravagant litter left behind by Khalid, was fitted with a cocktail bar and armchairs of deep comfort. It had range and speed enough to reach the resorts of southern Europe which no doubt suited the taste of the former President. Today's ruler had no use for luxury; he sat upright at the cabin table with an open file in front of him. His Highness Suleiman ben Yusoff had sunk into an armchair and now kept his eyes closed. Hatim and the other aides had seats in the rear cabin. We lifted into the bright cloudless sky and beams of sunlight played across the cabin floor.

'Poor Khalid,' said Jason, as he made vicious notes in the file. 'He followed the same course as Caesar; he was seduced by sensual pleasures, and he died. We do him a further injury by using his aircraft.'

I was surprised to hear the old ruler mentioned as usually his name was barred from our conversation, just as it was from the press. Solly opened one eye.

Jason continued happily, rashly, 'He encouraged the worst excesses of Western idleness. He was photographed with his arm round a young white girl, who was without proper clothing.'

Solly grunted and settled himself still further into Khalid's upholstery. 'I do not regret his passing,' he said.

'Neither, of course, do I,' the President said, 'though the manner of it was a trifle abrupt. The flash of a sword in the sunlight, handled by a young officer from a noble house, and Khalid fell to the paving stones! Then — did you know this, Peter? the symbolism of it will not escape you — they separated his head from his body and placed it in a litter basket. It lay there with the dirty paper.'

I had not known how Khalid went but this account did not surprise me. Jason raised his eyes to mine and smiled wickedly. I saw an opening in which I might introduce Langley.

I said, 'Since the death of Khalid, foreign investment has nearly

68

ceased. These matters are nothing to do with me——'

'Indeed not! But in this country there are no terms of reference. The Presidency was nothing to do with *me*.'

'—but I suppose there is a need to encourage the return of business. I'm not an economist——'

'We are all amateurs in the matter of government, my dear Colonel. I am a soldier called to unexpected office when my predecessor was consigned to a refuse bin. We have every need for foreign exchange. Khalid gave all our money to a girl in Cannes.'

'—then you may be prepared to grant an interview to Mr Langley. He is anxious to re-establish tourism. He has been trying to see you.'

'I know, I know! The indomitable Mr Langley whose tours are brightest and best. He would have made a good non-commissioned officer in a transport regiment.'

'It would be wrong, I think, to underestimate his commercial importance.'

Solly spoke in Arabic, with his eyes closed. 'He is a scoundrel, with unclean hands, interested only in dinars.'

The Chief of Staff could not have served my purpose better. Jason's enthusiasm increased in direct proportion to Solly's disapproval. 'Peter, you are correct! The country needs money both in investment and in exchange. Like Mr Langley, I am interested only in dinars. So, admit the admirable man of business. Bring him to see me.'

This was perilous talk within earshot of Solly, who would have let the desert reclaim the orchards and vineyards rather than admit the Infidel with his camera and traveller's cheques. I wondered if I had done Jason harm. He was beaming at me, as if he took delight in walking the high cliff path.

'Bring him to see me, Peter! Throw open the door. Solly will serve intoxicating liquor.'

The Chief of Staff raised his head in solemn offence; then let it fall again. The engine note changed as the pilot lost height towards the airfield at Kezzan. I saw the airbrakes extending on the wing surfaces.

'Solly is not in his best humour,' Jason continued. (How I wished he would stop pricking this man of strange moods!) 'He has had

69

disagreeable information. He has not been on parade since his cadetship many years ago, and now, at this late moment, he finds that he is leading the parade through Kezzan. Of course, for the festival of Haraq Tedj, I was bound to offer the city our most distinguished soldier in the role of parade commander. He will ride a white horse with a gold caparison; he will be a most impressive sight. I shall take the salute supported by the other members of the Officers' Committee.'

So that was what Jason intended. I didn't like it at all. The aristocrat of royal lineage was to make his salute to the Nebanese fellah. It was an exercise in provocation carefully composed and certain to be effective. For the first time I wondered if Jason meant to rule wisely. He grinned at me as if at a fellow conspirator and his satisfaction seemed complete.

We landed a few minutes later at Kezzan and drove to the Hotel Majestique, a masterpiece of the colonial French, where the President and his retinue were to stay. When I had unpacked I went down to Jason's suite in no mood to be circumspect. If he dismissed me, that would be that, and I would have no further obligation to serve his dictatorship. I found him sitting on the edge of an Empire settee looking as though his confidence had suddenly run out.

'Mr President, your appointment of the Chief of Staff to lead the parade is irresponsible. The job belongs to the officer commanding the Kezzan brigade. Solly's place is on the dais beside you. He is bound to be insulted.'

He gave a dull smile. 'That is the truth. He will be insulted.'

'Then why on earth did you make this arrangement?'

'Solly is an ass.'

'So he is; but why provoke him? It can do no good to break the unity of the government at the highest level.'

He nodded without emphasis. 'My friend, you should see the horse! It's a fearful old nag.'

'Sir, my brief is to give you advice on military matters. I'm sure you detailed Solly for this duty in a spirit of playfulness. It's the sort of joke that British officers would enjoy. But it can do you no good to injure Solly's pride and to antagonize the powerful class he belongs to. I urge you to countermand the order. Tell him you were pulling his leg.'

He said distantly, with a fatalism I now suspected to be a dangerous fault, 'I have given the order. I cannot countermand it.'

'Of course you can.'

'Solly would regard it as a weakness.'

'Then at least give him a decent horse to ride.'

He shook his head.

'Why ever not? To mount an Arab on a broken-down horse will be regarded as the most damaging insult of all.'

He sat with rounded shoulders looking at some point in the centre of the floor. 'It will be a strange occasion, Peter. A denouement. Solly must accept the situation or resign.'

'I doubt if he'll do either. You will humiliate not only Solly but the Kezzanis as well.'

He looked at me from the corners of his eyes, as if I had stumbled on an obvious truth. 'So? What if that is true? There are forces here that would destroy me.'

'You cannot improve matters by making a mockery of the parade.'

'Oh, but it will be fun, Peter! Such fun!'

'You will weaken your position, sir. You will weaken the military government.'

'But it is an expedient, a farce! I really do not believe in dictatorship.'

I stood my ground, no matter that it might be hopeless. 'Like it or not, the military government is a fact. I accept that you didn't want to become President, but why destroy your opportunity of putting things straight now that you are?'

He sank back into the melancholy in which I had found him. 'I am sorry, Peter. I cannot reverse the orders I have given. Solly and the Kezzanis must acknowledge my authority. I am their ruler—I, the Nebanese bondsman! There is nothing more to be said.'

I left him then, without acknowledging his presence in the room. I may even have slammed the door. I went in search of Hatim.

71

I had no doubt what my next task must be. With my aide to guide me, I drove to the battalion stables, which were in the military cantonment and close to the mess. In this unit a mount was valued above a harlot or a personal servant and the officers liked to have their horses nearby. The stables were built to a scale, and with an attention to decorative refinement, another regiment would have given to their mess or place of worship; when I entered the arched doorway and saw the fine spread of stalls and boxes I was impressed by the wealth of the first battalion. Here were all the trappings of the old Royal Guard. I had never been in the cavalry but the quality of the Arab horses stabled here would have thrilled even the most dedicated infantryman.

I found the NCO in charge of the stables. I selected a white stallion whose shape would not have been out of place on the pediment of the Parthenon. I told the NCO that no matter what other orders had been given the parade commander was to ride this horse tomorrow: it was the President's private wish. I was exceeding my authority; I might lose Jason's friendship and my job; but I had the impression that he would not mind too much — any more than the luckless soul, pistol in hand, will resent the friend who takes the weapon from him. I said nothing of all this to Hatim and he did not seem much interested.

We drove back to the hotel through the crowded streets. On the eve of the festival all Kezzan was out of doors. I washed, changed, took lunch in my room, and then went out into the city.

# 7

Kezzan, Solly's kingdom. The Sultan's palace, the mosque and the
university lay within a white wall on the crest of the hill. There
had been a city here and some sort of enlightenment when Europe
still laboured in the Dark Ages. Arab scholars had founded the
university before the Renaissance: doctor and sophist had sat in
pious argument under the olive trees while the world about them
had carried their ignorance like a burden. Perhaps I walked for
an hour in the streets; I don't now remember. For years it had
been my greatest pleasure to walk in the cities of Africa and Asia,
to drift with the crowd and listen to the footsteps and voices. With
the failure of love, I had been content to be alone. Now in Kezzan,
where the streets were filled by merchants, by the young male
students from the university, by Arab, Berber and Jew, each with
a motive in life stronger than mine, I had to admit that I was
lonely.

My eyes searched in the crowd for a figure I did not at first put a
name to; only after a while did I confess that I was looking for
Carol Langley. I did not know with what blade she had been
wounded, but clearly it had been sharp, destroying dreams and
replacing them with implacable truth. Needless to say I did not
see her, though I knew she had driven to Kezzan with her father in
the hope of a meeting with the President that evening; I saw only
the nameless faces of the Kezzanis.

When I returned to the hotel I heard that Jason had been
looking for me. His entourage was to be received by the Sultan at
four o'clock and he wished me to attend. The Sultan had no
position in the Republic beyond that of former sovereign, but he
remained titular head of the Arabic-speaking people with great

powers of influence and both Khalid and the military government had shown him respect. He was eighty and said to be senile. In the hall, waiting for the cars, Jason introduced me to the commander of the Kezzan brigade, Rustum ben Yusoff, another son of the Sultan and half-brother of the Chief of Staff. He was a slight young man of remote demeanour with a skin so pale it was almost white; his dark eyes seemed to rest on some motionless object in the far distance. I would have said his mother was French. He looked far too young to have charge of a brigade.

Solly joined us then, in a dark humour. He greeted his half-brother but ignored the President. Jason on the other hand was in a mood for merriment; he spoke to me but in a voice loud enough for the Chief of Staff to hear.

'The old city of Kezzan, Peter. The seat of Kings! Did you know that Solly was born in the palace with fifty slaves to attend him? You will find it different from Dharat, where I was born under a wall with no one in attendance but the crows and a foul-smelling Nebanese midwife.'

Rustum gave a smile so fleeting I would have missed it if I had blinked an eye. 'The President will therefore find the palace a pleasant change of scene,' he said.

Jason turned more closely toward me, as if in greater confidence, saying, 'The strength of the royal house lies in their contempt for those of different origin, and in its very great numbers. His Sharifian Majesty has so many descendants they are in fact a political party. You could call them the party of exalted privilege, elected by stealth in the bedrooms of the harem, confirmed upon graduation from the military academy. The only divisions in the party are the rivalries between the different maternal factions.'

Steeped in some private gloom, Solly said, 'If the President requires a guide in Kezzan, an aide will be found from the brigade. It is easy to become lost in a city so large and complex.'

I wanted to weigh in with some insult of my own, so that the young commander with the icy calm of privilege, and his sour patron, would know that someone in Kezzan supported the President, but I remembered my advisory status and said nothing.

We left for the palace soon afterwards in the Sultan's limousine.

Jason and Solly sat side by side on the back seat, but they did not look a cohesive pair. Jason's eyes were lighted with some private amusement; Solly wore a grimace as if he were deeply troubled in the bowels. I knew the cause of his discomfort. Here in his own city, tomorrow morning, he must make a public acknowledgement of Jason's authority by raising his hand in salute.

§

The Sultan's palace must have covered twenty acres of the hillside. We passed on foot through the outer courts and gardens until we came to the inner palace, which was a high, square, battlemented building. Around these ramparts the young Solly had ridden on Hero's back striking the sentries with a wand. The doorway, like so much in Islam, was conceived in perversity: we entered through a narrow opening in the wall where we could barely walk upright.

His Sharifian Majesty, exalted of God, received us in his audience chamber. This was a high white room with pillars of green marble and a roof of ornate mouldings. The ceiling was so high it provided a home for a dozen exotic birds which flapped between the capitals and scattered their droppings on the carpet. The Sultan was a small hairless man whose white robe seemed too big for him; he looked like a convivial gnome who might display a prankish nature. At the moment of our entry I think he was asleep. He was accompanied by a tall grave figure whom I guessed to be the Iman, 'El Sharif', the descendant and representative of the Prophet and spiritual leader of the people. He was very much awake and regarding us with an interest I found disconcerting.

Invisible to me, an acolyte said, 'Praise be to God!'

We sat on low couches and an attendant brought tea, small wheat loaves and butter and honey. We took the tea and a little of the bread as custom required. The Sultan, who had wakened, meanwhile beamed at us in what might have been pleasure and pride, but my eyes were drawn not by him but by El Sharif who was seated on the Sultan's left and a little to the rear. I saw the long dark face where power had inscribed the lines of arrogant certainty; I saw no mark of charity or of things of the spirit. As a guide in the tortuous places of the world I would have chosen

75

Kemel al Marabout, clothed in rags and sitting on his millstone, rather than this august vicar of God.

After we had taken tea Jason made some sort of formal address to the Sultan which was long and elaborate in the tradition of an Arab-speaking court. I recall his opening: 'Beloved of rich and poor, source of all wisdom, exemplar of nobility—greeting and the blessing of God!' Thereafter, in a flourish of tributes, Allah and the Sultan were commended in about equal parts. Though I watched Jason closely, I saw nothing in his manner to suggest that he spoke in irony; he stood proudly erect, his brow solemn, his eyes resting only upon the Sultan. He ended with a peroration with which any courtier of the old persuasion could have felt satisfied. ' . . . in the dark of the night, in the brilliance of the noon, the wisdom and strength of God sustain you in peace, most excellent Lord Sultan.'

The Sultan had not given his closest attention. 'What did the young man say?' he asked.

Following the address the members of the President's retinue were presented to his Sharifian Majesty. He greeted each of us with a radiant smile but with eyes that did not see us. 'Which boy is President?' he asked.

The Iman received us next. He had long ceased to pay any attention to the Sultan's prattle. He did not shake hands; he gave a short bow that was little more than a nod. He must also have been a member of the Sultan's family: his skin was dark, almost black, but he had the same straight features as Solly and Rustum, and the same imperious presence as all the Sharifian princes. When it was my turn to be presented, I expected only a formal exchange of compliments, but El Sharif drew me to one side. He spoke in Arabic, courteously but with a lack of concern which may have been contrived. 'You will tell me please—I do not understand military things—General Khymer's position in the Army gives him complete control of all units? It is so?'

I said yes, he was Commander-in-Chief.

'And they would respond to his direction?'

'Naturally,' I said; but I felt no conviction.

'It is your duty to give advice to the President? I understand you were his instructor in England and that he values your opinion.'

76

I saw dangers here. I said, 'I give advice on military matters. I am not concerned with the politics of the country. As a stranger and an Unbeliever I must be careful not to exceed my directive.'

I had misjudged El Sharif in supposing he would be satisfied with a formal reply. His contradiction was swift and to the point. 'You cannot separate military from political advice in a country where the Army has power. It is as one! You are in a position to influence our affairs.' He did not require me to reply; he was satisfied with his own opinion, like one who habitually governed by edict. His next words startled me, not only by their directness but because they made it plain he had a fast and accurate intelligence service. 'Yesterday, at the Hotel Khalid, you agreed to sponsor the man Langley, whose interest in the country is not a military one; you undertook to introduce him to the President. Langley is now in Kezzan.'

His criticism was of course justified; I had no brief to support Langley's business interests. I saw the anger in the Iman's eyes and how his nostrils opened in distaste for me and my vulgar purposes. I knew I was speaking to a man of power and intelligence and a certain dark vision, and I was disturbed to find such a leader in the Arab hierarchy. Solly was too stupid to be dangerous; El Sharif was altogether different. I put as bold a face upon it as I could. 'I made arrangements for Langley to meet the President as a courtesy to a foreign visitor. What the President says in response to Langley's ideas is entirely his affair.'

The weakness of the excuse must have been apparent to El Sharif who held up his hand to arrest the untruth. He did not offer his own interpretation of the facts because argument was not his forte. He said only, 'Langley will destroy our society by introducing the refuse of Europe.' At least his words had that meaning; but he was speaking in High Arabic and not the Maghrebi dialect used by the soldiers and a better translation would have been 'the effluent of Christendom'.

Jason came across to where we were standing, recognizing that I was in difficulties. 'Eminence, the hotels in Sidi-bel-Said built by Khalid are empty or incomplete, and we can only recover our capital expenditure if we admit tourists to fill them.'

The Iman's strength lay in his disregard for small matters; he simply averted his eyes from the President.

'In addition, we have an acute shortage of foreign exchange,' Jason went on. 'The country has a history of violence and famine that can only be checked by a prosperous economy.'

'Famine? Violence?' The ·Iman spoke in surprise, as if these misfortunes were of no importance beside the service of God. He held the President in an unbroken stare. 'The hungry, the fearful — they are strengthened in their religion. The others run to fat and unseemly ambition. The oiled body of a man of wealth is offensive in the sight of God.'

'If your Eminence pleases, between poverty and wealth there are several degrees of affluence acceptable, I believe, to our God.'

In Jason there was a disregard for consequences which would have made him superb on the battlefield; the assault upon the defended position would have been well within his talent for war. Rather than respond to provocation, the Iman changed his ground, knowing that a challenge to the spirit was best met with a counter-challenge of greater emotional colour.

'The fabric of the country is being torn apart. In the south the non-Moslems have found a powerful leader who has already raised his hand against the Faith.'

'Eminence? What can you mean?'

'An attack upon a venerable Believer by the Nebanese.'

'There has been no such incident!'

'A foul murder, perpetrated by stealth. A deliberate act of godlessness.'

'If you mean the murder of Kemel al Marabout, the police are investigating the circumstances.'

'It was a soldier's work, performed with a soldier's weapon,' the Iman said coldly. 'There is a Nebanese colonel of great personal authority who must be called to account. As Commander-in-Chief you must take him by the arm ——'

'I have no evidence that Colonel Nathan was involved.'

' — by the throat, if necessary! You must devise the sharpest punishment.'

The Sultan, who had remained seated on his couch, now called across to where we were standing. 'You should make an end to all malcontents, young man. Where you cannot destroy them, you should detach their means of generation. This can be done by a single pass of the dagger.'

Supposing this to be a Sharifian revelation, the hidden acolyte said, 'Praise be to God, who makes straight the path!'

'It can also be accomplished with a short piece of cord,' the Sultan said.

The Iman was not to be diverted from his theme. 'It will fall to the Army to take action against religious dissidents whenever they make an attack upon the Faith. Islam has been a religion-in-arms since the Hegira. The Army must carry the Word, they must convert those who are in doubt or in rebellion; the police have no vision for these things and can deal only with the whore and the pickpocket. It is for this reason that the Army must be responsive to leadership.'

'If the cord is fastened to a long rein, and the rein to a moving horse, there can be little doubt of your displeasure,' said His Majesty the Sultan.

Jason had not the same height as the Iman, neither had he the fierce composure that invested this dictator of the true religion, but as far as I could see he was completely without fear of him. 'The Army is not wholly Moslem, Your Eminence; it contains pagans, Christians and men of no religion but that of self-interest. It is not a religious weapon but our guarantee of national security.' It was well said. He winked at me, but he did not drop his solemn mask.

I had expected the Iman to repeat his demands, but in fact he folded his arms within his robe, bowed briefly in the direction of the Sultan, and left the chamber. Solly and the brigade commander followed him and I felt a sharp relief at their disappearance. In this dispute between the ministers of God and the Republic I had little doubt that Jason had scored the greater number of points, but he had not strengthened his position in Kezzan.

We took our leave of the Sultan who raised his hand in some vague blessing. Before the door had closed behind us I heard him asking, 'Who were those people? What did they want?'

79

§

I met the Langleys at the Majestique that evening and took them to the President's suite. Jason received them with the greatest courtesy; he had beautiful manners when he cared to use them. He apologized for not having been available earlier and paid courtly attention to Carol, whose first visit to the Maghreb this was. Langley's good behaviour, always inclined to slip with me, was securely in place. I couldn't imagine that Jason would welcome an inflow of tourists; but he was a realist in economic matters and would no doubt strike some sort of bargain with Langley. Tourists seldom left the coast; they would explore Sidi-bel-Said to a depth of two or three streets and be satisfied; in my opinion the holy city of Kezzan was in no great danger.

Leaving Langley and the President in consultation, Carol and I went down to the garden. The evening sunlight was falling between the trees and painting every small surface with gold. The garden had been made years ago in French colonial times, but the olives must have been much older than that; so were the cedars and willows. The sculpture so much admired by the French had now turned grey and black and in places had been overcome by the vines, but for all that it was a charming place of fallen pretension; the lizards were as much at home as the hotel guests, and it was possible to wander for half an hour without repeating the same path.

We seemed to have nothing to say. I suppose each of us had desired our next meeting, but now that it had come we did not know what to make of it. I knew she was lonely, because it is easy enough to see one's own problem in another person, and I suspected her disaster had been as great as mine; but I knew nothing else. For the moment it was pleasant just to walk through the broken shadow, claiming no part of each other's past or future, listening to the doves in the trees and the movements of small creatures in the undergrowth.

Once she said, 'General Khymer is a charming man. He does not seem like a dictator.'

'He was the choice of the soldiers following the assassination. He is not a politician.'

'And he played no part in the murder?'

'No.'

'Will he welcome my father's business?'

'I imagine so. The country must have money from abroad.'

'I see. I'm glad. Then Father will leave.'

I asked the question that had always puzzled me about the rich. 'What does it mean to him to succeed? I mean, surely his interests are big enough already?'

She said, 'They are big enough. I didn't want him to come here.'

'He operates through the Mediterranean. In America. In the Far East.'

'He wished to dominate this market. I could not stop him.'

I don't know what guided me, but as we walked between the banks of hydrangeas, where the light was fragmented by the leaves, I was struck by the thought that the Langleys had some connection with the country deeper than the one I knew; perhaps it had come to me from the tone of her voice, which was resigned yet fearful.

I asked, 'What is it that makes this country different from the others?'

She hesitated; her resignation deepened. This girl had grown older as we spoke. 'I should not say. My father is an impulsive man who does not like to be frustrated.'

'I wish you would tell me. There may be dangers.'

'I had a friend who came from here.'

'A friend? Someone who mattered?'

'Yes, he mattered.'

An idea, at first distant, grew in strength until it filled the whole of my mind. Where it came from I could not say; perhaps she had wished me to know the direction of her thought and, in sympathy, my mind had taken the same path.

'Tell me about the man that you knew,' I said.

'I would prefer not to.'

'I believe he was like your father. I believe he was a man of power.'

'Yes, he had power.'

'He enjoyed his life, he played for the highest stakes. . . .'

81

'I suppose so.'

I found it difficult to go further; yet I had to, in a blind obligation to the truth.

'I think he was highly placed in this country.'

'Yes.'

'And luck was not with him.'

'No.'

I did not ask the next question; at that moment I could not bear to hear her reply. I had supposed, like every man who falls in love with an image, which in my case was the image of a girl in a market, that she had no separate life, that she belonged only in the moment of time when I had first seen her. A stupid illusion. I took two paces down a path which led away from her; and then, ashamed of my cowardice, I turned to face her. Her figure was against the glare of the sun and her features were not well drawn.

She was calm. She had the gift of stillness.

'Yes, it was Khalid,' she said.

Khalid. Poor murdered Khalid, who had toured the pleasure spots of Europe until the Army could stand it no more and had killed him. I did not at once ask myself how she came to be here; the fact that she had known the old potentate was enough to occupy my mind. My heart plunged into bitterness.

She was speaking again and I made an effort to follow her. The Langleys came from nowhere, out of the vast anonymity of northern England, out of hard poverty, but her father had made a great deal of money in the tourist industry. He was a big man with something of the force and vulgarity of Khalid. She had been an actress and model—a poorly defined occupation for which she had no gift but that of a striking appearance. She had given no thought to the manner of her life; it had simply happened. She had followed the exotic path from Montreux to Cannes because that was the direction in which people moved, and in Cannes she had met Khalid. He was exciting, extravagant, filled with generous laughter. She had been one of the girls in the sharp sunlight of the Midi with whom the President had spent his last days.

'Tell me something,' I said. I had now to know the truth, no matter how much it hurt me. 'There was a girl with whom Khalid was photographed. The girl he seemed most fond of, to whom he was supposed to have given the nation's treasure. One picture showed them together on the beach and it upset the Moslem order. Was it you?'

'There's no point in bringing back the past.'

'But was it you?'

'Yes. Me. It might have been one of a dozen others.'

So that was it. Carol was the obscene decoration that had so shocked the orthodox they had made an end to their President.

The sun went off the garden and her face became clear to me. She was more beautiful than I had seen her. But I was imprisoned by anger, by my loathing for the world of Khalid.

'You're disappointed, aren't you,' she said.

I could find nothing to say. I was wrapped in private distress—absurdly, of course, because I had no rights in this girl beyond those I had imagined, but the moment when the dream breaks and you are left with a merciless reality is painful enough.

'I am sorry,' she said.

'Forget it. It's nothing to do with me. I shouldn't be angry.'

'I was young. I could remember being poor. The life Khalid led was rich and silly, but it was different. I think I really liked him. When I heard how he died I couldn't believe it. Not at first. It was so violent, so cruel. Then I realized it was true and that I had helped to kill him.'

'What happened then?'

'Nothing much.'

'There was something.'

'I felt wretched and cheap; I was disgusted with myself and for a moment I did not wish to live. I——'

'You don't have to tell me about that.'

'Well, it's over now. Over.'

True enough, an affair ended when one party to it was placed in a refuse canister. I said, 'Look. About me. I saw you for the first time two weeks ago. I've spoken to you only twice. If I've got myself involved, it's my own fault and you don't have to worry about it.'

She smiled, but it did not last. 'If I've upset you, I'm sorry. It's been a bad year for you, too.'

'You knew that?'

'People talk in this country. My father asked about you before he came to your office. If I've made things worse——'

'No, not worse; the sight of you makes things better. But I wasn't ready for the bit about Khalid.'

I was recovering my better mind. I still did not know what Khalid's girl was doing in his country so soon after his murder. I said, 'The faction that killed the President is still in power. You were his friend. Should you be here, where you may be recognized, perhaps harmed?'

'Me? No one remembers the girl in the photograph. She lasts only as long as the newspaper.'

She did not know how bitter was the hatred for Khalid and his followers; she did not know how his friends and associates were shot in the sports arena.

'I think you have been unwise,' I said. 'You may not be safe here.'

She said nothing.

'There are people, forces that reject all Western ideas. General Khymer has been attacked for his decision to reopen the tourist industry and his position is by no means secure. If it were known that your father had a connection with Khalid, the President would be seriously damaged. Surely you can see that?' I spoke roughly, because I didn't want Jason hurt by these political simpletons, and also I suspect because the girl was beautiful and could give me the comfort I needed.

She said obliquely, 'My father is an ambitious man. He is like Khalid.'

'He may endanger the President. General Khymer is not the strong man they claim. He's a regimental officer with no liking for government and his enemies are getting the better of him.' My words were incautious; I did not know what ears were bent in our direction from behind the vines, but I was disturbed by the thought that I had introduced Langley to Jason. In the shuttered mind of the Iman, in Solly's bitter imagination, what visions of treason might spring to life if they knew the President had taken the hand of Khalid's girl and struck a bargain with her father? I drew her towards me so that no one should hear. 'Carol, who besides me knows of your friendship with Khalid? You must tell me.'

'No one, I think. When I was an actress I used another name.'

'Will your father be careful?'

'In this respect, yes.'

'Could he be persuaded to forget his business here and leave the country?'

'No.'

'Not even if the dangers were explained to him?'

'He's a determined man. The market is important to him.'

I saw the concern in her face: she had known political violence, it had passed close to her. She said without bitterness, 'You will think us very silly.'

I did, but I'd been rough enough already. I tried to be as gentle as the subject would allow. 'You will have to be careful, not only for your own sake, but for the President's. His enemies would exaggerate your friendship with Khalid into a conspiracy and then Jason would be in danger. I beg you not to mention even the name of Khalid.'

'I have not done so. I'm not concerned for my own safety, but I don't want to hurt anyone else.'

I still could not see what had driven Langley to come to the country which had dealt so sharply with Carol's patron. I said, feeling my way forward, 'Why did your father find it necessary to expand his business in Khalid's country?' My mind would have given me the reason if I had followed my own thought, but I wanted Carol to tell me.

After a moment she repeated what she had said earlier: 'My father is like Khalid.'

'What does that mean?'

'He has wanted the same things.'

Yes, he was like Khalid, he had the same ambition, he loved the same girl. Langley would succeed where the old President had failed. He would assume the leadership as a commercial dictator and rule with the same authority as Khalid. He would take the Republic into his hand and then he would give it to the same girl. And who could say this raw tycoon in a purple suit could not match the power and generosity of the man who preceded him?

'My father can be rash and impulsive and someone has to control his impatience,' she said. 'That is why I came. I did not want him to get into trouble; I did not want him to go the way of Khalid. I'm not important myself.'

'You may be more important than you think,' I said.

I looked at the girl who was touched with grace and wondered how much she knew of the forces surrounding her. Was it you, lady? I asked. Was it you who brought the country to revolution, for whom the old ruler died, and to whom the country is now to be given? Does it begin and end with you? A shadow lay across her cheek like a veil drawn in modesty but I could believe the origin of the struggle lay here.

We walked back towards the hotel discarding the shadows as we came into the brighter light of the terrace. On a balcony high up the President and Langley were watching us. They seemed in a good humour, as if their business had gone well. They waved when we did.

She said, with the pain of new experience, 'Is it possible my father will succeed?'

'I daresay,' I replied. But in this country I had already lost the power of hope.

# 8

Haraq Tedj, the festival second only to Aid el Kebir, opened at dawn the next day when a cannon was fired from the palace rampart. It marked the end of fasting and vigil. The Kezzanis filled the streets around the citadel where stalls dressed in coloured paper provided the ingredients of festival. Flocks of sheep and goats had been driven into the old town the day before to be penned and sold singly to the householders. Now, in the first hour of the day, they were slaughtered and opened; the alleys were sticky with blood underfoot and walls were stained where the first pulse had struck and dribbled down the whitewash. In the Medina the crowd gathered early.

I went with Jason and Solly to a short meeting at the brigade headquarters. Sadek Ali, the Chief of Police from El Desmara, and the local commissioner, were there; so were the brigade commander and his officers. We were concerned mainly with security, because Jason and the members of the Officers' Committee would be exposed to the crowd when they mounted the saluting base. We heard of the precautions ordered by the police, which included lining the route with armed policemen and the use of plain-clothes men within the crowd; the Army were to employ guards, largely of deterrent value, on the roofs and along the palace wall where it abutted the route. Jason made a good chairman, passing quickly from one subject to the next and permitting only essential discussion. Sadek Ali looked no less mournful than before, but he presented his plans effectively and they were adequate. At the end of the meeting Solly and Rustum left to join the brigade. I could see that Solly was still deeply disturbed by the part assigned to him; his mood was sombre and silent.

From the brigade headquarters we returned to the Majestique, where we had to wait an hour. The other members of the Officers' Committee joined us there. Old General Salam, the senior officer and father of the Republican Army, greeted us kindly. Colonel Abdul Aziz, the large, confident, boisterous officer who had never entertained a political philosophy and didn't intend to start now, was at his most ebullient, telling funny stories in the British tradition; indeed he could have fitted into a county regiment without comment. The last member of the Committee, Captain Ismael, whose inclusion in the circle of power had been a concession to the junior officers, said little. He was something I had not met with in a lifetime of armed service — the officer of extreme political commitment. Such a creature did not exist in the Army I came from where politics outside a vague conservatism were thought to be a disablement of the spirit.

Now General Salam gave us his briefing. 'We will conduct ourselves as officers should. We will show confidence and fellowship, so that the people will feel the country to be in good hands. After the parade the officers may wave to the crowds, but the wave should be consistent with uniform, the hand raised no higher than the shoulder. No matter what task we have taken upon ourselves, we remain soldiers with a loyalty to our customs.'

It was the father of the mess speaking to his juniors, setting the limits of good taste, continuing the old tradition. I cannot remember that we said much more until, half an hour later, we mounted the cars and drove into the Medina.

§

Jason had invited me on to the dais with the members of the Committee and the civil leaders of Kezzan, but I thought it better to decline: I had no business there. Instead I joined the crowd on the opposite side of the road where there were people of all races and one tall European in a canvas suit would excite no attention. Here I saw red-robed tribesmen from the Sahara, Algerian Jews, muleteers from Morocco who still drove this way in spring; I listened to the voices, the clipped Arabic of the Kezzani townspeople which was spoken always at a brisk pace, the Hamitic accent of Rifian Berber, French, Spanish, Hebrew. I moved through the crowd under the palace wall and beside the processional way.

I wished I felt in a better humour. I would have liked to match the cheerfulness of the crowd. Despite the sunlight, for me the scene was hung with shadow. I was angry and hurt. I was angry with Carol for getting mixed up with a man like Khalid. I was angry with myself for supposing her something she was not. To my shame, I was angry with the murdered President whose appetite for vulgarity had led to my present bitterness. I looked for Carol in the crowd but did not see her. She might have closed the wound, but I was as usual alone among strangers whose voices were not addressed to me.

Save one. A hand touched my arm with exaggerated gentleness. I turned swiftly and checked in disappointment. This woman was taller than Carol and her fair hair hung to her waist. She held me at the length of her arm and studied my face in mock enquiry.

'So pale? So drawn? I do believe the military adviser has a problem. Now what can it be?'

This was either guesswork or good intelligence. I managed a smile but it cannot have been well fixed.

'You are appearing in Kezzan, Miss Mason?'

'A few concerts. You will call me Osmani, if you please. Now tell me what is troubling you!'

I would do nothing of the kind. A woman of this kind would gulp other people's miseries like a favourite drink.

'Let me think, let me guess. It is love, is it not? Of course, the Langleys have not been inconspicuous in El Desmara and Kezzan. The girl is beautiful, I agree. Those dark eyes are particularly fascinating. I would not blame you for becoming entranced with her.'

I cursed every informer and Peeping Tom that had kept me in view since I came to the country, but I could not think what use Osmani could have for the information. 'I don't know what stories you have been told, Miss Mason, nor where they came from, but you would be unwise to believe all that you hear in an African city.'

'Yes? Well, you can be sure that I will not embarrass you. I can appreciate your political difficulties.'

I said, 'The help I have given Mr Langley in reaching the President is already widely known. It would not embarrass me any further if the muezzin announced it from the Golden Mosque.'

'Of course, of course. The tourist trade will not appeal to the old-fashioned but the country cannot do without it. I quite understand.'

She had something more to say. She held her head to one side as if asking herself whether she should confide in me. Then she said swiftly, 'Colonel Warfield, you will know that I have travelled in many countries. I try to take my songs where they will do the greatest good. Last year I was in the south of Europe where you find the particular problems of wealth. Believe me, wealth has its own distresses! I was in a hotel in Cannes where by chance Miss Langley was also staying . . .'

She let the words hang in my ear for better effect, but she need not have bothered; she had already found the point where I was unguarded.

'Her companion was a man I had never met but whose face was familiar to me—a cheerful man, who spent his days in laughter . . .'

I felt sick in the stomach, for my own sake and for Jason's. I had not wanted the past given clear detail. I had not wanted to see Carol and Khalid together before my mind's eye. And I did not want Jason hurt by every scandal-monger in the Moslem old guard who would twist this story into fantastic shapes. With her instinct for the sharpest weapon, Osmani continued, 'The girl was very pretty; I could understand Khalid's interest in her. They seemed happy together despite the difference in their ages. Needless to say, I've told no one in this country of what I saw. That wouldn't help matters, would it?'

All around us the crowd was moving. No one seemed interested in the two Europeans standing under the palace wall, but I could not tell if we had been overheard, if one of the figures moving away from us carried the news that Langley's daughter had been the friend of Khalid. I shrugged; perhaps I was shrugging away Jason's leadership. I imagined that her motive was blackmail but I could not guess what price she wanted me to pay.

'What can I do for you, Miss Mason?'

'Now then—I have not asked for your help! Last time I saw you I asked you to report the brutalities of Colonel Nathan and you declined. Why should you suppose that you will help me now?'

Because, dear lady, you can damage the Presidency, I thought; because you can hurt me more than I care to be hurt. 'Nathan committed no atrocities of the sort you described,' I told her. 'He executed two revolutionaries during the change in leadership, but he did not kill the Marabout. That was the work of someone else.'

She wore an indulgent smile as she listened to these platitudes of dictatorship. 'We will not argue. You have your opinion; I have mine. It is not on my own account that I ask for the government's co-operation. Believe me, I seek nothing for myself! I am concerned for the safety of the young people on the coast, those who have rejected traditional cultures and are in search of an alternative society. You will know that there are many of these idealistic young people in Sidi-bel-Said.'

'I have heard of them,' I said.

'They are dears. They ask only to be left alone to follow their instinct for peace.' She looked across my shoulder as if at a world improved; she drew her lids together the better to see the bright prospect. 'I have made my home in Sidi-bel-Said. My doors are open to all who would find a better way. I am privileged to regard them as my family. One boy in particular has become close to me—an Arab youth of great vision. Of course, a conservative society will attempt to destroy new ideas as if they were infections. A visionary becomes an object of suspicion and contempt. My friend has disappeared. I do not know where they have taken him.'

'His name?' I had to pin this down; I was in no mood for fantasies.

'Mahmet ben Daud.'

'Madam, there must be a dozen young men of the same name in Sidi-bel-Said.'

'He is the son of Daud, the corn merchant.'

'How long has he been missing?'

'Two days.'

'Are you suggesting he was taken by the police?'

'Yes; or the soldiers. A youth of imagination and charm.'

91

'What were his politics, his affiliations?'

'None, I am sure. The politics of beauty.'

'And you want me to find him?'

She dropped her head and looked at me through her eyelashes, knowing I had to comply. She spoke in the voice she might have used to woo the friendship of a kitten. 'I am sure you will help me. Mahmet is a fine young man, a poet, whose affection is important to me.'

Very well, I would do it, I had no choice. I would look for the lost poet because Osmani had the means to hurt my patron and me. I said, 'I will try to find your friend, but I can't be certain I will succeed. My powers are not great.'

'I know you will do your best.'

She left me then, walking away through the crowds; she was tall enough for me to see her until she disappeared behind a veil of dust at the end of the Medina. With my bruised mind I tried to look into the future but I saw only danger. Even if I found Mahmet I could not be sure she would remain silent. I wondered if I should tell Jason the whole story but I shrank from this; I would lose his trust and so would the Langleys. Meanwhile I was left with the task of finding a poet in a country where records were incomplete and the individual might vanish when he passed the next corner.

§

I changed my position in the crowd as if I could leave my fears behind me. The Kezzanis, their fast ended, were content to wait idly for whatever entertainments the morning might bring. They did not seem to care if this was provided by a circus or a military Junta of repressive cruelty. I doubted if any of these townsmen knew the names of the Committee or which of them held supreme authority. I found a position under the palace wall where I could see down the length of the processional way. At the side of my vision the great dome of the Golden Mosque was catching the sunlight; the minarets, twice the height of the dome, were reduced in importance by the glare. I shaded my eyes: the President's car was approaching the dais accompanied by motor-cycle police, without whose protection no dictator found himself secure. Jason alighted briskly, followed by the members of the Committee. There were no cheers; the crowd simply stared at the President as he mounted the platform. He lifted his hand in greeting but they did not do the same.

I turned to see Carol beside me. I must have been blind not to have noticed her before.

She said, 'I hope it's all right. I don't want to make things worse.'

For me, she did not make things worse; she laid a balm upon every hurt; but it was none the less stupid for us to be seen together. 'I'm not going to send you away,' I said.

She took that to mean there was nothing wrong and interlaced her fingers with mine. I knew I was already far gone with this girl who had been Khalid's plaything, and I did not know what would come of it, but at the moment I did not care.

'What is it all about?' Carol asked me.

'It's about a mystic eight hundred years dead. It's about a man who wants to humiliate a brother officer. It's about the damnable split between slave and slave-master.'

I couldn't explain; the origins of this fool's parade lay too deeply in the past. I simply stroked the inside of Carol's hand, where for all I knew Khalid had laid his kiss, and waited to see how the farce developed.

Unusually, the ceremony started on time when a regimental band playing western music and marching in fair order took post opposite the dais. The drum major handled his mace with a flourish, revealing his British training, and the musicians were about as good as those of a minor county regiment without a musical tradition. They played two pieces and stood easy.

Then the wide arena before the President's platform filled with Arab boys who danced the Toqtoqa, the music for which came from the northern Maghreb and which was played by a native band sitting cross-legged in the dust. The compulsive rhythm set the crowd in movement. The boys were followed by a troop of Nebanese dancers who performed to a wilder drumbeat. Their dance, the Gnawa, derived from the devil-chasing rituals of the far south, and so keen was the response of the crowd I could not tell where the dancers ended and the onlookers began; the dust

93

rose in a thick orange pall that stung our eyes.

This was the savage energy of the Nebanese which no one who ruled hereabouts could overlook.

I don't know who had planned Jason's pageant this morning but he had been alive to the need for contrast. When the Nebanese dancers ran away into the crowd, their place was taken by women in robes of indigo who knelt in a circle and performed the slow seductive dances of the desert concubines. I had seen the same mesmeric gestures in Arabia where the seated dance, decreed by the tent's low ceiling, had its origin. Jason and the Committee kept to their chairs during the dancing, clapping discreetly when the pieces ended. They looked benevolent enough to satisfy the supporters of military government. Indeed, they looked like a row of toy soldiers identically painted, and it was not possible to believe there could be problems between them.

A young man forcing his way through the crowds towards us proved to be Hatim. 'It is dangerous, is it not, for the President to show himself to the people? There are windows, roof-tops from which he can be observed.' He was not concerned; he was just making amiable conversation. He bowed to Carol with his hand upon his heart.

'There are police in the crowd and soldiers along the palace wall,' I said.

'They could do nothing against a determined man. Madam, you are enjoying the carnival? The President, I notice, displays no fear.'

'I don't think the President is concerned for his safety.'

'It would be as well if he were. Assassination is so easy. It takes only courage and opportunity. The former President was frightened of death; at the end his eyes were filled with terror. See, Miss Langley, these are horsemen from the hills!'

Had she heard? I did not think so.

I had looked forward to the Berber horsemen who rode with a daring equalled only by the Cossacks. They entered the arena from either end, uttering the cries with which they had defended their independence over the centuries. The two groups opened into extended line and faced one another. They were silent, still. Then without a word of command they charged at a gallop, passing in the centre of the arena. How collision was avoided I could not see. The mounted games that followed were violent enough for most tastes and they showed how this strange people, white beyond doubt, had held their own against the Arab tribes for so long; they fought with broadsword and whip and horses and riders went tumbling in the dust. At the end of the games the horsemen joined in a single group and rode at a gallop at the President's platform, halting within feet and firing their rifles in the air.

The sound echoed round the old walls, arresting the voices. Then the crowd broke into a frenzy: it was a moment when violence might have been done.

Carol said excitedly, 'Would they do that for the tourists? Daddy says tourists love being shot.'

'They will shoot anyone if you pay them enough money,' Hatim said. 'The President has been reckless, has he not?'

The horsemen left and the dust settled in the arena. The drum major called his musicians to the 'ready' for the march past of the Kezzan brigade.

'The brigade is not enthusiastic,' said Hatim, who had come from the barracks. 'One officer could not find his sword; another had forgotten on which side the sword is worn. They much prefer hunting wild animals. Only the horses are eager for the parade.'

'Nevertheless, I hope the Chief of Staff is satisfied with the arrangements,' I said.

Hatim spoke in Arabic, as if his message was too grave for a lady's ear. 'The Chief of Staff moves in a dark shadow. He has acid in his stomach, but his bowels are closed. It is as though he were trying to pass a bitter substance from his body but can find no outlet.'

'Does that mean he is satisfied with the arrangements?' Carol asked. 'I don't speak Saharan.'

'My lady, it does not!'

'But it is such a lovely festival!'

'It corrodes his intestines.'

'I see.'

The band now played a set of pieces familiar in the West perhaps ten years ago while the brigade assembled in the narrow

95

streets behind us. I knew from the past that the timing of ceremonial was difficult; when units had to converge upon the processional route from different directions a fault in timing, or a difference in pace, could bring the rear-most unit before the saluting base ahead of the parade commander. I hoped there was one good non-commissioned officer in the brigade. Jason took post at the front of the dais. He at least would give a soldierly performance.

The march past began with a unit of light armoured vehicles which drove down the processional way in excellent order. The officers gave their salutes from the open hatches and Jason responded with matchless precision. The guns followed, trailed behind Land Rovers, the vehicles holding their position and scattering the crowd left and right. I was encouraged: it might not be the disaster I had feared.

An interval—was it three minutes? it seemed as long—separated the vehicles from the soldiers on foot. Perhaps the parade commander followed the route with a reluctant step. I heard a shout from the crowd as the head of the column came into their vision but not into mine, and simultaneously the band played the regimental march: I heard the sound of the column, as familiar as life to the military man, the rhythmic tramp, the cries of the NCOs, sounds which had not failed to draw a crowd since armies began, as the brigade approached along the processional way. The children came first, driven by the column, raising their arms in a parody of the soldiers; then the colour, escorted; then the parade commander, Suleiman ben Yusoff, mounted on a fine white horse and leading the soldiers in obedience to his superior. The first battalion followed, holding the step, marching with something like regimental snap. . . .

I kept my eyes upon Solly. Even mounted on the white stallion he looked a large man, with his stirrups hanging below his horse's belly and his body loose in the saddle. His spirit was sunk in lethargy. In his right hand the bared sword swung left and right as if he had not the will to hold it upright. The horse at least had dignity; its arched neck and sinuous step carried the burden of pomp as the parade commander approached the President's dais where he must offer his salute.

I turned my gaze to the President. He was proudly erect while Solly was fallen in shame. He conducted himself with a confidence which made every movement in the drill-book seem natural to him. I saw him come to attention as the parade commander drew abreast of him and I think he smiled in private humour.

As Solly passed his President, he raised his sword to his lips and let it fall to his side in the customary salute, but the movement was so badly carried out he might have been using the sword to chase a fly from his nose: still, a salute had been given. The President returned the salute smartly. I told myself the moment was over, the son of the royal house had acknowledged the poor boy from the Neban, the slave-master had raised his sword in tribute to the slave. I told myself the whole stupid business could now be forgotten.

The first of the foot soldiers were passing the President, turning their heads towards him. Discipline had been maintained. The military government had not broken. I realized then that I was crushing Carol's hand in mine.

Hatim shrugged his shoulders. 'I had not thought he would salute,' he said.

§

The last of the soldiers had passed. The crowd had closed behind them, following the rearmost file down the Medina. The band had stopped playing and the musicians were ready to march off.

I could not say what happened then. Perhaps it was nothing, just a movement in the crowd by the mosque. A dog had snapped, a child had fallen.

'What was that?' Carol asked. I did not know what echoes of violence were in her mind.

'Nothing, I think.'

I could not be quite certain, though I strained my eyes to see through the curtain of dust left by the soldiers.

'It was nothing,' Hatim said.

Carol said, 'There was something.'

Something. The carnival wasn't over, a scene had still to be played. Jason and the other officers had not left the platform but stood looking towards the mosque, quite still. It may have been my imagination but I fancied there was an arrest of movement, as if for a tenth of a second time was frozen and the long fall of the dust was stopped.

'I wonder what it was,' said Carol.

'Only someone falling down,' Hatim said.

'I heard a sound. Not loud,' said Carol. She spoke with the certainty of fear.

'There was no sound,' I said. 'It was just that the voices stopped.'

'A cry, I think. It was as if — as if——'

'I can't see that it matters,' said Hatim, who wanted to go.

But it did. A minute ago was as remote as yesterday. I had learnt to trust my instinct years ago in Malaya when my regiment faced an invisible enemy that made no sound. I forced my way through the crowd that was still thick by the wall, crossed the processional way and mounted the presidential platform. I went straight to Jason.

'You must leave, sir. At once.'

He looked at me with eyes that might have been amused. 'My dear Peter, this is a ceremonial occasion; the President cannot scuttle like a rabbit.'

'There may be danger. A moment ago something happened in the crowd.'

'It did? What?'

That was my weakness; I did not know. When I put my hand to his elbow he disengaged himself. He was at a high pitch of excitement but his voice was calm.

'You must not concern yourself. What does it matter? A small disturbance, I think. My impression was that someone jumped down from the wall.'

'It was more than that,' I said. Carol had given him a warning; that was her abiding right; and he must accept it.

'And if it was something more, what then, Peter? It would be simply another entertainment for the people of Kezzan.'

'Sir, I urge you to get into the car. If you won't do that, then stand at the back of the platform.'

I spoke in the voice I had used at Eastleigh, when I was his superior, and for a moment I thought he might be moved by the

98

habit of obedience.

Then he compressed his lips, looked at the ground in front of my feet, and said, 'I make my own decisions, Colonel. No authority is greater than mine. You have already played a part in this ceremony that was not open to you. I will complete my obligations before leaving.'

I waited through several vast minutes while Jason said good-bye to the dignitaries on the platform and from the corner of my eye I could see the police accumulating under the wall of the mosque. Some violence, it seemed, had been done, but not to the President. At length the presidential car and the attendant vehicles were brought to the foot of the platform and Jason took his seat. I scrambled into a Land Rover and drove in the procession back to the Majestique. Hatim would have to take care of Carol.

At the hotel, we went up to the President's suite, where Jason and the members of the Officers' Committee took off their swords.

# 9

Colonel Aziz was in expansive mood following the parade.
'Excellent, excellent! A spirited occasion! I congratulate you on
the conception, Mr President. The parade did much to strengthen
your authority.'

'Indeed,' said General Salam, with benign satisfaction. 'The
military government has shown its resolve in public. I was
gratified at the enthusiasm of the people. It was most salutary.'

'But for the incident,' said Captain Ismael, who dwelt in some
darkened habitat of his own.

'Incident? What incident?' Aziz was startled; his cheeks actually
quivered.

'Someone was killed a moment after the parade passed.'

'I beg your pardon? Killed? By whom?'

'I cannot be quite sure.'

'Great heavens!'

'In fact he fell from the wall,' said Jason.

I had not thought that General Salam had noticed the incident,
but now he said, 'The fall was from the minaret. It was directly
within my sight. At first I thought it was a crow, as it seemed to
fly, but afterwards I reflected that it must have been a human
figure.'

'It is a matter of importance,' said Ismael.

'Whatever happened, it was not connected with the
Presidency.' Aziz saw the need to crush the opinion of a junior
officer, to establish a common front. 'The police will make a
report very soon; then everything will be clear.'

Ismael gave a bitter smile, like a gleam upon a dark sea, but he
said nothing more.

100

Salam had reached an age when he perceived no difference between matters great and small. 'The police will know exactly what happened. See, the servants have brought tea and little biscuits.'

We took the tea standing up, as though we were waiting for some important guest. Perhaps we were waiting for the truth. I might have been wrong in supposing there had been a threat to Jason's life but I had to believe the incident, whatever it was, had meaning for us. Jason showed his excitement in the swift movements of his hands. I could not be sure but I think he knew what had happened.

At first we took no notice of Sadek Ali standing in the doorway—stout, sweat-stained, deferential, his was not a figure to command attention in a gathering of soldiers. He was only a policeman whose stature was diminished because he had played no part in the coup. The Chief of Police cast a dull, sour gaze round the members of the Junta and awaited their pleasure. He came with news and they were not concerned.

At length he walked heavily into the centre of the room, bearing his parcel of truth, and addressed himself to General Salam. Salam inclined his head an inch towards Sadek Ali as if towards a servant.

Sadek Ali spoke and the General nodded briefly.

'Gentlemen,' said Salam, with little emphasis, 'the Chief of Police confirms that a man died in the crowd about a minute after the ceremony closed.'

'After a fall,' Jason said. 'A fall from a height.'

Sadek Ali had a policeman's regard for verifiable truth and spoke in the dull colours of fact. 'He had injuries consistent with a fall. They were of a multiple nature.'

'The minaret,' said Jason softly.

'I cannot be sure.'

'It must have been.'

'There are other possibilities. There is a platform at the base of the minaret at a height of fifty-five feet. Formal identification will be difficult.'

'But you know who it was.' It was hardly a question.

'As yet, no.'

101

'Then give an informed guess.'

'I would prefer not.'

'Come now, Commissioner! We will respect your confidence; everyone present is in a position of trust. I must believe you know who the man was.'

Sadek Ali did not care for this cross-examination, but he was none the less a servant of the regime. His shapeless body took on the lines of servitude. 'Mr President, I believe him to have been a young subversive from the coast. One of a number. I cannot be certain of his name.'

Colonel Aziz said abruptly, 'He was attempting assassination, was he not, Commissioner? He was trying to kill the President when he was interrupted?' He had only just thought of the possibility but it had hit him with the force of revelation.

'I rather think not.'

'But it must have been so! The Marxists have been opposed to the military government since the change in the Presidency. He was disturbed, disarmed, flung down by loyalists.' The old soldier's outrage sprang from a generous heart, and he put his arm round Jason's shoulder. 'My dear boy, I'm profoundly relieved at your escape, just as the nation will be relieved.'

For all his lack of seniority Captain Ismael was a veteran of contempt. He looked at Aziz coldly, then turned his eyes to a quarter of the ceiling where truth was better made. 'I suspect it was different,' he said.

'We will leave it to the police to enquire,' Jason said, freeing himself from the General's copious embrace. 'I thank you, Commissioner, for your assistance.'

I knew something had still to be revealed; a moment ago the truth had loomed close to me like a figure I might have recognized had my eyes become accustomed to the darkness, but now it had gone again. Jason knew what it was.

General Salam employed his gentle authority. 'I think it is necessary for us to know if an attempt was made upon the President's life. There could be consequences inside and outside the country.'

'Of course!' bellowed Aziz. 'No one can remain silent. This is monstrous!'

'The man was murdered,' Ismael said. 'There was no attempt upon the President.'

'We have no such evidence,' Jason put in quickly, as ever steering towards the shadows. 'We will not be helped by unsupported opinions of that kind.'

'Murdered? At a presidential ceremony? What an extraordinary time to choose!' Aziz had been pushed to the limits of astonishment and he gaped at Ismael, waiting for further evidence of the world's insanity.

'A ritualistic murder, of the type practised in the south,' Ismael continued.

Jason said, 'I do not see how you can know such a thing, Captain.'

Sadek Ali grunted an endorsement, but Ismael was not to be deterred by disfavour and with a slight increase in the level of his voice, he said, 'We gain nothing by concealment. The government may be damaged by this incident. Plainly it was a savage demonstration by the Nebanese.'

I was ahead of Ismael now. The dark figure which had approached me a moment ago came back to reveal an ugly face. I remembered the dull flat landscape of the Neban, as unlike the Islamic north as anything in Africa—the one place on earth you would have not thought it possible for the flame of inspiration to have burned. Yet it had, in the mind of an old holy man at Dharat, who sat on a millstone under an argan tree and dispensed a wisdom never before heard in that country. There had been no attempt on the President's life that morning; rather there had been an execution, an act of retribution for the murder of a marabout.

Jason was excited, but his words had the calmness of authority. 'Gentlemen, I must ask you to avoid speculation. Nothing is proved. Certainly no attempt was made upon my life, although I think it is fair to say that a challenge to my authority has been made. I suspect the incident was intended as a reproof, the raising of two fingers in the face of authority. The matter will of course be investigated.'

'I suggest we take luncheon,' General Salam said now. 'We will not allow this matter to destroy the harmony of the Officers'

Committee. As ever, we will act as one and overcome the difficulties together.'

That sounded a worthwhile sentiment and together the Committee went downstairs to the dining hall. At that moment they seemed a cohesive body, but they were incomplete. Solly had not returned from the stables. I did not know what had become of him after he had led the parade past the President's dais and delivered his reluctant salute.

§

My name had been called: I sat up with a start. It was quite dark but the door was open to the balcony where moonlight lay, and I supposed the voice to have come from the garden. The day had left my nerves disordered and my heart beat heavily. It came again, my name spoken quietly but jovially from some place near at hand. I got up and moved in the darkness towards the balcony, but I stayed in the shadows at a point where I could look down into the hotel garden without being seen.

'Warfield, old boy—did you enjoy the parade?'

Nathan: I had no doubt of it. Once before he had come by night to find me.

'I know you are there, old son. Come down into the garden. I want to talk to you.'

I wanted to talk with Nathan. There was much that I wanted to ask him. I had a dark robe which I wrapped round me; this time I could see no reason why I should not meet with Nathan on equal terms. I went down a side staircase which led I knew into the garden. I did not know what time it was but there was a dew in the air and the moonlight made a ghost of every tree as I crossed the nearer lawn in search of the Nebanese colonel. This was the same garden in which I had walked with Carol two days ago but in the darkness it was quite different, the olives had grown into strange shapes and the paths led in directions I did not remember. I had no hope of surprising Nathan here.

I paused in a patch of moonlight and said, 'Very well, Colonel, I am here. I will play no games with you tonight. If you want to talk to me, let me see you.'

I could not say from which direction he came but a moment

later he slapped me on the shoulder. 'My dear fellow, we meet again! Sorry to have disturbed your sleep.' His hand was at my elbow and I felt the enormous strength of his arm as he guided me into the shadows. 'A precaution, old boy. What chance would a nigger stand amongst these cavaliers?'

When we had passed into the darkness I took his hand from my arm and turned to him. 'Colonel, listen to me. I'm in no mood for trials of strength. I am the President's friend and I care what happens to him. If you were concerned in the hideous business this morning, you must tell me. It looked like a political murder of an atrocious kind.'

I could see his shape only in outline against the moonlit grass and could not have said what expression he wore.

'Politics? What does a soldier know of politics? What are politics but a meaningless rigmarole that any fighting man will despise. When soldiers turn to politics they lose their sense of action.'

'What you did today was not only a political gesture but as close to mutiny as you can go.'

'Wait, wait! I'm an African, not an Englishman. I come from the arse end of the country. Listen! I care for one thing only. I care for the Dharat brigade.'

'I know. I have seen your unit. But you are still under command.'

'I took men who had been slaves; I gave them a will; I turned them into soldiers. After centuries of slavery men have no power inside themselves and can only gape at action. Men can be made to accept misery and servitude as their lot and to bear the lash across their shoulders. They can be made even to enjoy it. Let me tell you this—there is a religion of pain that has spread through the Neban and which it has been my object to destroy. I put stuffing back into these creatures and taught them to stand upright.' Nathan made a hammer of his fist and drove it into the hollow of his other hand as he moved from one shadow into another. 'This was new, this had not been seen before in Africa . . .'

In this he was wrong but I did not correct him. In the Middle Ages a race of Turkish slaves had freed themselves from bondage and created a warrior caste that ravaged upper and lower Egypt.

105

The Mamelukes had founded a kingdom given to the worship of the military virtues, they had applied a spartan discipline, they had ruled in Egypt for three hundred years until they weakened and were broken by their former masters.

I said, 'Very well. You have created an effective unit. But tell me what happened today.'

He stroked his chin and I heard the rasp of the beard. 'Frankly, old sport, what happened today was between the President and me. A tap on the shoulder, a wink, a reminder of responsibility——'

'But a man was killed!'

'A man? That was a man? No, friend, you can lose the right to be called a man. That was a faggot of evil, a bundle of foul motives in the shape of a man.'

'So you destroyed him.'

'He would have destroyed the Brigade.'

'There are ways, means——'

'Brother, there were none but our own! The police knew the murderer of Kemel but they would not act. They preferred to see the Army carry the blame—they were prepared to go along with Le Ciel Rouge because the Army had left them out of the game of revolution. The President would not act, though I asked him to. To have ignored the challenge would have weakened the brigade.'

'Dear God, man, you are a professional officer with a duty to your Commander-in-Chief. You have behaved brutally, mutinously——'

'Listen, listen. The brutality is in the sunlight, in the rocks. All we had was pride, and that was threatened. The President will need a brigade with an unbroken spirit when these cavaliers decide to make an end to him. We could not ignore Le Ciel Rouge. Besides——'

'Besides what?'

'The President had failed in courage.'

'Who were you to judge? The murder of Kemel was a horrible act, but you were not justified in seeking private vengeance.'

Nathan laughed softly. 'Vengeance? I said nothing about vengeance, son.' He seemed to be giving the matter his whole mind and perhaps ten seconds passed before he spoke again. 'I cared nothing for the holy man. A mumbling, rancid old fool who filled the heads of the Nebanese with notions of immortality. I did not wish him killed, but I would not have taken vengeance for such a life. The injury done to the brigade was another matter. There a failure of will would have started a cancer, a sickness in the unit that would have destroyed it.'

I saw no point in argument. As before in the desert, when I had faced him in the dark, I felt powerless and wretched and like every defeated combatant I took refuge in the law. 'The President will order an enquiry. You are bound to be suspected.'

'He may, he may, but I doubt it. He knows the punishment was just. He knows that it met the demands of the Neban. He knows very well he should have sought out the murderer of Kemel and strangled him with his own hands. Had you heard that the President took his first instruction in religion from that old man?'

I had, because Jason himself had told me. I felt the coldness of the Saharan night that surrounded me like a bad dream. Someone should indeed have sought out Kemel's murderer, but not like this.

There was something as yet unsaid. 'You did not bring me here to tell me your motives, Colonel.'

'What makes you think I had something else to tell you?' He spoke from the shadows on my right; he had changed his position without my knowing it. Then in a voice he had not used before, the voice of a commanding officer giving orders with absolute self-confidence, he said, 'The Kezzan brigade is no good. The officers are effete and they no longer think of themselves as soldiers; they are slovens with loose bowels who have no discipline of any sort. The private soldiers have gone soft. A unit in this condition is open to political manipulation. I believe the Arab hierarchy will use the brigade to dismiss the President, set up an Arab administration and suppress the Nebanese people.'

I remembered my meeting with the Iman and the mastering ambition that had left its mark upon his face, and Nathan's fantasy did not seem unlikely.

'The Pan-Arabist, the anti-militarists, all the riff-raff of the left including Le Ciel Rouge will unite against the Military Government. The soldiers will be turned into demons. The

President will become the devil incarnate. The Iman will be presented as an enlightened ruler whose aim is to rid the country of Fascist tyranny. The Sultan's family, whose brigandage will be forgotten, will return to power and the repression and torment of the Nebanese will continue. There will be a tyranny worse than the soldier's tyranny. Brother, I had to remind the President of his duty.'

I could not have said what I thought, though it was true the Sultans had been rapacious rulers whose brutality had passed into legend; very likely the Sharifian family would exceed the Army in cruelty. These dour aristocrats were about as fitted for popular leadership as the Bourbons.

I stiffened; so did Nathan. We were not alone in the garden. Another figure had joined the moonlit conference, one that moved behind the foliage at the end of the lawns—a tall figure of sour disdain, whose troubled mind would not let him sleep but compelled him to wander in the dark. His Highness Suleiman ben Yusoff, scion of the royal house, had not seen us. The moonlight would have made my presence plain and I joined Nathan in the shadows of the trees. I did not care to meet Solly or to explain my meeting with Nathan, and I could not think what I could say to the President if my nocturnal activities were reported to him. Solly walked an uncertain path as if his thoughts were a great way off. He came to the edge of the lawn and stood looking at the bright dew. I knew very well what burned in his mind. It wasn't the shabby politics of the Republic nor the future of the Sharifian house. It wasn't the antics of the Dharat brigade. These things could not disturb the sleep of an imperious old prince with a conscience that might have been forged in the Dark Ages. No, his disquiet lay deeper than that. He was kept awake by the injury done to his pride when he was obliged to raise his hand in salute to a slave. Now I had no fear that he would see me: he could see nothing but the fierce colours of indignation. He crossed the lawn, leaving haphazard footprints in the dew, and vanished into the further trees.

Nathan was laughing. 'He cannot sleep! The President might as well have kicked him in the groin. By the way, was it you who switched the horses?'

I had nothing more to say to Nathan. I started back towards the hotel, but he caught my arm with a grip so powerful I had to stop.

'Wait, brother! One thing more.'

'Let it be short, then.'

'It will be short. Forget everything else but remember this. When the Kezzanis start calling the President names—when the Sultan's family make their bid for renewed power—take a look at the desert trade routes, ask the brigade what they are doing there. Then tell those who bother with these things what the Iman and his tribe are really like.'

'You'd better say precisely what you mean.'

He laughed again, letting go of my arm. 'Who would believe an ignorant nigger?'

'Your silence will not help the President.'

'I've helped him all I can.'

He was moving away from me into the greater darkness of the trees.

'You can't leave it like that, Colonel.'

'Maybe I'm not certain. Maybe I hope for war. If you don't believe me, then tell them I killed Kemel.'

I heard no more from Nathan that night. I cursed him for his reticence. He was a man who had to set his life against the fall of a card; he had to test and refine his nerve, as he had shown me when he had placed a weapon in my hand and invited me to fire it at his shadow.

I returned to the hotel, chilled by the desert night, and found my way back to bed.

§

We were to return to El Desmara the next morning. After breakfast I managed to speak to Carol on the telephone and to apologize for leaving her in the medina the day before: I told her I would see her in the capital, where she and her father were also returning. I was putting my papers together (I couldn't trust Hatim not to leave something behind) when Jason sent for me. I went to his suite, expecting a rebuke for the change of horses, but in fact he seemed to have forgotten all about it.

He greeted me affably enough, though his eyes were dull.

109

'We've completed our work here, Peter. The Kezzanis have seen their President; they have given him their salute. Now I have only to take my leave of the Sultan. I want you to come to the palace. I don't want you to miss the entertainment.'

I could not guess what entertainment he expected, nor the real reason he wanted me to go with him: later I came to the conclusion he had foreseen the way the morning would go and the need for an independent witness.

We drove to the palace soon afterwards, the members of the Committee following in a second car. Solly was not with them; I had not seen him since our paths crossed in the moonlit garden and I supposed him to be carrying his grievance elsewhere, perhaps walking the streets of his native city careless of his duty to the President. Jason, at any rate, said nothing. At the palace we were shown into the great courtyard where the Sultan was to receive us. This was a beautiful place in anybody's reckoning. A colonnade topped by horseshoe arches surrounded the garden on three sides; on the fourth there was a pavilion of pierced white stone. In the garden fountains played; I saw deodars, almonds and figs, and the air was sweet with the scent of jasmin. The Sultan awaited us in the pavilion with members of his court. I did not see the Iman.

His Sharifian Majesty seemed to be in some distress. In the white robe his tiny frame was taking one painful attitude after another as he shifted his buttocks in search of comfort. 'An aperient,' he explained to us. 'I am gravely hampered.'

Jason ignored the Sultan's affliction and began a formal leave-taking in the approved language of the court. 'May Allah bless our Lord, the Commander of the Faithful, the Exemplar of Nobility——'

'So far there has been no movement,' the Sultan said.

The members of the Officers' Committee stood erect during the eulogy, giving the whole of their attention to the President. Only the Sultan showed an imperfect concentration. When he came to the end of his address, Jason bowed and the entourage did the same. The court servants then brought tea and we were invited to take seats. 'There is wind but no easement,' the Sultan told us earnestly.

I wondered why the Iman was not in attendance; his failure to bid the President good-bye could surely be taken as an offence. Naturally enough Jason said nothing about this notable absentee but Colonel Aziz, whose instinct for a delicate subject was not of the best, broached it roundly. 'His Eminence is indisposed?' he asked, his voice so loud the Sultan could not ignore it.

'His Eminence has an enviable rhythm. I have often told him so. It is a blessing of God . . .'

'But this morning he is unwell?'

'He has sent me a note regretting his absence,' Jason said, which I was sure was untrue.

The Sultan said, 'He is not, of course, at prayer. Neither is it the hour for love-making. I do not know where he is. Oh, the torment!'

'It seems strange to me that El Sharif is not here,' said Aziz in honest bewilderment.

'He was profuse in his apology,' Jason explained.

'I see. It is unusual.'

'I must take my leave, at least briefly,' the Sultan said. 'There is a demon at work in my nether parts.'

'Should we interpret his absence as deliberate offence?' Aziz pursued. 'I mean to say, we are the effective government of the country. The Chief of Staff should also be here. Why, where has His Majesty gone?'

'His Majesty will return after a short recession,' an acolyte said.

§

Later we took our leave, backing with difficulty down the pavilion steps, and a chamberlain led us back through the courtyard towards the entrance. The fountains spilled their waters into ornamental pools and the sound of the falls was a continuing theme in the garden: here was the embodiment of the Arab dream that heaven is loud with the sound of many rivers. Above the gardens the ramparts of the palace still showed their defensive features, battlements that would have concealed a hundred riflemen, and I was reminded of the power and ambition of the sultans. No matter that the present Sultan was an abject clown, the Sharifian family had from this stronghold extended their rule

111

eastward to the Atlas passes and southward to the Skar, and a brutal rule it had been; they had reduced the Berber and Nebanese people to servitude or slavery and sustained themselves by banditry and the enforcement of tribute. Now I could not deny that the tradition of the Sultanate was still alive. His Highness Suleiman ben Yusoff stood blocking our exit from the courtyard, his face dark with anger. At his right side stood his brother, Rustum, Commander of the Kezzan Brigade; at his left was another officer whose name I did not know. Behind him in the shadows of the terrace I saw the figure of El Sharif.

'My dear General, I could not wait for you,' said Jason, showing no surprise at this meeting. 'I have already taken leave of the Sultan.'

Solly did not move, did not speak; in his mind the process of thought seemed to have stopped.

'You will have to let me pass,' Jason said.

I did not know what form the challenge would take. I could only wait, as did the other officers.

At last Solly said, 'What action do you intend against the Dharat brigade? The Colonel is guilty of mutiny.'

'We do not know that the brigade is guilty of anything. Certainly they have not mutinied.'

'They murdered an Arab in the holy city. They chose the most sacred festival in the Islamic calendar. It was provocation of the most deliberate kind.'

In the seclusion of the terrace El Sharif made no movement, but I knew well enough that these words were his and that they had their origin in the darkest part of his mind. The murder meant nothing to him; he planned on a larger scale.

Solly continued, as if in sleep, 'It was a pagan ritual, a foul profanity in the face of Allah. You must punish the brigade with the greatest severity.'

'Come now, Solly, you would not wish me to jump to conclusions. The police have shown me no evidence that the brigade was implicated.'

But Solly had not listened; he could hear only the voice of his own wounded spirit. 'The Nebanese must be proscribed. They are a primitive, godless people. You must disband the brigade and

112

court-martial the officers. Their punishment must be public and salutary.'

'That is an absurd suggestion. Our control of the Neban depends upon the brigade. You would divide our country——'

'Better so than offend our God.'

The effrontery of this remark surprised even Jason, who said nothing for a moment: I think he was already aware that Solly's anger arose as much from private offence as public indignation. 'I suspect, friend, it is not the Nebanese as a whole who have offended you; it is one Nebanese in particular,' he said.

I expected the members of the Committee to intervene but in fact they drew back a pace. Had he been an English officer, old General Salam would surely have used his age and seniority in rank to quieten even those who were his political superiors, but Salam was an Arab of the old stamp who clearly believed there was no arbiter but individual strength in a struggle for leadership. With his liking for blood sports, Aziz gave the same close attention to this conflict as he would have given to a cock-fight. Solly's two companions had plainly been briefed to say nothing; they stood to attention in recognition of a formal occasion.

Solly raised his head, wakened by Jason's words. 'The parade was designed to insult me. It damaged my position in the Army and in the state.'

'Nonsense, Solly. As parade commander you were much admired. Colonel Warfield found you a splendid horse.'

'Such a thing was incompatible with my rank.'

'I do not think so. Every soldier must acknowledge a superior. Every soldier but one, that is.'

'You degraded the Sharifian family. It was a deliberate act.'

'You speak as though the President had no right to your salute.'

There was no answer to that. In military terms Jason was Solly's Commander-in-Chief and entitled to his respect. It was all in the book. Beyond doubt, this was the entertainment Jason had asked me to witness. I could see that Solly was deeply angered, not only by the indignity done to himself but by the manner in which he had been trapped.

General Salam ventured to raise his voice. 'Perhaps we should conclude this matter elsewhere. Here there are servants,

113

gardeners . . .'

'I do not care what passes in the mind of a servant,' Solly said.
Then he used the sharpest blade he could find. 'Even Khalid
would not have ordered me to head the parade.'

'I suggest that is not a proper remark,' said Aziz. 'We do not
speak of the former ruler. You cannot quote the manner of his
Presidency in support of your argument.' He was concerned only
that the conflict should not be spoiled by the use of an illegal
weapon.

Ismael laughed, as if the whole process of succession was no
more than the play of shadows, but there was no mirth in it.

'We cannot conduct a matter of importance, where the
outcome may affect the entire nation, other than in private,' said
Salam.

But the dispute was in being, the conflict joined. It was nothing
to do with me, but as the legality of the Officers' Committee was
in any case open to question I could not see that I was prevented
from giving an opinion. I said, 'There is nothing to decide. The
death of the Arab boy is being investigated and if members of the
Dharat brigade are responsible they will be charged. The parade
was in order. A salute is the universal greeting between soldiers
and implies mutual respect.'

I might as well have kept quiet; no one paid the smallest
attention to this voice from Northern Europe, where such things
were understood.

Solly said, 'I performed the duty given me no matter that it
demeaned me in the city of my birth. I have not been disobedient
of orders no matter that they were conceived maliciously with
ridicule as their purpose. But you have challenged a soldier whose
tradition does not permit him to suffer insult without seeking
redress. I therefore ask for your apology.'

The Iman, standing in the shadows of the colonnade, had not
spoken, but now I saw him nod his head in solemn approval.

Jason dropped his flippant manner. 'I am sorry. As
Commander-in-Chief I cannot give an apology. As you are aware,
to ask for one is an impertinence. You must withdraw the request.'

'I will not do so.'

'Then you are guilty of prejudicial conduct. These officers are witnesses.'

I did not know if I had any influence remaining from our days at Eastleigh, when I had been Solly's instructor; at any rate I said, chancing my arm, 'Better withdraw, Solly. The President is right.'

He paid no more attention to me than to the twittering of the sparrows in the lemon trees. The violence in his nature had closed his mind to caution.

'An apology is necessary if the Military Government is to continue,' he said.

'That is the judgment of a self-important fool,' the President replied. 'Still, if you are prepared to offer your resignation from the Committee, I am prepared to accept it. I will also require your retirement from the Army.'

'I cannot resign; my authority is traditional. I am Caid and Kalifa.'

'You are forgetting that we have abolished hereditary responsibility.'

'The Sultanate is still in being.'

'The Sultanate is no more than a sack of dry bones. The Army alone has power.'

The resources of Solly's mind were at an end. He could only turn to violence. He took a pace forward.

'If you will not apologize, I insist that you fight me. I cannot be humiliated in this manner.'

'My dear chap, you are making yourself ridiculous. The President does not fight to defend his legitimate orders.'

'You must! You must!'

'I entirely decline.'

'Then you are not worthy of your office. You are a menial, a sweeper!'

To give endorsement to his point Solly caught Jason a swinging blow across the mouth which brought us all to silence. The movement was made with savage contempt as a prince might have struck a slave. For a time the only sound in the courtyard was the falling of water in the fountains. Then the Iman, his purpose accomplished, moved away behind the colonnade and disappeared.

Aziz said, 'There can be no further move on either side for the

115

time being.'

General Salam nodded: the conflict had been worked out to a formal conclusion.

Jason spoke next; somehow he had kept control of his voice. 'General, you are suspended from duty. You will return to El Desmara in the company of these officers and there you will be confined to your quarters. Colonel Aziz will succeed you as Chief of Staff until this matter is decided.'

I don't think Solly heard any of this. He was swaying on his feet as if concussed by his own explosion of temper. Salam and Aziz had sense enough to recognize the inevitability of the President's order and they approached Solly, laid their hands upon his arms and escorted him out of the courtyard. Ismael followed them with the two Kezzanis.

Jason looked at me, and smiled without humour. 'There you have it, Peter. I had thought he would kill me.'

'At least things are plain, sir. You were obliged to arrest him.'

'Obliged? Yes, I was obliged to do that. But, as you will have realized, the idea was not mine. Now let us leave the holy city.'

116

# 10

I was glad to be back in El Desmara, which was home to me as far
as I had one. The Military Government might be in disarray, but
for a time I could forget it and enjoy the seclusion of my home. I
could not tell how long I would stay here. If Jason fell, so would I;
if the Military Government was torn to pieces I would be lucky to
get out of the country with my suitcases. But my years of service
had taught me to enjoy each day as it was given, to disregard the
voices raised in fury, to keep hold of what little I had until that too
was lost in the developing storm.

I hoped that some day I would find the words—the honest
words—to describe Jason's Presidency of this strange country. So
far I had only a few pages of notes to tell of the conflicting motives
that divided the leadership. I needed time to fix the images in
words and to decide what was true, but just now I had no notion
where the truth lay. Truth had the imprecision of the clouds; it
changed shape and direction as I watched. I knew only that Jason
had a core of honesty. I knew only that he was a better man than
Solly. Tonight Solly was confined at his home with a military
guard. The terms of his arrest were no doubt as ambiguous as his
future was likely to be; he was in that limbo of disapproval known
best in Arab countries where he might rest for a day or a year
depending on the whim of those in authority.

At sunset the sky burned with a rose-red glare as it mirrored the
desert and in the courtyard of my home the air was infused with
the scent of orange blossom. Carol came to join me, looking more
beautiful than I had seen her, or perhaps she was painted by my
fancy to meet my own need. At any rate she was here, a part of a
familiar scene, a part of the blessing I had been allowed and

which would last as long as the peace continued. I didn't deserve it, but that didn't trouble me now. Ravi had built a grill on the terrace on which we laid kebab sticks; we threw aromatic herbs into the ash; we sat under the white wall as the sunset was overtaken by the warm dark and enjoyed the smell of the wood-smoke and the sharp taste of the meat. Ravi had brought a big-bellied jar from the market filled with the strong young wine that came from the western foothills of the Atlas, and this stout servant stood between us now, a benign third person whose company was the least objectionable in the whole society that I knew. I did not have to share the scruples of the Officers' Committee nor submit to the austerity of Allah; I could nod my appreciation to my own more tolerant God and hold on to each perfect minute in the knowledge that, once lived, it could not be taken away.

Carol remained quiet; she had her own need for peace in Jason's country. But there was a part of her mind that had to revisit the past in obligation to the man who had died.

At any rate she said now, without telling me whom she spoke of, 'He was such a generous man. He was always giving things to the people he liked.'

Yes, Khalid—it could only be Khalid—who gave away the people's sustenance, who might have given her the country had he lived. She was beautiful enough to deserve it. With the wine to help me, I could bear the thought of it now; I could remember without too great a pain how the hands that had squandered the nation's capital had been laid upon this girl's cheek.

'I suppose—I suppose——' she began.

'It would have been quick,' I said. 'He can have felt nothing.'

The old story, which every fighting man knows to be untrue because terror can halt the bullet in flight, seemed to comfort her.

'Was it near here?' she asked me then, urgently.

'It doesn't matter.'

'No, of course not.'

Another lie from the soldier's bag of comfort. The place mattered, his shadow still lay upon it, the dust was still in movement; the violence would not be gone from there until the years had weathered it away.

I said, 'I think you should forget it now.'

118

I had consigned him to the past, which is the proper place for the dead: I had dismissed old Khalid to whatever part of the nether world is occupied by the spendthrift emperors. I believed that the living had an overriding claim to the earth. I believed that Carol could be forgiven for her lapse into the world of vulgar politics. For the first time in months the bundle of rags I carried within me, and which I called my heart, felt near to wholeness as the ash fell in the fire and the darkness became more complete.

§

I had never known how many people lived in my house. The number in the rear quarters seemed to change daily and very likely my evening meal would be served by a stranger. It was the way of the Hindus and it would have been impolite if I had questioned it. I was therefore hardly surprised when, in the light from the kitchen entrance, a small figure I had not seen before joined the familiar figures of Ravi and his wife. Probably it was his sister. I was conscious of a small sympathetic countenance, very dark, but I did not give her my attention. Only after some minutes watching Carol and me did she come forward to the place where we sat.

'Forgive me if I speak to you. . . .'

The voice was soft, sweet, but with the edge of determination. I could not be angered by this diminutive person who had been reluctant to disturb us. Now that I could see her clearly I knew her to be Negro.

'I hope you won't mind me coming into your house. I came to the rear entrance and spoke to your servant.'

Our visitor was clothed in the headcloth and patterned robe worn by West African tribeswomen, but her voice had the accent of education. I invited her to sit down.

'At first I didn't have the courage to speak to you,' she said. She still did not have the courage to look at me. 'I have been several times, only tonight did I knock.'

'I think you'd better tell me who you are,' I said.

She gave a lovely African smile. 'It might be better if I didn't.'

I was inclined to trust her no matter who she might be; even in this country of perilous friendship I could not believe that such a

119

person could be a danger to us.

'Then tell me what I can do for you.'

'Honestly, I don't think there is anything you can do.'

'Are you in danger?'

'I'm not sure. In any case, it doesn't matter. I'm not very important myself.'

The light that burned in the doorway was catching the side of her face. I could see that she was a pretty Negress, perhaps about thirty, with the high cheek-bones and narrow chin that you can see in the royal houses of the Akan. Our visitor was no mere beater of millet, of this I was certain. Her voice was clear, her English exact and with none of the lazy slurring of the West Coast.

She said now, in concession to our vulgar curiosity, 'My name is Helen. I am a graduate of Achimota. I am a Christian.'

I liked her for that. I was sure the earliest Christians had announced their faith with just the same ring of pride.

'And what is it you wish to tell me?' I asked. Carol had meanwhile poured the coffee that Ravi had brought.

She did not answer me precisely; she took another direction. 'I do not know if I should interfere. Perhaps a man should be allowed to do what he wants to do, no matter where it leads him. But if you see him getting into danger . . .' She giggled, as an African does when the subject becomes too close to the heart.

I said, 'This man, is he known to me?'

'Yes.'

'It is the President?'

She nodded. 'Of course, I would not approach him directly. He would not wish me to do that. Besides, what notice would he take of me?'

'It would depend who you are,' I said.

'I have said that I am no one.'

'I find that hard to believe.'

She smiled, but the smile fled past me into the shadows; she still had not looked at me directly. 'I am a teacher, I work in Sidi-bel-Said. My identity is not important.'

'But you are concerned for the President's safety. Are you a friend of his?'

'I have not seen him for more than a year.'

It was Carol who got to the point of it. 'I think you and the President have been close at one time. That's so, isn't it?'

The black girl looked at Carol, I thought gratefully. A secret was shared between them.

'You'd better tell Peter,' Carol said.

'Do you think I should? I don't want to involve him in anything deceitful.'

'I think you must be Jason's sister,' I ventured.

Carol glanced at me with friendly contempt. 'She's his wife, silly. Haven't you any sense?'

I believe I started. I had known Jason for two years and had supposed him to be a celibate dedicated to his profession, following the tradition of Gordon and Kitchener; he had never mentioned a wife to me.

Helen was entirely composed. 'I am the President's wife. I have two children living with me on the coast. They are six and four. Jason and I were married ten years ago in Mogalor.'

'I had no idea,' I said, and no doubt my surprise showed in my face.

'I am sure you had not. In a Mohammedan country wives are not important; it is unlikely he would have mentioned me. In any case, he asked me to live separately when he became President.'

'I don't understand. Why did he do that?'

'As you know, Jason is not wholly Nebanese. When they made him Dictator he felt he had a better chance of holding the two sides of the country together by being identified with neither. Naturally I did what he asked me.'

'But everyone knows where Jason came from.'

'It was what he wanted. As you suggest, it was politically naïve. But he may also have seen the Presidency as an occupation for a celibate, perhaps as some sort of martyrdom.'

'I see — I see.' The images were coming slowly into focus. 'Tell me — I have never known for certain — tell me where Jason came from.'

'He came from a village near Dharat, the son of a Nebanese stall-holder who traded in almonds and dried herbs. His mother was a Berber woman from the Haut Atlas; a mountain woman, I believe of some culture.' Helen paused, as one does when the subject has remained a long time unspoken; then she continued in the same quiet voice. 'She must have been white-skinned as many of the Berbers are. She may even have been beautiful. Certainly Jason resembled his mother. His father died when he was three and his mother left him in the care of an eminent Berber in El Desmara. A man of wisdom, an elder amongst his people. A man whom the Berbers called the Pasha of El Desmara.'

'Helen, Jason told me he was born in a ditch, that he was sold into slavery, that he worked a bellows in an iron-master's forge. . . .'

She gave an affectionate smile as if the sound of these tales was familiar to her. 'Those are metaphors he uses to describe poverty. They are not actually true. His father certainly came from a family that had been in bond to an Arab merchant in Mogalor, and Jason was very poor, but his stories are the work of his imagination.'

'I should have guessed that, perhaps.'

'His patron was a man of much kindness. He had great influence over Jason. He may have still. He gave him his education and sent him to the University of Achimota, where I met him. In those days Jason was anti-militarist. Only later did he find virtue in the soldier's profession.'

'I had supposed Jason to be a soldier from the start.'

'He is ascetic. The restraints of the Army are like those of Islam. I think he found peace in the disciplines of the military life. At any rate, he forgot that he had been opposed to violence and the things that soldiers stand for.'

'And you have been distressed by his dictatorship?'

She paused; then she gave an answer that would no longer be possible in Europe. 'I have faith in the infinite mercy of Jesus.'

I asked her now the question that perhaps only she could answer. 'The leadership is in a state of crisis. It is partly Jason's fault. The attitudes of both the Arabs and the Nebanese are hardening and a determined man is needed. Is it Jason? Can he find the strength to save the country from a struggle over the leadership?'

She spoke carefully, as if she had considered the problem and found no certain answer. 'Jason is very brave. He does not fear for his own safety. And he has a genuine concern for the future of the poor people. At college we were Socialists. I am certain that given time Jason could introduce the reforms that are necessary for the development of the country. But——'

'But what?'

'There is a difficulty.'

'What is that?'

'I do not know that I should tell you.'

'I think you came here to tell me.'

'Very well. Perhaps I did. Jason has decided to die.'

From her lips it did not sound so strange. I urged her to go on.

'Such a thing is not unknown among the Nebanese. A man renounces the gift of life when he sees no point in living. It is a part of their fatalism. Naturally, as a Christian, I cannot accept this rejection of God's gift. I do not suggest that Jason will take his own life but I do not think he will make any attempt to save it.'

She did not have to persuade me of this as I had seen the marks of it in his face, just as I had seen them in the faces of Japanese soldiers after their defeat.

'We must take him out of himself,' Carol said, with all her father's confidence. A tonic, a holiday in Majorca, there was a cure for every malady. It was written in Langley's brochure.

Helen continued, 'The Nebanese are simple people but they know that, if you seek death, it will find you. I am African myself and I share that view.'

So did I; and I could see the forces assembling, occupying the most favourable ground, and I did not know what dispositions Jason would make against them. I said, 'Jason has enemies whose dislike of him is cultural as well as personal, but he has much on his side. The country does not want another violent change in the leadership now that trade is beginning again. He has proposed sensible reforms which will be popular. At least one of the brigades—the best in military terms—will probably support him.'

'And you think these things will make a difference?'

'I don't know, I don't know.' When I thought about it, the future looked about as predictable as a tropical storm. 'They will make a difference if Jason can be persuaded to use his forces wisely.'

'It is your job to advise him?'

'Yes. But he may pay no attention to me.'

'Do you think he will deliberately misuse his authority?'

'Probably not. He's a trained soldier who will follow a rational plan. But in leadership much depends upon the leader's manner. You can throw a battle away by giving the right orders in the wrong voice.'

'I see. It will go like that.' Her next words were spoken with a private conviction so strong I had to share it. 'There are terrible people in the country. They are without mercy. They will take some violent action against the Military Government.'

'Who are they, Helen?'

A figure was passing the courtyard gate, it seemed no more than a tired old woman, but one could not tell if her ear was alert for the sound of our voices. Helen looked into the house, suggesting we go in. We got up and went into the small living room where I sat with Helen on the settee and Carol brought close one of the stools.

Helen said slowly, calmly, 'You will understand that I am opposed to the Junta. It is a repressive regime that came to power violently and has no legal basis. But I do not wish to see Jason killed. That is why I came to see you—to save his life, if that is possible.'

'You must tell me who wants to take it.'

'There is a group of young people in Sidi-bel-Said who call themselves Marxists. They say they have a dream—but in fact their dream is of violent death, for themselves as well as for others. They are rich young people from the merchant class; they have become bored with schooling. As a teacher, I have knowledge of them, I have heard what they say. Of course, they have always been passionately opposed to the Junta.'

'You mean Le Ciel Rouge.'

'That is the name they use.'

'And they plan some form of violence? Of what type?'

'I cannot be sure. It will be designed to attract the world's attention. Last night someone spoke under my window. No, that's not strange, it has happened many times before. Whoever it was told me the soldiers had executed a young revolutionary at a festival in Kezzan and that the soldiers would be required to account for it. There will be a flamboyant gesture of some kind.'

I said, 'The fact that the revolutionary was guilty of a hideous crime against a marabout would not dissuade them.'

'I am afraid not.'

'Nor that the President was not a party to his murder.'

'No. To Le Ciel Rouge the soldiers are not people but symbols of Fascism. In their uniform they are all alike. That is, all of them but for the officer who opposed the killing, who turned upon the Junta, who struck the President's face——'

'Oh no! Not that! They can't make a hero out of General Yusoff. His motives were personal. He's a venomous scoundrel who would never appeal to Le Ciel Rouge.'

'They have marked him for heroism, just as they have marked Jason for villainy.'

'But he would have no more use for Marxism than he would for a creeping pestilence!'

'It makes no difference. He will be what they want him to be.'

'Helen, Helen, is the truth always turned inside out? What do you want me to do?'

'I want you to persuade Jason to take care.'

'You didn't come simply to ask me that. I will do it, of course——'

'Very soon he may have to take refuge outside the country.'

'He may enforce his leadership. It may not come to that.'

'Is that what you really believe, Colonel?'

'I don't know what I believe.'

'I want you to persuade him to go when you think he will lose his life if he stays. Will you do that? Can I count on you?'

I hesitated to say yes: I had come here to give the President military advice, not to secure his exit from the scene, and I doubted if he would leave the country even if the mortar shells were falling on the Tamran Palace. I said, 'I will tell the President when I think his position is hopeless. But I cannot guarantee that he will leave the country.'

'No one can do that. Now tell me this—is there anywhere he can go, anyone that will help him?'

In fact, I had thought this one out already, I suppose accepting that I might finally have to help Jason over the border and find it imperative to go in that direction myself. We had one strong card which I would play in the last round. Jason was a graduate of Eastleigh. There were presidents, princes and the commanders of armies throughout Africa and Asia who acknowledged him as a fellow student and who might be disposed to save his life if not his dictatorship. General Kitonga was Chief of Staff in the most powerful military state in West Africa. Air Marshal Abdullah ('Trigger' Abdullah) commanded an Air Force in an adjacent country; Suradin Khan and 'Dicky' Almena were the leaders of their countries: and all were Pelicans, as we called the graduates of the College. I thought it likely they would provide an aircraft, allow staging and over-flight, and that one at least would give asylum to the refugee dictator who shared their military fellowship.

'I think there are those who will help him,' I said cautiously. I did not want to raise her hopes too high.

'And you will speak to them when the time comes?'

'I will.'

'It may not be necessary, of course. Jason may choose to give his life. But I have done what I can.'

§

Helen said she must go. I did not like to see her pass unescorted through the streets at night but she told me she would be safe. Naturally enough, she did not want Jason to know she had seen me, as he would not approve a woman's interference in the matter of his safety. She did not know if she had been watched in El Desmara.

I took her to the gate. There was no one in the street outside but I could hear footsteps at a distance; probably it was nothing. I took her hand. At this moment she was the one person in Jason's country for whom I had sympathy. There was a question in my mind I had not thought to ask before.

'Who will tell me the name of the boy who was killed?'

'I don't know. I'm not sure. How much does it matter?'

'It may matter a great deal.'

'Le Ciel Rouge hide their identities. They are young, they are

126

handsome, they are all alike.'

I said, feeling my way, 'The police will not say his name. They have reasons of their own for not wanting to serve the Presidency. And maybe they really don't know it.'

I had forgotten I still held her hand. Now she withdrew it calmly. 'Can the soldiers not tell you his name?'

'Colonel Nathan may know it, but he will say nothing.'

She said, as if reading from a secret part of her memory, 'There is a man in El Desmara who perhaps has the means to find out.'

'Take me to him, Helen. Jason's safety is important to us both.'

I cannot be certain which way we went through the streets of the old city that night — Helen, Carol and I; I remember only the labyrinth of alleys. In El Desmara trade continued until after midnight and the streets were still filled with people. We passed through the wall at the eastern gate, where the path turned at right angles; here the defenders of the town would have halted the cavalry and caught them in the flank with their cannon. Inside the wall we were in the quarter of the cloth and leather workers. I looked into one lighted interior after another where each scene — the tailor with his needle, the saddler with his tree — was etched so sharply I seem to remember it now. We took with us a following of beggars and children whose hands tugged at our clothing. Soon I did not know which way we were heading; Carol and I simply followed Helen as she turned left and right, taking us to the man who would give me the name I sought.

Finally we stopped at a doorway in a wall which was no different from any other door we had passed but for the elaborate brass fixtures. We beat upon it with our hands but we might as well have knocked at a tomb. The beggars had halted with us and I felt a military man's unease at their encirclement. I kicked at the door and heard the dull echoes inside. I do not know how long we stood there while the harassment from the beggars continued and the house remained closed to us. At last, to my great relief, we heard the bolts being drawn back as someone responded to our knock.

An old man in a threadbare robe admitted us into the dark interior, which had the chill of a windowless building. When the door closed behind us, silencing the voices outside, I could see

127

nothing at all and I could not guess where we were: this might be a
house of wealth or of abject poverty. I took Carol's hand and
followed the footfall of our guide as he led the way forward. We
were walking upon tiles and the resonance of our steps told me we
were in some large vestibule. I guessed then that Helen's
informant was a man of substance.

'Who lives here?' I asked her. 'What is his name?'

'He may tell you,' Helen said. 'He may not. It is for him to
decide.'

A further door, a shaft of light across the floor, and we entered
an arched hall lit by kerosene lamps. I was astonished at the size of
the place. The walls were covered in plaster mouldings done God
knows how long ago and the ceiling was so high it disappeared
into shadow. We were taken up a staircase so narrow I had to
incline my shoulders, and at the top we entered a small chamber,
where there were narrow windows covered by wrought iron and
the night sky gave a faint illumination. Our guide lighted a lamp
and invited us to sit on leather cushions. The greater light filled
out the old lined face of our attendant, which I saw to have the
fine features of the Berber people; there was distinction here, the
grave contemplation of the scholar; and with a stilling of the heart
I realized this was the master of the house who had himself come
to the door and seen to our comfort.

I took a chance and spoke to him in Arabic. 'Master, you are
kind. It is late in the night for strangers to call.'

'My house is yours.'

This courtesy belonged to an earlier age, before the massacres
of Munich and Lod; I had heard the same words from a Libyan
prince and a Qatari sweeper.

To conclude the courtesy, I said, 'Peace to this house!'

A Berber girl, clothed in the brilliant colours the race
preferred, who might have been our host's grand-daughter, now
brought black coffee which we took in silence, our host declining
to ask what had brought us until we were refreshed.

At length Helen said, in the formal Arabic used by the
instructed, 'My friend, we are concerned for the safety of the
President. These guests to your house, who are Nazarene like
myself, do not wish to see him harmed.'

128

Our host nodded. He did not suggest that such things were in the hands of Allah, as an Arab might have done. The Berbers had been Mohammedan for centuries, but they did not share the deeper fatalisms of Islam; they had survived in the mountains of the Maghreb, challenging their pre-destined end; and this old man was disposed to think that a man's life could be saved by an effort of the will. He said now, 'I do not care for the rule of the soldiers, but I will help you save the President's life if I can. There are ways, means . . .'

'What ways, Master?' I asked. As an English officer, I had also to believe that the will of Allah could be thwarted.

'I have some influence in El Desmara and the mountain villages. The Berber people have not forgotten that the President shares their blood and they will help him if there is need.'

'I think the President may already be in need of help.'

'Tell me in which way.'

'He has enemies amongst the Arab people, but more particularly I am concerned with another enemy, one who can also do him harm.'

'And that is whom, my friend?'

'A stranger, a Nazarene.'

'What do you wish me to do?'

I was afraid to ask the question; I was afraid of what the answer might be. I said, 'Two days ago in Kezzan a young Arab was killed by the soldiers, when he was thrown alive from the mosque.'

The old man dropped his eyes, which told me he had heard the story.

'Master, I need to know the name of the man who died.'

He did not move for some time; then without further word he got up and left the room. I could guess what happened next. He spoke to a servant, telling him to go into the street, into the market, to find the water-carrier with the cast in his eye, who would lead him to a seller of hides, who knew a man, who knew another. . . . In a while our host came back and invited us to relax while the enquiry took place in the night outside. I do not remember that we spoke much: the hospitality of the house included the gift of silence, in which a guest could follow his thoughts without the intrusion of voices, but at that moment I

129

could not enjoy the company of my own thoughts.

Once Carol pressed my arm. 'What's happening?' she whispered.

'Just getting some information. It won't be long.'

'Do you know who the old man is?'

'I think so. I will tell you later.'

I was grateful she did not speak Arabic. I did not want her to hear what came next.

Perhaps we waited half an hour until, at a footstep outside, the old man left us and I heard voices at the head of the stair. He returned, he looked at us kindly; he could not know how much hung upon his next words.

'He was a young man of privilege, of wealth ——'

I had thought so: he had been described to me before.

'—who was given to the making of verses.'

I said nothing. I was stunned by the perfect pattern that violence always made.

'He lived in Sidi-bel-Said, one of three brothers. He was the son of Daud the corn factor and his name was Mahmet.'

So there it was: I had found Osmani's poet. His broken body had lain at the foot of the minaret where Nathan had thrown it. Osmani had wanted him returned to her, and she had charged me with finding him, but all I could offer her was the news of his violent death at the hands of the soldiers.

I suppose my face showed my dismay, for now the old man said, 'I offer you such apology as I can for being the cause of your distress.'

'My distress is for others. The man himself was not deserving of pity.'

'It was so? It is not said—it is not known—why the young man died.'

It would serve Jason not at all if Mahmet ben Daud, the young revolutionary poet, became a martyr. Accordingly I said, 'Master, you recall a Marabout named Kemel who taught a knowledge of Allah to the Nebanese.'

'I recall him well. An abiding flame, which death has not put out.'

'I believe the son of Daud to have taken the life of Kemel.'

130

He was too familiar with the ways of violence to be much surprised, but he looked at me closely. 'He was said to be a youth of great beauty — beautiful in manner, in the ways of his mind. Is it conceivable he could have taken the life of a holy man?'

'It is barely conceivable, but it happened. You will know, you will have seen how the spirit of violence can touch young people like an infection. They call it war, revolution — they will find words to give it a moral purpose — but really it is just the violence of their natures. These young people are dangerous, Master. Their beauty lies upon them like a mask.'

He nodded gravely; he had taken my point. But his next words showed me the quality of his mind. 'Mahmet's life was taken violently. It is difficult to distinguish between one killing and the other.'

I could only fall back upon man's oldest excuse. 'The first blow is more guilty than the second, Master.'

He did not answer this, letting the silence offer its own contradiction. An Arab would have seen nothing wrong in retribution. Then he said, 'You see a danger to the President in this exchange of lives? There is one who would use the incident to harm him?'

'I believe so. A lady who was enamoured of Mahmet could do him a great injury.'

'And the weapon that lies in her hand is one that she might use?'

'I cannot be sure, but I think the temptation will be one she cannot resist.'

'Then tell me how I can help!'

'My lord, I have not been told your name, but I believe you to be the Pasha of El Desmara.'

He bowed to me then. 'My name is Abdul Haq. The Berber people sometimes call me El Pasha. I was Jason's patron when he was a child, and I have offered him my help in more recent years.'

'I know it, Master. And I believe that Jason holds you in affection as if you were his father. Some time — I cannot say when — it may be necessary for him to leave the country if his life is to be saved. When the moment comes, Madame Khymer and I may ask you to use your authority with the President to persuade him to go. He will not wish to, but the voice of El Pasha, whom he

131

reveres, might persuade him where others cannot.'

Helen raised her eyes to me, I think thankfully, and she got up from where she sat and kissed the Pasha's hand, in silent endorsement of what I had said; and Abdul Haq, himself saying nothing, nodded in what I knew to be a promise that he would come to our aid when Jason's life was threatened, as surely it would be.

As we rose to leave, Carol said, 'He gave you his promise, didn't he? What did it mean?'

'He is the President's friend. He will give his help if Jason should get into trouble. Nothing more.'

She wasn't curious, she didn't press me—she couldn't know what damage would be done, to Jason and to us all, if Osmani said what she knew about Carol and Khalid. But, stung by the death of Mahmet, could we count upon her silence?

Abdul Haq took us back to the street, where now the moonlight lay and no one was about but a sleeping beggar. We thanked the Pasha for his kindness and started back through the streets towards my home.

§

I had to insist that Helen stayed at the bungalow for what was left of the night, and I gave her my room. Until dawn, there would be no way of getting Carol back to her hotel; so she and I took blankets into the courtyard and wrapped ourselves up in the garden chairs. God knows what Ravi thought about it all.

I must have been tired; I think I slept. I was aware of the chill of the desert night, the brilliance of the stars. I listened to Carol's quiet breath and from somewhere outside the garden the sound of a donkey coughing. For an hour I stayed awake watching the stars disappear behind the wall. I didn't know what would happen, but I was happier than I had been at any time since I came to Jason's country. I had friends, I was in love.

Then I slept until the dew woke me. There was a white light in the sky and from every tower in El Desmara came the call to the faithful. I got up, together with the townsmen. I had a lot to do.

# 11

Jason sent for me as soon as I reached the Tamran Palace that morning. He was brisk and cheerful, showing how well his British instructors had taught him; in the tradition that shaped us both one may not show a sad face when the heavens are falling.

'Greetings, old boy. Take the weight off your feet. What an idle soldier you are! I have been here since six o'clock using the telephone.'

It was true Jason kept the most punishing hours which must have been trying for his staff. His desk was clear of paper and you would not have thought the country he governed had any real problems.

'I will tell you something to amuse you, Peter. The Kezzan brigade will not answer the telephone. A big laugh! My aides have rung the headquarters, the mess, the laundry; they can raise no one higher in rank than a corporal.'

If the brigade was unresponsive to the Officers' Committee we had reached the point which had proved fatal to every military government in the past: the moment when the Army divided.

I said, 'Let me try to reach them, sir. Perhaps they are playing truant for some reason other than political insolence.'

I went into my office and fought with the telephone for an hour. The system was a poor one and not improved by the Tuareg habit of stealing the lines, but at an expense of time and patience I finally got in touch with a sergeant at the brigade headquarters. Where were the officers? I asked him. They were hunting jackal. When would they be back? Soon, he told me. In the Maghreb 'soon' could mean anything from an hour to a week and I was not encouraged.

They were skulking, of course. No commander would leave his headquarters bare of officers. If they intended to show a degree of insubordination without resorting to mutiny the measure was finely judged. I suspected a mind more astute than Rustum's and gifted in the ways of ambiguity: El Sharif's, no less. I rang the three other brigades commanded by Arabs, those at El Desmara and the single brigade at Mogalor. All were present, but there was what seemed a studied slowness in the response from Mogalor.

I didn't like that. If the Mogalor brigade changed sides the President would be dangerously weakened.

I returned to Jason's office. 'The Kezzanis still don't answer and we must suppose they are in some form of disobedience, probably not total. The Mogalor brigade seems to be vacillating. I'll go there if you want.'

Jason stood up, the instinctive movement of a man who is challenged, and went to the window as if he might see his enemy there. A commander-in-chief can receive no message worse than the one I had given him — but his step was as light as it had always been. 'It can't be Rustum. He's an amateur soldier, interested only in pleasure and horse-racing. Someone has got to him.'

'Sir, I must believe that the Chief of Staff's attitude towards you, and the disobedience of the brigade, are part of the same design.'

'You're right, Peter. I can see it clearly. They wish to restore the Sultanate. Solly as king; El Sharif presiding over an Oulema, a religious council. What a party!'

'You have still the greater part of the Army, sir, particularly if Mogalor remains loyal. You have one excellent brigade in the Neban.'

He turned to me, smiling faintly. 'My dear Peter, what is the truth? I am a weak military dictator, recognized by no major state, reviled by the liberal conscience everywhere. Without the Army I am just a Fascist refugee fit only for the firing squad.' He turned back to the window, beyond which, in the palace garden, I could see that the strong points had been manned. 'I intend to court martial Solly,' he said softly.

I had already prepared my piece where Solly was concerned. I said, 'Sir, the Chief of Staff is undoubtedly guilty of assaulting you, but——'

'But what, Colonel? There are no alternatives. He must stand trial.'

'I urge you to find some other means of punishment. Ask for his resignation. Put him on the retired list. You have many ways of showing displeasure. It can only make matters worse if you put him on trial in the present situation.'

'He struck a superior. Every soldier knows what to expect if he does that.'

'I don't have to tell you that El Sharif has engineered the whole thing,' I laboured on. 'He drove Solly to accost you. He wants him put on trial. He means him to become the focus of Arab nationalism, a popular hero behind whom all the Arab interests will rally. For God's sake don't play into his hands.'

He seemed not to have heard me. He turned from the window with a radiant face. 'Peter, Peter, can't you see it? That pompous ass escorted before the court without his cap? There is no doubt they would find him guilty of striking the Commander-in-Chief. I will confiscate all his women and palaces.' He was intoxicated with the idea of putting an end to Solly, but I knew his exuberance would be followed quickly by depression. I did not have long to wait. He walked back to his desk in a mood of gloomy rectitude. 'You do not understand African politics, Colonel. The leader has to sustain his position in the state, if necessary by severe means. Solly must stand trial.'

I knew Jason well enough not to oppose him once he had made up his mind, but I had to be sure he would do something to mitigate his recklessness.

'Everything depends on the Army, sir. We must be certain of its loyalty. Show yourself to the troops. Speak to them. We'd better forget the Kezzan brigade for the time being, but the other units may still respond to you.'

He was too good a tactician not to have foreseen this need. He knew that every leader since the Roman emperors had shown himself to the Army when his power waned. He resumed his place at the desk and folded his hands as if to display a tidy mind. 'I am inspecting the two brigades in El Desmara this morning. I shall ask for the loyalty of the officers and make an exhortation to the troops. I do not expect trouble. The brigade in Mogalor is a different matter. The commander is a pious-minded creature, weak in discipline, who might be attracted by the idea of a theocratic state. I want you to go there: form an opinion of his intentions, judge the loyalty of the men. Naturally I shall respect your judgment.'

I took what comfort I could from this plan of action. I had one other thought. 'We should warn Nathan to be ready to come forward. If the Arabs force a show-down, he will be your best security.'

His head rolled on his shoulders; the focus of his eyes grew long as if he were looking into the ambiguity of the Neban. 'He might save my life. I don't know. I suspect, if the Arabs take over the north, the Neban will secede. It has no natural unity with the rest of the country.'

'Tell him to stand by. He'll come if you ask him.'

'Very well. Send him a warning order. Tell him to load his vehicles. Tell him to keep quiet until he hears from me.'

I came briefly to attention and left. Jason was gazing at the further wall, looking small behind the vast presidential desk. I wondered what hope there was of saving him and could see little of encouragement. I went to the signals office and sent a warning order to the Dharat brigade: the commander was to bring his forces secretly to readiness and await further orders. Then I went to my own small office and put things together for a trip to Mogalor.

§

In the car with Hatim, on the long road to the coast, I asked myself why I should be propping up a military government which had many of the trappings of Fascism in a country not my own. Warfield, the mercenary soldier, the friend of dictators! The claims of friendship did not extend this far. I told myself I would help Jason restore his authority, if that were possible, and then I would leave the country with Carol if she would come with me.

I admired Hatim's detachment from the matters in hand; I imagined it to be supported by a foreign bank account handsomely in credit. Once I asked him, 'Hatim, what do you

136

believe to be the power of the Iman in the country as a whole?'

'Oh, he has gall in his stomach and a foul smell upon his breath. As a child, I hid from him in cupboards.'

I had to be content with that — that, and the undoubted beauty of the littoral. Here the road was lined with eucalyptus, and the land on either side was turned and red and the young maize was a foot high. When we entered the old sea port of Mogalor I could see traces of the British builders who had established the place in the eighteenth century for the export of slaves. They had left a church whose spire would have looked better in the Home Counties. To the north along the dunes was the great suburb built by Khalid as a trap for the international tourist — Sidi-bel-Said, where now Osmani had her home. Hatim gathered together the resources of his mind and directed us to the brigade headquarters.

The commander, Brigadier Ben Talun, proved to be a long-faced apparition whose eyes spilled sadness. I could not imagine how he would behave if the brigade had ever to go into action. As far as I knew he was not related to the Sultan, which was about the only thing to commend him as an ally. He took my hand in his thin dry fingers and murmured something that might have been a blessing.

I said, 'I would like a word with you, sir, and then a sight of the brigade in training. May we go into your office?'

'Whatever your will directs. . . .'

I was not impressed. The headquarters, plainly built by the British Army, was in poor repair and the soldiers I could see in the corridors were slovenly even by Arab standards. Ben Talun conducted me to the brigade commander's office and invited me to be seated. The chair offered doubtful support but I chanced my weight upon it. A chicken was perched on the commander's table.

'My purpose is liaison, sir. The Commander-in-Chief may wish to exercise the brigade in a few days' time, so it will be helpful if I can assess your readiness for combat.'

It seemed unlikely that the Mogalor brigade could fight its way out of a paper bag, but none the less I looked at him in sober enquiry.

He cleared his throat. He waved a hand at the chicken, which rose into the air in sudden disquiet, shedding feathers and pieces of straw. 'The brigade is not at full strength; there are difficulties in supply, I have a malfunction of the kidneys. . . .' He realized that this was not a sufficient account of his battle order and he sought for some evidence of readiness, such as might please the Commander-in-Chief's principal aide. 'I will call the brigade adjutant and he will give you a return of the ration strength; I am sure we can make up a good company if the Commander-in-Chief desires an exercise.'

I said gently, 'Sir, you are established for three battalions and a company of armoured cars. Standing orders require you to be ready for combat at full strength after a three-day mobilization.'

'That, as you say, is the requirement.'

'Well, sir?'

He looked at me with his sad, pious eyes. I felt a brute for pressing him but his negligence was obvious. 'You do not understand, Colonel Warfield; the government pays the soldiers very low wages; there has been some discontent. I am obliged from time to time to grant the soldiers some extra leave so that they can work on the fruit farms and make a few fils. I could not call the brigade together in under three weeks. You understand, it is a matter of charity.'

And charity was one of the most cherished principles of Allah! Out of the goodness of his heart, and no doubt to prevent desertions, he had sent the brigade on leave; it was an astonishing admission for a commander to make at a time of military uncertainty. I had to nail some facts to the table.

'How many soldiers are there in camp?'

'I cannot say—perhaps three hundred. I was grieved to see the men so pale, so little provided for.'

'And they are at battle readiness?'

'Well—no.'

'What is your programme of training?'

'Why—drill, fatigues, fasting, prayer. We observe the Mohammedan calendar. Is there something else we should do?'

I was no stranger to the holy soldier; the British Army had bred them in abundance since the days of the Ironsides; but they at least combined their prayers with a vigorous discipline. I felt certain this devout old man was telling me the truth and I could risk the next subject.

'It will not have escaped you, sir, that the Officers' Committee is passing through a period of difficulty. There has been—some disagreement.'

'I will pray for unity, for accord.'

'I am sure the Commander-in-Chief has your undivided support. It would however strengthen his position if you were to send him a message reaffirming your loyalty and that of your officers.'

'I will give the matter my earnest consideration.'

'But will you do it, sir?'

The chicken, which had come to rest on the top of the door, now took off like the Brigadier's startled conscience and flew into the opposite wall. I watched it fall to the floor, apparently stunned.

He said, 'It is not my habit to act upon impulse. I need to reflect, to seek the guidance of heads wiser than mine. I have to ask for the confirmation of God.'

'In a matter of primary loyalty, sir? I would not have thought it necessary.'

'Dear friend, I took my original oath to the Sultan. When Khalid came, I was obliged to renew my oath to him, though he was an obscure solicitor I did not know. Then I was asked to acknowledge the Officers' Committee. Can you tell me which of these is my primary loyalty?'

I could not. I could only wait for him to continue.

'It is a difficult matter. It has encouraged me to use my discretion when granting leave to men who were hungry. I obeyed the will of Allah, there being no other directive. I have now received a message from Kezzan asking me to acknowledge the Iman as a spiritual director of greater authority than the military government. I do not know what to do. I must seek enlightenment. I must wait for the inspiration of God.'

This was no way to run a brigade, but I knew better than to interrupt the process of Arab mysticism. I took note that the Kezzanis had approached him and had no doubt got the same equivocal answer.

139

I made one last attempt at securing his allegiance. 'I suggest that a soldier can have only one loyalty — to his Commander-in-Chief. If the Commander-in-Chief happens also to be the Head of State his claim upon your loyalty is doubled, particularly in difficult times.'

He nodded slowly. 'That is a persuasive point. I will think about it. I will commend it to Allah.'

I said, 'Come, sir; let's have a look at the brigade.'

In more than a quarter of a century of soldiering I had seen nothing quite like the brigade's quarters in Mogalor: the condition would have destroyed the sanity of my late regimental sergeant-major. The Brigade Commander saw nothing amiss as he led me from the headquarters to the barrack square despite the market in livestock that was in vigorous life under the acacia trees. On the square itself, where in Britain none but the pure in heart may set foot, some form of public entertainment was in preparation: rugs stretched across the asphalt, lamps hung from the flagpole and the peddlers of refreshment had set up their tables. The soldiers I could not see, though men in parts of their uniform were here and there relaxing in the shade. The barracks seemed to have been taken over by the soldiers' women; there were children at the windows and playing in the dust outside. In the guard room, where the defaulters should have been detained, a herd of goats was impounded.

Ben Talun said, 'We are at a low state of training. You understand, it is not the season for operations.'

I doubted if it ever would be. As a military force the brigade did not exist. I was not as disturbed as I might have been.

I went into the signals office and encoded a message to Jason: *Loyalty obscure but brigade could not be brought into action in under six months, supposing the soldiers could be found. Suggest omit from all calculations. Remedial action should wait upon the re-establishment of your authority. Back this evening.*

When I said good-bye to him, Ben Talun wore the expression of an elderly don who had been detected in a· philosophical falsehood. He was too honest to pretend the brigade was present. 'I will send out recall parties if you wish. I will have a company by the end of the week, though their equipment will be incomplete. . . .'

I couldn't help liking this grave old gentleman who could no more command a brigade than he could perform the acrobatics that were now in rehearsal on the parade ground. 'I'll come back in a few weeks,' I told him. 'We'll sort things out. Meanwhile I should find some good NCOs and get the place cleaned up. You can't start from a mess.'

He seemed encouraged by this offer of modest help; at any rate he smiled faintly and murmured some words of Arabic which meant 'God will bring you back'.

I left him to his prayers and to the nearly impossible task of rebuilding discipline in a unit where it had collapsed. At present I didn't care. Better a brigade of absentees than a unit of doubtful loyalty. In the arithmetic of rebellion, we could discount the Mogalor brigade. There were still some hours of daylight and I had another job to do. Leaving Hatim and the driver at headquarters, I drove myself into Sidi-bel-Said where, if I was not mistaken, there were greater dangers.

§

Khalid had planned his pleasure dome at Sidi-bel-Said with an ambitious hand and it had been his undoing. He had laid a boulevard along the shore with gardens on the inland side. Behind the gardens he had foreseen hotels and places of amusement, but today these were no more than empty shells or abandoned building sites. Certainly, he had placed his folly in the best position, for these sunlit beaches with the Atlantic rollers breaking against them were among the best in the world.

Osmani had given me an address in the Avenue Atlantique, a street of older houses behind the esplanade. It was in this district that the wealthy of Mogalor had made their homes in the years before the development of Sidi-bel-Said; now it had the look of all places from which fashion has passed. Many of the houses were boarded up, their gardens overgrown; others had been taken over by the poor.

The address I sought proved to be an old house within a walled garden that might have been beautiful once. In the garden the fig trees were stifled by an overgrowth of convolvulus. The house

141

itself was beginning to dissolve, which is the lot of any house built of mud brick and lacking maintenance.

I paused on the verandah. Indoors I could hear voices speaking English and French. I knocked on the outer door and a young Arab girl of startling beauty came from inside the house. No doubt she was surprised to see me standing in the light of the entrance, but her eyes were clouded with an absence of interest I found disturbing. When I asked for Miss Mason she invited me into the house in good French.

The principal room was wide and like every Arab endeavour out of the true square. The tiled floor was covered with rugs, cushions and fleeces; the walls were hung with Moroccan blankets. Osmani was seated on a couch at the far end of the room; her head was turned towards me, her eyebrows raised in criticism as if I were late in keeping an appointment; she had been about to rise but had checked in the moment of recognition.

I said, 'Miss Mason, you gave me a job to do when we met in the Medina at Kezzan. I have done it.'

Her mouth opened; it was her only concession to surprise. Either side of her, seated on cushions, were two young Arabs who were alike in the fineness of their heads. They must have been boys not yet twenty. They rose at the sight of me and bowed with a remote unsmiling courtesy. I guessed them to be brothers close together·in age, and like the girl they were plainly young people of education and privilege. Osmani sent them away with a gentle movement of the hand.

She rose from the couch; she did not let me speak. She was clothed in a white robe which fell from one shoulder without constraint and she had about her the heavy scent of jasmine. 'This is a house of unashamed affection, Colonel Warfield. These children are my family. We have only one principle, that of love . . . No, don't speak to me yet. I'm not prepared for the news you have brought.'

She put her fingers into the corners of her eyes and worked them in a little circle; she was preparing her vision for the foul images I had brought from the world outside. One thing I knew from the manner in which she had received me: she had already heard of the death of Mahmet.

'You must listen to me, Miss Mason. I have to speak plainly.'

She said obliquely, 'Aissa and Haida are charming boys. Their minds are dedicated to the improvement of society. You understand me, their conceptual thinking is of first-rate quality.'

'Please listen; I'll put things as clearly as I can ——'

'And Leisha, the girl—what a lovely nature! She has the same universal charity, and she is only fifteen.'

'I have to tell you that Mahmet is dead.'

I did not know if Osmani had any real fondness for Mahmet but it would have been ungenerous to suppose she had none. At any rate, she now seated herself and dropped her head into her hands, not, I suspected, from grief for the lost poet but in a graceful semblance of tragedy.

'The soldiers killed him; it was a brutal thing . . .'

I had to tell Osmani the truth. I had to start from the lawless situation in the Neban at the time of the change in leadership, admit Nathan's executions, tell her of the poet's terrible counter-stroke, and carry it through to the death of Mahmet. Any distortion of the truth could only injure Jason. I had little hope she would admit to a belief in my story: I guessed her to be a woman of powerful physical appetite who had been deprived of her satisfaction, for the violence in Mahmet would have appealed to her, and I could think of no more dangerous adversary for the man I served.

When I had finished, she raised her eyes, and they contained more of anger than of pity for the dead Mahmet. This was a powerful nature that had been challenged by the working of fate. My only hope was that she would recognize that there had been violence enough.

'You expect me to believe this, Colonel?—I, who knew the grace of his mind?'

I had nothing to lose now. Truth was my only weapon. I said, 'I think you will believe me, but I doubt if you will admit it.'

Osmani was artist enough to know that restraint is the better part of indignation. She rose in a muted fury, seeking her voice, her fingers closing as if to strangle the false witness. 'I told you before that General Khymer was a blood-stained tyrant and that the lives of free people would not be safe while he was in power.

143

Soldiers have no beliefs; therefore they must destroy the beliefs of others. They must eliminate those who are working towards an alternative society, those with a genius for love . . .'

There was more in the same vein. I let it flow over me, old mercenary that I was, wondering indeed what beliefs my life had left me. I believed you must take the knife out of the assassin's hand. I believed in the warmth of the sunlight, the chill of the night. I believed, too, in the stench of the cesspit. God, was there nothing else?

Osmani had a swift feminine intelligence and she knew well enough where I was most vulnerable. 'It does not become you to attribute cruelty to those who are its opponents, Colonel. Mahmet believed in universal charity. You are a tool of the Junta.'

Aye, so I was — a lackey, a running dog. I let it go. 'Madam, you asked me to investigate the disappearance of Mahmet. I have done so. I can't change the facts.'

She was deeply angered and a yet sharper weapon lay close to her hand, one she had not used. She made her next thrust with an exactness of aim that only a woman could execute. She turned from me, towards the window, and she spoke with a rapid inconsequence.

'The Langley girl was an international whore. I suppose you know it.'

I did not answer.

'Khalid preferred his girls white. Carol must have been greatly to his liking.'

She was not the first woman on earth who wanted to destroy the messenger who brought bad news. I heard the breath escaping from her lips in savage satisfaction. And she had found my weakest point: I did not know, I had not dared to ask just what Carol's relationship with Khalid had been. I got up to go.

'No, don't go. Not yet.'

'I can't believe we have anything else to say to each other, Miss Mason.'

'I have hurt you. I am sorry.'

She was not actually crying. She was too proud for that. But there was a sob upon her breath that did not go away and her head was in small movement from side to side. Perhaps after all she had cared for Mahmet.

Somehow I found my voice. 'Any death is a tragedy. I won't pretend that this one was other than violent and cruel. I would only ask you to believe that the President had nothing to do with it.'

The swinging of her head increased in emphasis; there was a force within her that had to reject my words. Even in my desolation I felt afraid, and I made a last attempt at reaching her.

'Miss Mason, you could hurt General Khymer a great deal by revealing his connection with the former President. Those who oppose him might use it as an excuse for his assassination. And I have to admit that you could hurt me as well. If the General goes, the man who would replace him would set up a regime more cruel, more oppressive than anything we have seen so far. Therefore, if you please ——'

She raised her head. She might have laughed.

'— if you please, act with restraint.'

'I see. That is what I must do.'

Her laughter was unmistakable now — deep, mocking laughter torn from her distress. I could not continue my defence of Jason; I was not that much a tool of the Presidency. We sank into the lethargy of unresolved antagonism. Once she ran her fingers across the back of my hand — in affection, in contempt, I could not say which — and then expelled her breath in a long shuddering draught that ridiculed all military strong men and those who served their repressive purposes. I wanted to go but I could not. She held me there with the strength of her displeasure. I knew beyond doubt that this woman had a part to play in the undoing of Jason's Presidency. I could not count upon her silence; I had to plan for this further threat to the military government. The Langleys, too, would need protection. At last I broke out of my trance and told her I must go. She did not rise.

When I reached the door her voice halted me. She had resumed the soft notes of universal harmony. 'We have lost a poet, Colonel Warfield, but there are other voices to carry his message. Aissa and Haida, for instance. Did I tell you they were Mahmet's brothers? Did I tell you they too are sons of Daud?'

She had not, but I saw her point.

I went out into the sunlight, into the overgrown garden, and walked quickly back to the car allowing time and distance to intervene between Osmani and me. I drove back into Mogalor to pick up Hatim before returning to El Desmara. I wondered how the day had added to the political equation. I had found a brigade in weakness, a woman in strength, and in the terms of military expediency I would have said that the one equalled the other and that the dangers facing Jason were no less.

I urged the driver to make his best pace back to El Desmara.

# 12

We arrived in the capital in a blazing orange sunset of the type that excited the writer in me, but I could not think of it now. Something was amiss in the old city. In the nearer streets I saw people hurrying towards the great market as though an urgent summons had passed through the crowd; others stood looking in the same direction.

'What is it?' I asked Hatim.

'A rich man has collapsed under the weight of his dinars. They run to pick his pocket.'

'What would take so many people to the market?'

'Only an entertainment of some kind.'

I told the driver to follow on the heels of the crowd and within a minute we had entered the market where the falling sun threw long shadows and there seemed to be a great many people about. At the far end of the square, where the crowd was thickest, I could see movement which a moment ago might have been violent, but I could not say what they were doing. I stopped the car under the old wall, jumped out and caught the man nearest to me. He was a fat man stained with sweat, and he was laughing.

I said in Arabic, 'Tell me what has happened.'

'A scene of great amusement. I laughed heartily.'

'But what was it?'

'I laughed until I made wind. I do not know exactly what it was.'

I started across the dusty market towards the congestion of people on the opposite side. It was over now, whatever it had been, and the people were walking back towards me.

Hatim's voice followed me. 'What does it matter? They torment a beggar; they carve a political message on his rear parts. It is a game they play.'

There were soldiers in the square—soldiers carrying their arms but under no control that I could see. I laid my hands upon a corporal and turned him roughly towards me. His mind was stimulated by some powerful emotion.

'A spectacle such as in the old days, lord. I have seen nothing like it since I was a boy. A scourging, the punishment of a criminal.'

'Who are you? What is your unit?'

'My name is Zakiel. I am of the headquarters company.'

'Where are your officers?'

'I do not know. They are not here. It was an engaging sight.'

I still held his wrist. Now I gripped it strongly in an attempt to cut through to his intelligence.

'Listen to me, Zakiel. Who was it the people tormented?'

'No one that matters. A man stripped of dignity. They have taken him away.'

'What was his name? You must tell me!'

'When a man is forced into the dust, and his mouth stopped with offal, he does not have a name. He is part of the world's excrement.'

I was getting nowhere. There was no firm evidence in the square but for some crazy scarring of the dust. I ran back to the car and told the driver to take me at once to the Tamran Palace, but in the streets near the market we could move only slowly and we were twenty minutes in reaching the palace. I went straight to the President's office and let myself in without announcement. I found Jason strangely complacent, as if he were privy to a secret I did not share.

'Ah, my dear Peter! Did you enjoy yourself in Mogalor?' He hastened on before I could answer. 'I have visited the regiments in El Desmara, as you advised. They are fretful, vacillating and given to disorderly behaviour. The officers were surly but obedient. I lectured them on the rudiments of discipline.'

But it was not the ill-nature of the Army that was at the centre of his mind; rather some part of his day's work appealed particularly to his sense of humour.

I said, 'Sir, what has happened in El Desmara this afternoon?'

'Why do you ask me that?'

He looked smug, and I wondered for the first time if he had sent me to Mogalor to get me out of the way while he took some action of his own.

'Well, the day has not been without interest,' he said.

'Will you tell me what you have done?'

'It is not within your competence to question the Commander-in-Chief.'

He would tell me if I waited. He took a file from a tray and leafed through the enclosures, but he was not reading it. He was letting my curiosity grow. He did not know that I had been in the market at the conclusion of a savage ritual. A terrace lay beyond the garden door; I went out into the raging sunset knowing that he would follow me. After the heat of the day there was a pleasant coolness in the garden and I walked slowly towards the end of the terrace. I heard his rapid footstep on the pavings behind me before I had gone twenty paces.

'Wait, Peter! You must hear my story, it is very amusing, I know you will laugh. . . .'

I came to a soldier's halt and turned. 'Sir, what have you done? Have you taken some action against the Chief of Staff?'

'Dear friend, I have done nothing! It was the indignation of the crowd, spontaneously expressed.'

I waited grimly for the next stroke of the pendulum, wondering what time we had left. Jason took my arm and led me to the edge of the terrace where cannas were in bloom. 'You are tired, you are depressed; the realities of African life are distasteful to you. Nevertheless I will tell you what happened this afternoon. It is not without humour. You see, I ordered Solly into close arrest this morning.'

'That was unwise, sir.'

'Wise—unwise—it does not matter. It was inevitable. Solly has to stand trial for an offence against the President. He was taken from his house by soldiers and conveyed to the detention barracks. On the way, when they passed through the great market, the townspeople demonstrated their anger—the Chief of Staff was taken from his guards and roughly handled. He was abused, he was scourged, he was spat upon.'

So that was the scene of which I had caught the last moments. The soldiers had dragged the tall disdainful figure through the market, the crowd had gathered, their mood of curiosity had changed quickly into anger as government agents showed the way with gestures of derision. In the hot countries, where there was much to condemn, a manacled figure was always the object of hostility: here walked the culprit, the author of all misfortune. I saw the figure struck down and beaten as the soldiers stood aside and the dust rose about him. Poor Solly, he'd walked a strange path since his days at Eastleigh.

Jason said, I thought with a certain relish, 'The people recognized his offence and they required him to pay the penalty. It was a great popular demonstration in favour of the President. Of course, the soldiers intervened to save his life.'

I moved away from him on to the lawn where the shadows were losing their definition as the last of the sunset flared out behind the cypresses. I wondered if there was anything left to stay for in Jason's country: Osmani had lacerated my heart when she called Carol a whore, and Jason seemed no better than a vulgar tyrant who took pleasure in the torment of his enemies. He had followed me on to the grass.

'You must not look so shocked, Peter. He was not badly hurt—a few cuts and bruises, nothing more. He has received medical attention.'

I no longer cared what I said. I would leave the God-forsaken country tomorrow. I spoke without acknowledgement of his rank or our former friendship. 'It was a stupid, brutal vendetta. It wasn't necessary to take him through the market; the people would not have attacked him without encouragement; the soldiers were obviously briefed to stand aside. You want the world to regard you as an enlightened leader and you behave with primitive vindictiveness.'

I expected him to take lasting offence but in fact I do not think he caught more than the tone of my voice. 'You are angry, Peter. I can tell that you are angry! But really I had little to do with it. I simply instructed the escorting officer to show the Chief of Staff no particular favour. I did not expect him to be molested.'

'I don't believe it. The officer would not have allowed his prisoner beaten unless he felt he had your authority.'

'On the contrary, I have reprimanded him.'

'Then you are behaving with inexcusable despotism.'

He understood me now. He looked at me sharply, his lips compressed. 'You may not speak to me like that. You are my adviser, not my spiritual director. Plainly you think I am no better than a bully.'

'The scourging of Solly was a hideous mistake.'

'But he was guilty! He was planning an alternative government under El Sharif. He had raised his hand against me.'

I said, with sudden utter weariness, 'It would have been better to have treated him with restraint. Even the guilty have rights. I suppose he is now imprisoned in wretched conditions.'

His mouth snapped shut. He would not tell me in which of the states of confinement known to the world's dictatorships Solly now lay.

'Is he fettered, manacled, confined in a small space?'

'I do not know.'

'Will you let me see him?'

He shook his head.

My next words came unbidden out of my tiredness. 'I had supposed you incapable of things like this. I had supposed you a soldier.'

His eyes widened; he might have been looking at an assassin who had stepped into his path. I knew I had angered him deeply.

Now I saw no point in withholding my opinion. 'What's more, you have played straight into the hands of El Sharif. The world press will make a monster of you. Had you tried, you could not have turned Solly into a hero more effectively.' I opened my hands to let my frustration fly, then dropped them in exhaustion. Who could say that power in the Saharan Republic had not been transferred at the moment when Solly was struck down into the dust?

Whatever his shortcomings, Jason did not lack dignity. He didn't abuse me. He didn't even speak. He turned away from me in a movement that would not have been amiss on the parade ground and walked back across the lawn to his office. I watched

151

him go. He was enough of a commander-in-chief not to slam the door. Then I was alone with the expanding shadows and a sense of futility that sank into my heart's core. The sunset fell out of the sky; the darkness thickened. After a while I dragged myself awake and went off to find the car.

§

The day had been long and I was tired. By the time I reached home the dark had a shine upon it and there was a stillness of the air that magnified every sound. I poured myself a tumbler of whisky and sat with it in the courtyard. I listened to the cats in the neighbouring gardens. I wanted to sleep but the misery that lay like a corpse within me kept my mind in sluggish movement. The things I had been given were now, it seemed, to be taken away. Osmani's abuse of Carol, which had put form to some suppressed thought of my own, returned to my head again and again. Did I have to believe that Carol had been the paid bedfellow of the lascivious old potentate who had once ruled the country? At the moment I could not say, and jealousy flowed like acid through my lower body. Perhaps I had lost the girl I loved. Certainly I had lost Jason's friendship, because I did not think he would have the means to forgive me. There was a mocking laughter in my ears, that after a time took on the quality and pitch of my poor, lost, angry wife, who had told me I would make an ass of myself. I wondered where I would go, what I would do.

It was silly to drink, but I had no other comfort. I must have depleted the bottle, hoping the whisky would smother the pain I felt, which of course it did not, while about me the cats played in the darkness. I did not see the robed figure come into the garden. I did not put a name to him even when he compelled the direction of my eyes. I did not hear the first words spoken.

' . . . . do not get up, there's no need of formality, I shall be gone in a moment.' The voice was crisp, with a military inflection; he spoke with the lack of consequence of a man not deeply concerned.

I struggled to my feet: I could still stand up for the President. I had not seen Jason out of uniform before and the grey jellaba, the raised hood had deceived me. He must have walked all the way

152

from the Tamran Palace. I felt a lift of the spirit, to which my loneliness gave an absurd emphasis, to see him at my house. He would not sit down; he was obviously still angry with me.

'So, you are alone! You console yourself with spirits. You are cast down because the President is wanting as a soldier and as a leader of his country.'

'I was angry, sir. I should not have spoken as I did.'

'You plan your escape from a country that is irredeemably wicked. You say to yourself, let it dissolve into barbarism, into the black night! You form the opinion that there is nothing here worth saving.'

I did not know why he had come; it was not simply to complain of my behaviour. I drew forward a chair but he did not take it. Instead he moved into the shadows by the wall and continued his rebuke as if I were elsewhere. 'Colonel Warfield, who has never felt a lash between his shoulder-blades, who has never begged his food, knows best how to rule in Africa! He comes from Wimbledon to teach the Army how to dig their latrines and all at once he is a sage, an oracle.'

Why Jason associated me with Wimbledon, where I had never been, I was unable to say; perhaps he saw it as a symbol of English respectability. I had to speak out then. 'I have offended you, sir, and I am sorry. I am prepared to resign my job if that is what you want. Indeed, I don't know how to go on if we are seriously at odds over policy.'

'My friend, in Africa there is no policy but the sunlight, no law but the bad temper of the Arabs. You do not understand our people.'

'You may be right. I have said I am prepared to go.'

I had laid my resignation before him but he had not picked it up. He came forward to where I was standing and took a chair—not the one I had offered, but another, of his own choosing. I sat beside him.

Now he spoke across my shoulder, as if he were instructing a subordinate in whom he had no interest. 'Colonel, in every Arab country there are many eyes and ears. Khalid, of course, set up a system of intelligence that forewarned him of every danger—that is, with one notable exception! There were government spies in every town and village prepared to sell information for the price of an oatcake and a measure of syrup. When the Officers' Committee took power, they also took over Khalid's information service, every turnkey and scullion, and the system has operated no less effectively under the dictatorship. You cannot really have thought your visit to a house in Sidi-bel-Said would go unreported.'

I might have known it. This was the Maghreb. I waited for him to go on, which he did at an increased pace.

'Naturally, the house is known as the home of an American lady where Le Ciel Rouge receive entertainment. Indeed, the lady is Miss Iris Mason who wanted to sing songs to the Officers' Committee but who, despairing of their conversion to the dream of universal peace, transferred her support to the revolutionary Left. She has no love for the Army, nor for its Commander-in-Chief, particularly since her friend and protégé, Mahmet ben Daud, was killed by soldiers during the festival of Haraq Tej. She would destroy the Junta if she could.'

I said, 'I will tell you the whole story, which I should have done before now. Needless to say I was not giving help to your enemies.'

He gave no sign of having heard me. He continued to address the shadows in the same featureless voice he had so far used. 'Now what would Colonel Warfield, the trusted aide of the President, be doing in a hotbed of revolutionaries? Had he defected to the enemy? Had he some other purpose?'

'I will give you an exact account,' I said.

'Of course, he may have had some quixotic intention comprehensible only to an English gentleman of persuading Arab revolutionaries to behave with decency. He may have been trying to save the neck of his friend and superior officer. He may have said to them, "Good fellows, just play the game, as we do in Wimbledon — the President's not such a bad chap!" Or perhaps — it is possible — he is in love with Miss Iris Mason and he goes there to receive her most intimate favours — '

'Good heavens!' I said; and I must have laughed.

' — which may appeal to him, even in the high temperatures of afternoon.' I could not be sure, but I think Jason himself had smiled. 'It then occurs to me that Miss Iris Mason has some hold

154

over the Colonel which causes him to seek her out when he should have been inspecting establishments. Now what can it be, I wonder. What is it that the Colonel cannot tell his friend and fellow Pelican? It must be very terrible.'

'Not terrible, but bad enough,' I said. 'Will you let me explain.'

He held up a hand, he had not finished. For the first time he turned towards me, speaking now with sad intimacy. 'Old fellow, I have told you of Khalid's obsession with information. He compiled a library of written material that now lies in the cellars of the Tamran Palace—the work of an Algerian misanthropist who was paid highly for his services. But Khalid should have feared the thing he had created. An intelligence service develops ideas and motives of its own. Very soon the Algerian had opened a dossier on Khalid. His work was painstaking; every feature of that extraordinary life was written down and placed in the file, which grew as fat as the subject—the countries he visited, the entertainment he received, the dishes he consumed. He recorded details of all the malevolent people who crossed the President's path—yes, and the harmless too—and above all he kept an account of all the vast sums of money that spilled from his pockets on to the gaming tables of Europe. You may wonder what became of this conspectus. It is not difficult to guess. Damaging material will always find its way into the hands of those who can use it. The Algerian sold his dossier to the Army who, as you are aware, gathered together their small courage and destroyed the tyrant before his wicked influence could spread.'

The wound I bore had worsened even as he spoke, and my guilt had deepened. I said, with barely strength enough to make it audible, 'I see. Then you know about Miss Langley.'

He was too sensitive to pursue the point. He drew himself upright in his chair and spoke next in his business-like voice. 'The file remains in my keeping. In it there are many names. That one of the President's companions is the daughter of the gentleman who now wishes to set up a tourist industry in the Republic does not concern me deeply. But the fact could be used to my disadvantage were it known to my opponents.'

'I know it. I have tried to prevent that happening.'

He nodded briskly, like a general assessing danger in the field.

'Of course, Miss Mason has told you that she is aware of Miss Langley's relationship with Khalid. She would have seen them together in Menton, when she sang songs to the President's entourage. And now, with the Left coming into collusion with the Iman, she will tell her story to the Sharifian Arabs.'

'I think it likely. I asked her not to, but she will persuade herself it is in the interest of peace.'

'I see. I understand.'

The General had made his appreciation of the battlefield with a coolness of mind his instructors would have approved.

It was too late for apology, but none the less I said, 'I am sorry about the Langleys. I would have spared you this one if I could.'

'It was not your fault, Colonel. You could not have guessed they were connected with the late ruler. However, you should have told me as soon as you discovered the relationship. In that respect, you were seriously at fault.'

He spoke as we had taught him, delivering his reprimand without heat, and it was justified. I was utterly in the wrong. What is more, I had gravely underestimated his intelligence, for he had torn through my pretence without hesitation. When Jason used his best mind he was formidable. I left unsaid the things I might have said, following the tradition we both acknowledged, which did not permit excuses. He rose as if to leave, and I got up beside him.

He said, in a voice not wholly steady, 'These are difficult days. The trial of the Chief of Staff will open divisions in the country, but at least we will know where we stand. I will be grateful if you will continue your duties for the time being as I cannot afford to lose your experience.'

I did not hesitate in my reply. In a world bereft of loyalty it was better to offer one's service than to withhold it, and just now Jason was the only friend I had.

'I shall be there in the morning,' I said.

We did not shake hands; we were conducting ourselves with military decorum. I escorted him to the gate, where I came to attention as I said good-night. He went a dozen paces down the unlit road, the regimental step looking odd under the peasant's garment, the darkness beginning to cover his figure; but he did

156

not disappear completely. He stopped abruptly, facing away from me, a thought seeming to strike him. Then he turned and came smartly back to where I stood.

He spoke impatiently, as if I were wasting his time. 'The girl Langley was a friend of Khalid's for about six months. She was with his entourage in Cannes, Menton and Rome. From the record, it would appear that he had a genuine affection for her; certainly he treated her with great respect which was not his custom with women. You understand, a Mohammedan gentleman does not feel the need of ceremony unless the woman has meaning for him beyond the satisfaction of his appetites.'

Perhaps my eyes had shown my distress, even in the darkness; at any rate I now waited for him to continue, saying nothing, my heart quite still.

'My friend, I am unfamiliar with what you term love. What is love? Perhaps it is no more than the illusion of a romantic heart. From a ditch in the Neban, love looks like the luxury of an overfed nation. No more than that! Still, I am sure you feel what you call love for the beautiful Miss Langley and it is not for a Nebanese peasant to say otherwise.' He turned on his heel, as if he meant to resume his walk into the old town, and his last words were directed away from me.

'If it matters to you, I do not think Khalid ever laid his hand upon her. His need of her was different. She was the illusion fulfilled, the angel shape. In any case, in the last years of his life, when he was glutted with admiration and the confections of the dinner table, he had lost the power to make love. That was his penalty. That was his penalty until the soldiers imposed a sharper one. I have told you what I know.'

Now he left me at a quick pace, the snap in his stride making plain his displeasure, and I watched him until he vanished. A sweet relief stirred in my dull mind. I wondered briefly if I had deserved this gesture of friendship and it looked unlikely. I had kept the secret of Carol's friendship to myself to spare my own embarrassment. One thought only was clear to me: whatever his weakness, I would see things through to the end of Jason's Presidency, no matter what form that end might take. He had earned that scrap of loyalty.

# 13

The steps Jason took to rebuild his authority in the next days were sound. He required the remaining members of the Officers' Committee to renew their obligations to him; he made changes in the command of the two brigades in El Desmara, appointing officers of no political or religious persuasion; and old Ben Talun at Mogalor was sent off to find his troops.

One of the new battalion commanders particularly appealed to me. Lieutenant-Colonel Zarahid was a tough professional whose face looked to have been forged on Vulcan's anvil. I asked him frankly if the Army would fight to defend the President.

'Can't say, old boy,' he told me. 'Arabs are not moved by regulations, like the British; they prefer symbols. Read him the articles of war and an Arab soldier will spit in your eye. Show him a magnificent illusion and he will fight for ever.'

'The Kezzanis will use the power of illusion,' I said. 'They will make a hero out of General Suleiman.'

'The illusion must be destroyed if the Army is to be obedient.'

'I know,' I replied. 'We may have the means to discredit him. At least, I believe so.'

A plan was taking shape in my mind but I could not have said how effective it would be.

After the first days, at my earnest request, Solly was removed from the lightless cellar where he had been thrown and confined in decent conditions in the officers' mess. Jason had charged him with striking a superior, and evidence had been taken from the officers present which would support the charge to the satisfaction of a court martial, but Jason did not at once convene a court, perhaps on the grounds that more serious charges might be possible: letting the accused languish in disfavour, which might thicken as time passed, had been the practice of the Sultans and Jason saw nothing wrong with it. But others did. As it chanced, a journalist had photographed the scene in the market, and the picture was reproduced in the world's press as an example of Jason's brutality. The single picture drew the attention of those who had otherwise forgotten the Saharan Republic to the nature of the regime, and protests to the international agencies followed. Solly was accorded the status of a political prisoner. Many of the world's newspapers found their way into the Tamran Palace and I read of General Suleiman's stand against tyranny and his martyrdom in the great square.

I had to act at once if the myth was to be arrested. I needed help, and it was help that only Nathan could give. I telephoned Dharat and after a number of wrong connections I heard the thick familiar voice over an appalling line.

'Hi there, soldier! What do you want with the big nigger?'

'To meet you, Colonel. Urgently.'

'Can't think why. How can I help Warfield, the adviser from Europe? I've already told you I can get my brigade to El Desmara in ten hours if you want me to thump the Arabs.'

'I must speak to you. You have information I need.'

'What was that?'

'We must talk.'

'Well, go ahead.'

'I mean privately. Can you come to the capital?'

'Nope.'

'Look, the President's in a great deal of trouble——'

'I don't doubt it, old son. He has provoked the Sharifian Arabs deliberately. I can't help you there.'

'But you'd help the President if you could.'

He paused.

'After all, you are under command,' I said, a pointless remark at which he snorted.

'You are right, soldier. I'm under command, and I'll fight any obvious enemy. But I'm not going to get mixed up in the filth of politics. Speak up, Peter. What can I do for you?'

'Meet me within six hours.'

'I'll come to the Skar. I'll be there at noon.'

He rang off.

Noon. It was now nine o'clock; I would have to move swiftly. I took a Land Rover from the MT yard and drove towards the Dharat road. On the outskirts of the town the road was lined with eucalyptus and Berbers in bright colours sat in the shade of each tree. I passed donkeys bearing baskets of oranges and amphoras of wine. The crowd thickened; it might have been a festival. I saw an archway leading to an enclosure where there were stalls and a press of people. Here a Berber market was in full vivid life. I stopped the car and went to buy wine and fruit; I felt sure that Nathan would bring only bread and water and I saw no need to get stuck with that.

I enjoyed the colour and vitality of the market and would have stayed there had it not been for the distance I had to travel. I was leaving by the archway and avoiding the outstretched hands of the beggars when my instinct warned me that I was being observed. I could not say what provoked this sensation. I paused in a shadow; I took money from my pocket and pretended to count it, at the same time searching the nearer crowd with my eyes. I could see nothing to confirm my suspicion; only the trinket peddlers paid attention to me, as they would to any European with money in his hand. I might have been mistaken but I didn't think so.  I had served too long in the Malayan jungle, where there were many eyes behind the foliage, not to know that I was being followed, marked, but at present I could not tell if my attendant was friendly or malign. I went back to the Land Rover and started the engine, but no one emerged from the market to note my departure.

The long road to the Skar was empty but for the travellers on foot, tribesmen who walked in the dust apparently undismayed by the vast distance ahead of them. The sun burned in the rimless plain. After half an hour, when I looked behind me, I could see a wedge of dust hanging over the road which kept the same distance from me no matter what my speed. Why should he draw close? From five miles back my movement across the desert would be clear to see; he would simply follow my dust and when it subsided he would know that I had stopped. I had covered about a hundred

160

miles when I saw the line of stunted trees which marked the river.

Nathan waited for me there, sitting on a milestone. He was alone.

He spoke first, without a greeting. 'Listen to me, Warfield! If you've come on a political errand, if you want me to sing the praises of General Khymer and his nanny-goats, you're wasting your time. Got it? I'm not the sort.'

'I didn't think you were,' I said. We moved into the shade of an argan tree. 'I'll be brief. The Arabs are getting the upper hand. The Left will support them.'

'Well? If you're flogging a doctrine, I won't buy it.'

I had to pin him down; only he had the information I needed. 'Colonel, we have to choose between General Khymer and General Suleiman.'

He squatted in the shade of the tree and drew with his finger in the dust. He said, 'The stronger will win. It doesn't matter which. All I care about is a formation of bush boys and pig stealers just out of bondage.' His finger described the conventional sign for a brigade of three battalions. 'Hell, Peter, what is the rest of the country but a stew of cultures ready to fall apart as each new government reveals its weakness?'

'We have to tell the truth about General Suleiman. We can't let him become a hero.'

'Well, go ahead. Tell them all he's a randy old goat who wants to rule the country.'

'Once in the hotel garden at Kezzan you told me the Sharifian family was involved in a dubious venture. The brigade was being misused. It had the makings of a scandal. General Suleiman is the most prominent Kezzani soldier and Colonel-in-Chief of the First Battalion. He is certainly involved. You must tell me what you know.'

'Want to bet?'

'This is not the moment for keeping things to yourself.'

He rose from the ground and faced me squarely. A laugh came up from his stomach. 'Brother, don't ask me to make it too easy. I don't play like that.'

'Then give me a point to start from.'

'Very well. This is it. The Kezzan brigade is engaged in an

161

operation in the desert west of the Atlas. Don't ask me what it is. I don't know for certain. Certainly it's a commercial venture from which the Sharifian family draws a large profit. Guns, illegal merchandise, minerals—it may be any of these. The one sure thing is that the Army should not be engaged in work of this kind, but then the Sultan's family have always regarded the brigade as a private force to be used for their advantage.'

'Right. The brigade is being misused. But where's the proof of corruption?'

'Steady, old boy. I didn't offer you proof. However, some months ago three soldiers joined my outfit who had earlier service in the First Battalion of the Kezzan brigade. Two were not thinking men; their brains were forged in the Neban and were as thick as the baked earth. The third was a corporal whose brain was at least on the move. He told me they had been used to close intersections on the camel tracks; they had held up travellers so that they should not see what traffic was passing on the old trade routes.'

'And what was it?'

'I'm not sure. They've found something valuable, that's certain. In that area—the Fahdia Waste—there are disputed mining rights. Perhaps the brigade is holding an illegal frontier to protect the shipment of ore. Work on that one.'

It could be so; the mineral wealth of the Sahara had only recently been defined. Something precious was being moved in the vast territory beyond the Atlas.

Nathan was looking across my shoulder and his eyes had hardened upon the desert across which I had driven. He said softly, 'The game goes on. I suppose you know you were followed.'

'I saw the dust behind me.'

'The vehicle has stopped now. We'll get him if you want.'

'Forget it. What's one spy in a place like this?'

'He could be within three hundred yards. He could have us in a line of sight.'

'So what, Colonel? I imagine your own soldiers are nearer. You know more than you're telling me.'

Nathan drove his fist into my shoulder. 'Now why should I hold out on you, brother? I've no love for the Kezzanis. They're a bad lot, particularly that boy-loving creature Rustum.'

'There is something unsaid.'

'Nothing of fact.'

'But you have a theory.'

'I don't deal in them. If I told you every possibility the game would be spoilt. It's up to you now. Find the truth. Tell the story. Wreck General Suleiman. If you want any extra muscle let me know.'

'This isn't a sport.'

'Friend, there's nothing else in the wide world that's worth a minute of your time. Toss the coin and chance your arm; find the limit of your strength. The rest is so much vomit and stale breath. Perhaps I really don't know any more.'

He took my arm and conducted me back to where my vehicle was parked, speaking as he did so. 'The corporal who had been in the Fahdia Waste I later dismissed. On parade one morning he couldn't stand. He was drunk. He was through the gate the same day in civilian rig and I haven't seen him since. Not a bad soldier, but in drunkenness he was a sloven. I don't remember his name. It may have been Ayub. He's the one man who can pinpoint the area in which the Kezzanis are active.'

I took my seat behind the steering wheel. 'That's fine, Colonel. I start by looking for a man whose name and whereabouts are uncertain.'

'I'll shorten the odds against you. The man came from Kezzan. By trade he was a dyer of wool and he went back to that work in the dyers' market. . . . You're not satisfied? You want more? Very well, I'll tell you this — he was a dyer in crimson. Good luck, Peter.'

§

As I drove away from the Skar I looked left and right in the empty desert for a sight of the attentive spirit who had followed me from El Desmara and watched my meeting with Nathan. I saw nothing but the broken ground where any depression could have hidden a man and a vehicle. I saw only one other human being: by a well, a mile or so back from the river, a tribesman robed in black was seated by the hoist, but he paid me no attention and I noticed nothing about him but that he seemed tall for a Tuareg or a Nebanese. After an hour I stopped by a ruined house that might have been the home of a road mender. I sat in the single patch of shadow with the wine and cheese I had brought from the market and took my lunch. No one passed in either direction. Nothing moved under the hard sun but for a rim of mirage at the limit of my sight. God, how I loved the desert, where the sun lay like a curse and the despoilers of the world had not thought it worthwhile to enter! One day I would write about the desert if I could find the words.

I was back in El Desmara at the moment when dusk fell and evening prayer was announced with a white flag on every tower and the harsh cry of the muezzin. At my office I found a message from Carol, asking me to call. I rang at once.

'Carol? This is Peter. What's the matter?'

'Nothing really. We're going.'

'Going where?'

'To England.'

I was silent. I had not thought she would leave so soon. Jason's country would be a barren place without her.

'Look——' I began.

'I want him to go. He should not have come here.'

'Of course not.'

'He plans to reopen the tourist industry. We leave in ten days.'

'It's not the best moment to bring tourists into the country.'

'He believes that General Khymer will keep the peace. He believes him to be a strong man. There will be a pilot scheme next season.'

I had to say something, a question, a promise; the opportunity would not come again.

'I am going to Kezzan,' was all I said.

'I see. When?'

'Tomorrow, at dawn.'

Then, not a word. We were adrift in a wide sea.

'Carol, we met at a strange time. For both of us the past is very close.'

'I made a mess of things. I wouldn't blame you for thinking badly of me.'

164

'I don't. Not now.'

Silence. A car started outside my office window.

'Why are you going to Kezzan?'

'Wild-goose chase. It may help Jason.'

'Is he in danger?'

'I think so. But the other side can be dented; that will even things up.'

'I want to help you. I want to help him. I've done so much damage already.'

'This won't be a picnic,' I said.

'Let me come.'

'That's absurd.'

'You can't say no.'

My mind was drifting into insanity: it had nowhere else to go.

'You want me to come, don't you?' she said.

'Yes. But I don't think you should.'

'I have to do something. Try to understand me. This time I have to get things right.'

'O God!'

'What does that mean?'

'It means I'm out of my mind. You can stay at the Majestique. I don't promise to take you any further than Kezzan.'

She said, 'It's settled, then.'

'Be ready at six in the morning,' I said, and rang off.

I had to find a robust vehicle without military trappings. I rang the Public Works Department, using the President's authority, and borrowed a white Range Rover belonging to the Superintending Engineer. When it came, I drove to the MT yard and waited while the sergeant fitter effaced the government markings. I filled two ten-gallon jerrycans at the petrol pump and secured them inside the rear door. With the tank added, I had fuel enough for six hundred miles, or a 300-mile penetration of the Fahdia Waste. I went next to the stores where I drew a tent and camp gear; I also drew a revolver and a box of ammunition which I locked in the glove compartment. I was home by ten o'clock. I rang Carol again and told her the whole thing was crazy. She told me she was coming none the less. Now her voice was clear and firm and stronger than mine.

I rose before light the next morning, when there was a dew and the cool air was sharp with the smell of the desert. The city had not yet wakened but I could hear dogs barking as I put food and water into the back of the car. I drove through the lightening streets where the townspeople still slept on the pavements and the dealers in meat and vegetables were taking down their shutters. Carol waited for me at the Hotel Khalid: there was brightness enough in the sky above the mountains for me to see her clearly. She said nothing as I helped her up. Then I drove north towards Kezzan, leaving the town behind, watching the mist disappear from the date gardens on either side of the road. I made a good pace, slowing only for the herds of goats that were being driven across the road on to lower ground.

We had covered twenty miles when we spoke together.

'Look——'

'Look——'

I said, 'You don't have to say anything. I'm in love with you, if you want the truth. I think I can stick to it.'

She looked at me in confused sympathy; then she closed her eyes upon a vision of the past. 'I'm not worth it, Peter. I've caused one disaster. You'd better forget it.'

'God, I suppose you know I'm in my forties and a failed husband.'

She nodded. I think she was happy. We didn't say anything else. We didn't even touch each other. But I had made some sort of promise that I thought I might keep. The mountains were on our right, blue and clear and rising into snow.

§

I had no brief to visit the Kezzan brigade, but while I was in the holy city I could not let slip the opportunity of a word with Rustum. I wanted to judge the level of his courage. I wanted to know how deep was his disobedience. The command of troops in rebellion required a steady nerve and by this time Rustum might see the merit of loyalty. I therefore made a private call upon the brigade that afternoon. I simply turned up alone at the headquarters and let surprise work for me. The brigade had never declared itself in revolt and Rustum could not decline to see the

166

President's aide without confirming his position as a rebel, which I was sure he didn't yet want to do. I flashed my official pass at the gate and didn't wait for the guard to check it. Rustum was plainly on the unit: a car bearing a brigadier's plates stood in a marked space outside the headquarters. I marched into the building and allowed the reflex of experience to guide me to the Brigade Commander's office. I banged on the door and when no answer came I let myself in.

Rustum lay in an easy chair and he looked as if my summons had wakened him. He wore the white uniform of the old Royal Guard, which the Republic had made obsolete, and if I needed evidence of a rebellious intention it was here. The office contained many fine wall-hangings and the floor was covered with a deep carpet. Rustum must have been surprised to see me but he contained his shock and rose to his feet. He could hardly do less.

I had decided to attack frontally. 'Good afternoon, Brigadier. You have broken communications with the capital, you have not responded to orders, you are wearing an inappropriate uniform. The President would appreciate your explanation.'

Rustum took his place behind the broad desk, his face showing a patrician disregard for the small details of revolution. He said calmly, 'The Kezzan brigade has always enjoyed a position of independence; it has a traditional loyalty to the Sultan.'

'That's idiotic. You report directly to the Commander-in-Chief.'

'Communications have been poor. We have been exercising outside the city.'

'You have not answered my question.'

'We have offered no defiance, conveyed no insult.'

'I should hope not.'

'We have done nothing to divest the President of his dignity.'

This was Arab thinking at its best: if you hadn't actually put a bullet through your leader's head you were guilty of no intransigence.

I said, 'Your state is virtually one of mutiny. If you wish to redeem yourself, you will go to El Desmara and confirm your allegiance to the President.'

The Brigade Commander, a spare young man with the well-cut

features shared by all the Sultan's descendants, knew the weakness of my argument. He knew that the President could command only the grudging loyalty of the two units in the capital and that Ben Talun didn't count. He knew that the Iman could impress the vigorous forces of Islam to his cause. But a soldier in breach of his oath is a divided, disintegrating man, and I knew that despite his off-handedness Rustum was unhappy. He laced his fingers together and undid them again.

He said without arrogance, 'You must remember that the President arrested the most prominent member of the Sharifian family. His Highness Suleiman ben Yusoff has served in the Royal Guard and is our Colonel-in-Chief. After his arrest he was beaten and humiliated in the market place and confined in a cellar. It was an insult to the brigade, as the President knew.'

'General Suleiman had assaulted the President. The attack was witnessed by three members of the Officers' Committee and by yourself.'

Rustum did not speak but I knew the way his mind had gone. So what? he thought. Prince Suleiman laid his hand upon the Nebanese upstart as he would have scolded a thieving donkey boy. It was part of Sharifian privilege.

I saw no point in presenting a logical argument as such things do not appeal to a high-born Arab who thinks himself aggrieved. With the greater emotional force of Arabic, I said, 'An officer who has broken his pledge has broken his fighting arm and put himself upon the outside of dignity.'

He raised his chin sharply, as if I had opened a part of his mind he did not wish to explore. 'There are many loyalties,' he said in high Arabic.

'For an officer there is only one.'

'There is birth, tradition——'

'There is only the Commander-in-Chief.'

'It is so?'

A wedge of doubt, perhaps not a large one, had entered the mind of Rustum ben Yusoff, and I wondered if I had gained an advantage. I knew the Arab soldier well enough not to be surprised by a gesture that would have embarrassed an English mess. Rustum got up from his desk and walked to where his sword and belt hung across a chair. He wanted the sword in his hand, as evidence of his commission in the Royal Guard. He withdrew the blade half its length from the scabbard; he looked at the quality of the steel, as he might have looked at the quality of his own metal; then he slammed the sword home again. He did not evade my question.

'General Khymer has spat upon us. I cannot offer him a proof of loyalty.'

My next question I let fall as if I knew the answer. I was speaking English now, the language of harsh reality.

'You will not, of course, use your force against the President.'

'I can give you no assurances.'

'It would be treason.'

'Better that than suffer insult.'

We were accompanied by the shadow of El Sharif. I no longer doubted his power in Kezzan when an officer could pass such a message to his superior and head of state. Ben Talun had at least offered to accept the arbitration of God. To my amazement, Rustum now turned a charming face upon me, resumed his Arabic and spoke with the indestructible courtesy of his race.

'You are our guest. We will give you refreshment. You will come with me to the mess.'

'I regret that I cannot come.'

'But you are tired! We will give you pillows, we will give you rest.'

'It may not be. I will leave you now.'

I went out. I would not take tea with troops in mutiny. I found the car and drove back into Kezzan. I was confirmed in the opinion that Jason had no hope of recovering the Kezzan brigade, but soldiers could be disarmed by other means than force: I had now to try the power of scandal. I wound my way through the streets where the Kezzanis covered the road like a litter and the light had thickened with afternoon. At the Majestique I called for Carol and together we drove into the Medina.

§

At this hour the townspeople, wakened from siesta, were pouring into the souk. I gave a boy fifty fils to protect the car and, to keep

169

him at his post, promised him another fifty when I returned. Then we passed under the arch which marked the beginning of the souk and entered the long dim barrel-vaulted market. At first we were in the street of the sandal-makers. We moved at the pace of the crowd while the beggars tugged at our sleeves. Soon the sandal-makers were replaced by the tin-smiths, then by the workers in brass, by the haberdashers, the silk merchants, the makers of nails. We stopped in a booth selling Berber jewellery and I bought Carol a necklace worked in silver and coral. I had said things to her I must mark with a precious metal of some kind. As I gave it to her, I wondered how it compared with Khalid's gifts.

I could not have said where the dyers' market began. I remember seeing first some skeins of rough-spun wool, coloured emerald, hanging from a pole; then more and more booths had wool on display, spun or raw, the skeins hanging like fruit from the rafters. Beyond these, where the street widened into an open space, where the sunlight lay brokenly in the dust, my eyes were drawn by the successive colours of the dyers' market. Here on each side the booths opened like dark caves, each given to a different colour. The first we looked into was working in black; the dyers themselves were stained the colour of pitch; we could barely see them as they turned the heavy skeins in the cauldrons. The next worked in indigo, and the blue footprints fanning out from the doorway merged with the succeeding colour, which was sepia. I did not know how to find a corporal in this strange place where the dye obliterated the features of the workmen, but I looked for the splash of crimson that would give me my direction and saw only that orange merged with red, and red with purple, at the end of the market.

I asked the dyers in blue if they could help me. I asked for a soldier who worked in crimson. But they only laughed and flicked their dye towards me, telling me they were not soldiers. Further down the street the dyers did not look up from their work but told me to go away. I was looking for someone who bore the mark of a military man. The stride, the straight back, the carriage of the head — any of these might have revealed him to me.

I did not find the corporal; the corporal found me. I had

forgotten that I too had worn a uniform and carried the imprint of the Army. Where the market ended in the derivatives of red a man stained bright crimson left his work and ran towards me offering his hand.

'Captain, Captain!' he said in the Maghrebi dialect.

I said, 'Greeting, and the blessing of God.'

'Thou art a soldier.'

'So are you, my friend.'

'My life is yours.'

'Equally. I have come to see you.'

'Who is it?' Carol asked. 'Why does he know you?'

'He's an old soldier. He doesn't know me, but he can see that I've been in the Army.'

The dyer in crimson who had once been a corporal took us into the back part of the booth where the colour was less pervasive. He talked all the time, but I couldn't catch much of it. We sat on boxes and inspected, one after another as he took them from his pocket, his discharge certificate, a medicine and duty chit, and a citation from his unit commander. From these I learned his name was Ayub ben Hamun and that he had been a good rifleman but given to drunkenness (a serious offence in a Mohammedan regiment). Then with the same eagerness he handed me a paper that had once committed him to a corrective training establishment and I realized that he could not read. The odds against me lengthened: if he could not read print it was unlikely he could read a map. None the less, of the two soldiers I had met this afternoon I would have trusted my life more readily to Corporal Ayub, the drunken defaulter, than to Brigadier Rustum ben Yusoff of the Royal Guard.

I spoke in bazaar Arabic. 'Fellow soldier, the Commander-in-Chief has sent me to find you because he needs your help. He has still a trust in you; he conveys the warmth of his heart.' I told him then of the Commander-in-Chief's interest in the Fahdia Waste, of which he, Corporal Ayub, had an unique personal experience. Only he could help his old friend, the Great General. These would have been lies in English but in Arabic they were an acceptable version of the truth. I asked him then if he remembered the place where he had turned back the travellers so that they should not see

171

what traffic was passing further down the path.

'I well remember, my Captain.'

'Then tell me where it was.'

'In the Red Sands, of course.'

He meant that it was in the Sahara.

'How far into the sands?'

'An infinity of miles.'

'Tell me what you saw.'

'The sunrise, the sunset.'

'There was a crossing, a well, a village?'

'Only the ill-tempered Tuareg.' He struggled with his memory; he slapped my knee in sudden recollection. 'I remember now! It was hot beyond imagining.'

I took out a map of the Fahdia Waste that I had found in the map store. It was the work of a local survey team and it displayed the camel tracks and place-names with a confidence I found suspect. I showed it to Ayub and he stared at it with a bright incomprehension. At length he brought down his crimson thumb in the centre of the map to suggest that the place I sought was somewhere on the world's surface and that, with diligence, I would find it.

I liked Ayub no matter that he had disappointed me; he had a friendly nature and he had done his best. When we rose to leave, he shook hands with Carol and gave me an untidy embrace that left me well smudged with the colour of his trade. We were walking down the market almost beyond sight when he called me back.

'Captain, the cloud has passed from my memory! Everything is clear! The travellers were carrying rock salt and crystal. We took it from them, but it was worthless and we threw it into the sand.'

I thanked him again. We left him standing in the path and watching our progress along the crowded street. Not until we had taken a dozen paces did I realize that the odds against success were now much reduced. The salt deposits which the Tuareg had worked since the earliest times were at Amiri, and if the travellers were carrying the raw salt they must have been bringing it towards the mountains, where they would sell it in the market at Quazetta: there was a chance that the area I was looking for, which the brigade had been at pains to isolate, lay on the path between these places.

I stopped and spread the map against the surge of people. I saw that a camel track joined Amiri to Quazetta and that it was crossed by two other tracks running on the north-south axis. At one of those distant crossings a traffic had passed and perhaps still did which the world was not supposed to see.

Carol said, 'What are you looking at?'

'A path in the desert.'

'Is it important?'

'I don't know. Yes, I think so.'

'Are you going there?'

I didn't have to make up my mind. 'Yes, I am going there. I will leave in the morning.'

'I am coming with you.'

It was not a question. She held me in a firm gaze.

'I don't know that you should. There may be danger.'

'Will it help the President?'

'Perhaps.'

'Then you cannot prevent me. This matters to us both. I didn't exactly help the last President.'

I had not seen her so determined before. I wanted her with me, and I needed a separate witness, but I doubted if she knew what it was like in the desert. I hesitated.

'You are not going to refuse,' she said.

'I suppose not. It won't be easy.'

'I'm tougher than you think I am.'

'I daresay.'

'What will we find?'

'I can't be sure. Probably nothing. Possibly enough to wreck Solly Yusoff.'

'Then it's settled.'

'I suppose it is,' I said.

We went back to the Majestique, where I had taken rooms earlier in the day. I made the car ready for the desert.

That evening I danced with Carol in the small club in the basement of the hotel. She made me very happy and I nearly lost my head. But at eleven o'clock I said good-night to her and took myself firmly to my room, telling myself that I was a middle-aged divorcee who was supposed to have learned his lesson.

I needed to bring some order into my mind. I took out the map and studied every feature of the Fahdia Waste until it was engraved in my memory. Given luck, I could destroy Solly and sustain Jason as President. I might even give Rustum a wallop. Then I went to bed and watched the moonlight falling on the wall and wondered how Solly was spending the dark hours. At last I fell into a dream-filled sleep in which I saw the Red Desert and it revealed nothing but its own barren face.

# 14

The road from Kezzan to Quazetta crosses the Southern Atlas and reaches six thousand feet at the head of the pass. We were climbing for two hours. The pine trees that grew along the foothills threw their shadows over the road; here there was only a slight gradient and I kept the big car in top gear as we took the bends and gained a little height. Above the pines, in the higher folds of the mountains, the Berbers had long ago made their homes, having sense enough to fortify their houses and granaries against the bandits who came up from the plain. Each village adhered to the mountainside as a martin's nest adheres to a wall, and the fields were incised into the face of the hill. Like the people, the trees had grown small; I saw ilex, thorn and tamarisk where the contour offered shelter from the wind. Above the villages were the rocks, and the road narrowed and the bends became more acute; the air was cold and sweet upon our lips. There was no movement but for an eagle turning in the sky far above us. Higher still and we entered the snows where the road was marked by wands, the wheels slipped and the sun was bright beyond bearing. We continued for another thousand feet. Now the eagle turned far below us, just visible against the floor of the valley. We stopped at the col and looked back at the road falling for thirty miles.

Carol said, 'There is a car behind us. It has been there for an hour.'

I was surprised. I had thought we were alone. I looked down the long road and saw, two thousand feet below, a car emerge from a crease in the mountain and disappear again.

'It may be nothing,' I said.

'We are being followed, aren't we?'

She wasn't frightened, just curious. After all, her father was buying the country.

'I think so. Two days ago I was followed to the Skar. But he doesn't come near.'

'What does he want?'

'It could be anything.'

I didn't think he wanted our lives: there was a reticence about our guardian that marked his activity here as in the Neban.

'Can we hide?'

I looked at our vehicle tracks in the snow, the only marks in the road; he would know that we had passed the col and that our destination was Quazetta and the desert. I suppose I was angry.

'This isn't hide and seek,' I said. 'The country is in a state of revolution and the car behind us may contain violent men.'

'Never mind,' said Carol. 'It's lovely here.'

It was true: Jason's country was beautiful beyond description. I kicked the snow left and right in the road. I was angry because I had brought her into danger and she wasn't frightened when she should have been.

'Come on,' I said irritably. 'It's a long way down.'

On the far side of the mountains the earth turned red and there was little water. After the Atlas the world grows poor. Shallow red hills lay all around the eastern horizon, and beyond them were the sands that we must reach.

We came into Quazetta at midday. It was not much of a place: a street of mean houses, a weak growth of palms about a single well, a mosque, a dusty space that might have been a playing field. I stopped at the petrol station, waked the surly attendant, filled the tank and topped up the jerry cans. Ahead of us for all I knew the nearest petrol was somewhere on the Nile; the Sahara, as broad and empty as the Atlantic, lay between here and Egypt, and somewhere in this wilderness was the evidence I needed. The notion that I might find it began to look optimistic to the point of insanity.

The road continued well made for ten miles beyond Quazetta, and then we were on the camel track, the haphazard path beaten by the nomadic tribes who had somehow found the means of life in the desert. I saw the tyre marks of heavy vehicles which might have been those of the Kezzan brigade, but lorries were known to reach Amiri from time to time. We were climbing now, not steeply but on a long gradient into the hills of red rock. The track was well marked and I kept to a steady pace, a little above twenty miles an hour. After three hours the path was falling and ahead I could see the level plain they called the Fahdia Waste.

Then we were in a world of sand and the path followed the firm ground, bending this way and that, but keeping the same mean direction, two degrees north of due east upon which bearing lay Amiri and the salt deposits. Darkness and the cool of the desert night were still four hours away. I wanted to reach at least the first intersection by nightfall where I might find traces of movement on the lateral path.

Towards evening the path grew less distinct and twice I lost it, after which I had to turn the car and follow our tracks backward until I found traces of the road. The mountains grew small behind us until they vanished, and then we were alone in the desert with no guiding mark but the falling sun. At sunset, when the shadow of the car lay exactly along the path, a second track came in from our right, joined our own, then broke away left-handed on a northerly bearing. The ground was pitted with the footprints of men and camels. A pile of rocks supporting a wand, the ruins of a rest house, some litter and sump oil—these marked the first intersection. I examined the north-south track for evidence of recent traffic, but such traces as I found were blurred by time and the path did not seem to have been much used.

We were a hundred and twenty miles from Quazetta. We had seen no one at all. I wondered if we were wasting time.

§

I drove forward a mile and left the road. I stopped near some rocks where the desert was unmarked by any footprint. The sun was touching the horizon and the sky flared with red and amber. In the short dusk we made a camp under the rocks and drank the beer the flasks had kept cool. Carol had been intimate with men of power and she had tact enough not to ask me how close we were to failure. The darkness spread quickly and the stars came out in

177

all the fullness of the Saharan night. In the huge desert there was not a movement, not a sound.

An infantryman learns to draw the utmost value from each minute; for him the greatest peace lies between one shot and the next. I lay on the blanket next to Carol, not touching her, enjoying the coolness and the silence after the fret of the day. I should not have been happy but I was; for once in my life I had all that I needed. I know that Jason's country would probably break apart, but just now that didn't disturb me nor prevent me from hoping the night would last for ever. For an hour the only sound I could hear was the breath upon Carol's lips.

Then far away there was another sound which at first was so soft it did not beckon my attention. At length I raised myself on one elbow and turned my ear to the road up which we had travelled. We were not alone; somewhere a car was moving. In this great silence it could be five or fifty miles away. I climbed the rocks behind me and looked into the western quarter of the desert, and at a distance I could not judge I saw the loom of headlights and heard clearly the beat of an engine. I watched for a long time as the lights drew closer, keeping the same direction, following us along the old camel track. I saw the beams rocking as the vehicle plunged over the rough ground. At length I saw the lights swing off the track and go out as the car stopped for the night. I guessed it to be three miles short of the crossing.

I returned to Carol. 'He's some way back. I don't think he will come near.'

'Is it the same car as before?'

'I believe so.'

'Is he a friend or an enemy?'

'I can't say. But had he meant to harm us he would have tried by now.'

This fellow traveller who kept himself at a distance had no doubt a strong motive for following us across the Red Sands, but what it was I could not think. None of Jason's petty agents would have stomach enough for a journey of this sort. I was certain of only one thing—that he knew we had seen him, for were it otherwise he would not have let his headlights blaze across the desert. We were travelling, as it were, by mutual consent.

Now in the starlight which illuminated the rocks and lay like a dew across the sands I took Carol's hand in mine and raised her to her feet. We walked across the yielding desert, going nowhere, just moving together towards a star-filled horizon. Perhaps we went a quarter mile; then she turned towards me as though we had reached the place we had searched for, laid her arms about my neck and let her head fall so that her lips, now parting ever so slightly, were only a small space from mine. The starlight which came from nowhere, making the sands as bright as the sky, threw no shadows; her face revealed its moulding only to the tips of my fingers. I cannot say how long we stood there while the seconds slowed to the point where time had no movement and the whole of my life, that which was passed, that which was still to come, led surely to and from this long still minute in the Fahdia Waste.

We were moving again, slowly, as time resumed a gentle pace. I don't think we spoke; there was no need for that. We could never recall that first moment when life had the power of dream and which was now set firmly in the past. I don't know where we went. It might have been a mile, perhaps only a few paces. We came to the brow of a tiny hill that was no more than a billowing of the sand. Here then; it was as good a place as any we would know. About us was the soundless desert which turned this strange stylistic ritual into a play of symbols that was no more than the fulfilment of rhyme, of pattern. In the gentle light which allowed no colour Carol was as pale as the sands with a remote, lost identity. Then we were returned to the familiar, and she took my hand, I think a little shyly, and together we walked back towards the car.

§

I was certain the north-south track was not much in use and that we had to continue eastward to the second intersection. The map showed it to be about forty miles away at the foot of an escarpment. We started early, but I had no doubt our companion in the desert would have seen the plume of dust on the horizon and put his vehicle on the same path. We drove into the blazing early sun which dissolved every feature of the desert; we hobbled forward over soft ground, making little more than ten miles an hour, feeling the first heat, keeping our lips stopped against the dust. After three hours I could see the escarpment like a pencil line drawn midway across my vision. Later it assumed detail and I knew I was looking at a band of rocks at the head of an eastern-facing cliff that stretched north and south for a hundred miles. The map showed the second intersection to be on the far side of the escarpment and on the lower ground. When we reached the head of the cliff, where the track found a perilous route down into the depression, I turned north and drove for half a mile along the top of the escarpment until I found a cleavage in the rock large enough to conceal the car and where there was some shadow.

Here I took the binoculars and studied the lower ground. I was looking into the first miles of the Fahdia Depression which had been known since the explorer, Admiral Eager, first reached the escarpment in the eighteen-sixties, but which no doubt the Tuareg had known long before that. Sure enough, I could see the second track, which clearly was in greater use than the first, running parallel with the cliff at a distance of perhaps a hundred yards; the crossing was below me and a little to the south. Beyond the track the floor of the depression reached away into mirage. We could not have found a better place from which to observe the road.

I stretched canvas from the roof of the car to the rocks, to give us shelter when the sun climbed to the vertical. I off-loaded the camping equipment. I reckoned we could stay here for three days before our water ran out. I watched the dust of the other observer as he advanced towards the escarpment and turned south; then it disappeared and I knew he had stopped. He was less than a mile away.

We waited through the long hours while the sun beat on the canvas and nothing stirred on the road below but small changes in the mirage. At midday it was hot almost beyond bearing; by four o'clock the sun was losing its fierce strength and the shadow of the escarpment was creeping across the floor of the depression. For all I could see there was no one in the Fahdia Waste but ourselves and that other watcher whom I had almost forgotten. It grew dark; we were again invested with all the wonder of the desert night. Now we slept on a bed of sand beside the car. I held Carol's hand, then

180

dropped it; we were too exhausted by the heat of the day to make any claim on our new fresh love. In the hour before dawn, when there was a moisture in the air, I listened for the sound of traffic on the road, the beat of an engine, a call, a footfall, but there was nothing but the stillness of an empty land.

At dawn I left Carol sleeping and took my post in the rocks. The sky whitened; I could see the track receding in both directions. It was bare of movement, of any life whatever. I wondered what sort of idiot I had been to come this far on such a slender hope. The sun rose steeply and the fierce impact of the light in the rocks stung my eyes and forced me back into the shelter. I do not know how we endured the hours of the sun's greatest strength, but in that endless period, when the hands of my watch seemed to be stationary, I learned that Carol had a fortitude greater than I had a right to expect. She made no complaint; she did not suggest that I had made a mistake in coming here. We took it in turn to watch the track, but nothing passed and I doubted if it ever would. When the sun declined and I could breathe more easily, I climbed back to my place in the rocks, extending my vision to the horizon, and waited without hope for the evidence that whould show Solly and the Kezzanis to be the crooks I had supposed them. I knew we could not bear another day in the desert. Failure lay upon my mind like a sick shadow. Then, in the south, at a distance so great I could not at first trust my eyes, I saw a feather of dust.

I blinked and it did not go away. I closed my eyes and counted twenty seconds: still it was there. I called Carol and she confirmed that many miles down the path something was moving. A little later a second feather of dust appeared behind the first; later still and there was a third. I watched for half an hour as the shards of dust crept towards us, growing in size and colour; I had no doubt that a convoy of three vehicles was travelling northward on the old track, taking the outermost route, keeping far beyond sight.

There was an oblique sunlight in the depression that would last another hour. With luck I would see what the vehicles contained. I made certain we could not ourselves be seen, either from the track below or from the path leading to Quazetta, as the convoy might turn west at the intersection: if the Kezzanis were running an illegal traffic they would deal abruptly with onlookers. We

181

waited behind the rocks while the vehicles came up the road about a mile apart. At length I could hear the engine of the first vehicle as it laboured across the surface of the desert.

I kept the binoculars steadied on the rising dust, watching the vehicle take form at the base of the cloud. A lorry hard-pressed in the clutching sand. A lorry with hooped canvas at the back. A lorry painted khaki with an emblem on the off-side wing. It crossed the intersection and continued northwards towards us, throwing a long shadow. I held the binoculars on the cab. I could see men — men wearing forage caps and clothed in denim. It was a military vehicle driven by soldiers. I studied the emblem on the wing and saw the figure 1 superimposed on a sprig of lilac.

Then the lorry had passed me, going up the road.

'Who are they?' Carol asked.

'The First Battalion of the Kezzan brigade. The Royal Guard. Solly's regiment.'

'What are they carrying?'

'I can't see.'

The canvas was lashed hard down over the ribs and the slit at the back was laced. But of one thing I was certain: the lorry bore a heavy load, one that depressed the springs through half their movement. I watched the vehicle recede up the path and disappear behind a jutting face of the cliff. This was a frustration I had not expected and I cursed myself for my lack of foresight. Of course they would cover the load if they meant to keep it secret.

My anger got the better of my sense of caution. I left Carol in the rocks and, clumsily, without seeking the best path, scrambled down the face of the escarpment taking my binoculars and camera. The second vehicle was within half a mile and I had simply to hope they would not see me. At a point thirty feet from the base of the cliff I started a fall of rock that raised a tell-tale dust, but the air was still clouded from the passage of the first vehicle and I told myself that drivers long at the wheel were unlikely to be watchful. From the foot of the incline I ran forward fifty paces and ducked below a screen of rock. I was now close enough to the road to get a better look at the vehicles.

The second lorry bore the same regimental markings as the first and the back was likewise covered. It passed me with the same

182

laboured beat of the engine and was clearly carrying another heavy cargo. Before the dust intervened, I saw something I had not noticed in the first lorry: there was movement under the canvas, as if the load swung with the rocking of the vehicle. The rear curtains were drawn tightly together and laced. Again I watched the lorry pulling away from me up the path as the sun made rainbows in the dust.

The dust hung for a long time in the windless air. When it thinned and cleared I saw with a surge of the heart that the first lorry, now returned to my sight at a great distance, had stopped, and that the second lorry was drawing to a halt about half a mile behind it. In something like panic I realized that the last vehicle in the convoy, were it to follow suit, would stop close to where I was hiding.

I waited with fear plucking at my nerves for the third lorry to reach me. It came at a languid gait, a wisp of steam escaping from the radiator, and when it drew level it had slowed to a walking pace as if the driver were looking for some firm ground on which to stand. It stopped at a hundred yards and the driver and two other soldiers jumped down from the cab. They were armed. They were going to unlace the back.

I turned the binoculars on to the rear of the vehicle, where the soldiers were dividing the canvas; with an effort I kept my hands still so the picture should not be blurred by movement. The soldiers looked young; certainly they were Arab. They peeled the canvas apart and let the tail-board fall. At first I could see nothing inside the wagon but shadows — restless black shadows — but as the soldiers off-loaded their vehicle I had a sight of the cargo they had tried so hard to conceal.

Men. Black men. Men so crushed and suffocated they could hardly stand. Men with their wrists joined by chains, who bore themselves with a lethargy of spirit, who fell into the sand as if their bones could no longer support them. Men the Maghrebi Arabs had tormented for more than a thousand years.

So that was it. Here in the Fahdia Waste was the evidence that should ruin Solly and sustain Jason's Presidency when I made it public. The Kezzanis were slaving. The Army was using the desert tracks to raid the black south, conducting a trade that has never been finally abolished in Africa. Below the Atlas was the enormous area of the Neban where the villages were far apart and it would be a simple matter to make captive the young men and women who still fetched a high price in the markets of Arabia. Somewhere to the north they would be taken to a desert airstrip and from there flown eastward.

I set the camera for the reduced light and crept forward until I found a place with an uninterrupted view. I took a sequence of photographs, the first I believed of Nebanese slaves in transit, though I had seen similar pictures taken in Chad and the Sudan. Then I closed the camera and waited for the vehicles to move off.

I was confident I had the means to discredit Solly, to cashier Rustum, to embarrass the Iman and the Sharifian family, and to put an end to the Kezzani rebellion.

§

When I climbed out of the depression I was dusty and tired and sickened by the things I had seen. Carol met me at the head of the escarpment. I suppose I was short-tempered.

'I hope you saw that,' I said. 'We will need the statement of a separate witness.'

'Were they convicts? Their hands were chained.'

'Nebanese slaves. The brigade is working the old routes.'

'What on earth for?'

'Profit, private service, an age-old habit of exploitation.'

'But those men were dying!'

'They always did. Of heat, of misery. When you take a tribesman from his village he will sometimes die from loneliness.'

Carol's world had contained no slaves and she could not adapt quickly to this frightfulness. 'Can they *really* have been slaves?'

I said, 'This was a well-planned operation showing all the signs of experience. They used the most easterly route where no one goes but the Tuareg. They kept the lorries well apart so that the groups of slaves should not join. They had separated the women and children from the men to break the women's spirit more quickly and to deprive the men of strength. The women and children will have been in the leading vehicles.'

'You mean there were children in those lorries?'

184

I was callous in my disgust. 'Children fetch high prices in the markets of Arabia, particularly well-shaped young females. But then, they would not have taken the old or the deformed or the ugly. Those they will have killed to prevent them from speaking.'

'You are telling me the truth?'

'The utter bloody truth.'

My anger had gone to my head. I had now to know who had followed me to this place and what had compelled him to endure the sunlight in his own lonely vigil. I took the pistol belt and fastened it round my waist, but I did not undo the holster strap. I left Carol at the car and walked along the head of the bluff, not troubling to conceal myself. Whoever it was would have seen me in the depression, would know that I had photographed the slaves with their captors; I had to know his identity and to whom his loyalty was given. The light was vanishing off the face of the desert. I found the tracks of his vehicle where they had veered south from the Quazetta road and followed them for about five hundred yards. I was too angry to be much frightened.

I saw his vehicle first. It was a small saloon car built for Europe. The driver had needed courage to bring such a vehicle across the Red Sands. Great courage, or perhaps an unalterable obligation.

I rounded a shoulder of rock and found him standing on the path looking in my direction, waiting for me. There was light enough for me to see him clearly.

There was only one greeting appropriate for a meeting in the outer desert. I said in Arabic, 'Peace and the blessing of God.'

He did not respond. The enormous black frame was quite still, neither menacing nor fearful. The habit of service, the constraint of the fetter, the blows across the shoulders had left in him a sort of repose.

'Master, what are you doing here?' he asked me after a time, the voice soft for so large a man.

'Seeking the truth.'

I sat on the rocks which were beginning to cool. I meant to show him, in the way of the nomad, that I had come to talk, not to fight, but he remained standing in the manner of the servant.

'Come, sit by me!' I said.

'It is not fitting.'

'We are in the desert, where there is no difference between one man and another. Your arms have twice the power of mine.'

'The desert does not change the orders of men.'

'Friend, you followed me to the Skar and you saw my meeting with Colonel Nathan. Now you have followed me many miles across the Red Sands. What is your purpose?'

The giant Negro, who had been bound to the young Prince Suleiman, who had carried him upon his shoulders, kept his eyes upon me but did not answer my question. My mind was beginning to clear.

'Hero, I will tell you why you came here. General Suleiman is your suzerain, is he not? Many years ago you were given to him. Your hand was never to be raised against him, your great strength was to protect him from harm. You accepted a role of thraldom and obedience.'

I could not be sure, but I think he nodded.

'I believe you are obedient still. When I came to this country your master told you to keep watch over me. He would have put you into my household the better to see what my life contained. He was afraid of what I might do, what I might discover. I dismissed you from my house, but you have kept to your master's word. He knew that he held your loyalty in his hand like a golden coin, and that once he had given you his command you would follow it no matter where it led, even to the ends of the desert.'

I had expected him to show a trace of pride, but his face was without expression. Perhaps a loyalty of this strength did not seem remarkable to him.

'Well, fellow traveller, you have found me here, you know what I have seen. You know also, I am sure, that the royal family is behind this trade in human lives. What will you do?'

His mind was on a different course. He said slowly, 'I was in Kezzan for Haraq Tej. My master was humiliated when he was made to raise his hand in submission to the Nebanese President. It was an insult I could not bear. Later I was in El Desmara when the soldiers brought Prince Suleiman to the great market. I saw them beat him, and spit on him, and force him to the ground where he lay in the filth of the market. I saw them take camel droppings and foul meat and rub them into his face. Why, master? Why was it done?'

'The Prince was guilty. He struck the President.'

'But the President is drawn from the menial order.'

'Even so, Hero.'

I had to try the path of reason because that was the way I was made, but I hadn't much hope that Hero would follow me. I looked for the simplest Arabic, the better to convey my point.

'Old man, you saw the lorries and what they contained. Those were Nebanese people taken from their villages and forced into slavery by the Kezzani soldiers. They were dying from the cruelty of it. Your master is a leader of those soldiers and a merchant in human lives. You are Nebanese. You have felt the manacle and the lash. How can you defend the slave-masters who have tormented your people and kept you in subservience?'

Well, I had made my gesture to the prophets of logic and sanity but the futility of it was already plain. Hero turned away from me and looked at the road up which the lorries had travelled. He smiled in private wisdom.

'Master, I came this way many years ago. There were no lorries then; we came on foot and many died before we reached our destination. I was taken into the Royal Palace at Kezzan where there were more than a thousand slaves and placed in bond to the young prince, who was then three years old. It was my duty to love him, to serve him. I carried him upon my back and felt the strokes of his whip. He abused me and called me a nigger and a slave.'

'Did that not change your love for him?'

'It was changed. It was deepened. A slave loves his master as part of his obedience. The harsh word is his endearment. I was filled with love for the young prince who was the only human being visible to me.'

'You did not have to love him, Hero. You could have felt hatred for him.'

His next words had a meaning in formal Arabic which did not translate exactly into English, chiefly because the key words were missing; I could only suppose thoughts such as these had never entered an Englishman's head. His meaning was something like this. 'I cannot hate, because hatred has not been defined for me. Love reaches its fullness only through degradation and

187

endurance. I do not understand another love, nor do I need to.'

I said helplessly, 'You are big, you are strong. You could have broken away from slavery.'

'Why should I, Master? A slave is at peace.'

I clung to what was left of my Christian accountability. 'No man has the right to enslave another,' I said; but here on the old slave road, in the failing light, the words had lost their proper sense.

Hero did not answer this.

I stood up. I had spent long enough in Islam to know how simple it was for the truth to become reversed and still to have the ring of certainty. I had work to do. I had to demolish Solly and the Kezzanis. I had to enlist the forces of Christendom with all the outrage of which they were capable, and this I could not do if I listened to the language of slavery. I was turning to go when a new thought struck me.

'You have fuel? You have water? It is two hundred miles back to Quazetta.'

'I have fuel for ten miles, and no water.'

'Then you came all this way with the knowledge that you could not return.'

'I was bidden to follow you.'

'Hero, no obligation requires you to die of thirst. Your master would not have wished it.'

'The Prince would not have known.'

So, he would have died under a cloth with no one to mark his passing but with an intact heart.

'I will give you what I can,' I said.

I went back the way I had come, stumbling over the rocks. It was dark now and the first stars were showing. More than once I lost my way and had to shake my mind awake before I could recover my direction. Likewise my mind was lost in a strange territory where there were no firm bearings. When I got back to Carol I was not in the best of tempers.

'Who was it?' she asked me.

'An old slave of Solly's following a promise that Solly had certainly forgotten. He would have died here.'

'He must be mad.'

188

'Yes, mad, I suppose.'

'What else can it have been?'

'Nothing else,' I said, but with more force than certainty. 'Nothing else at all.'

# 15

I went straight to the President's office when we reached El Desmara two days later. We hadn't much time. Hero would have told the Kezzanis that I had seen the slave traffic and they would need to take some sort of initiative. I asked Jason to call a meeting of the Officers' Committee, which he did for that evening. We sat in the ornate reception room where once the Sultan had given his unalterable judgments. Jason was flanked by General Salam — asleep, I thought, but his white head giving authority to our proceedings — and the jovial Colonal Aziz. I sat at the foot of the table with Captain Ismael and a secretary.

I gave them an account of my findings in the Fahdia Waste. Beyond doubt the Kezzanis were slaving in the Neban, using the brigade for the purpose. As Kezzan was in rebellion against the Military Government and aimed to set up an alternative administration under General Suleiman, we could put an end to their activities by discrediting them in the outside world. I urged telegrams to the United Nations Commission of Human Rights in New York, to the Anti-Slavery Society in London, with a simultaneous release of the photographs to the press agencies. I concluded, 'We must act quickly. The Kezzanis will know that the trade has been discovered and they will try to distract attention with an initiative of their own.'

Jason had listened attentively. He looked tired, but his mind was as lively as ever. 'Very well, Colonel. You have presented a convincing argument. You have made it possible for the Committee to take action against Kezzan while retaining a progressive image. We are much indebted to you. Of course, the trade must be stopped at once.'

190

'A vile business,' said Colonel Aziz, but his voice broke upon the untruth. He turned the palms of his hands upward. What if the Kezzanis do bag a few Nebanese? he seemed to say. They've always done so. It's their particular sport.

Captain Ismael didn't speak but his bitter smile, which illuminated the foot of the table with a cold light, said clearly that he had predicted as much in an unreformed society.

Jason pulled at the undersides of his eyes, keeping them from closing. He had taken the winning card into his hand but he showed no relish in playing it. 'Gentlemen, we are agreed that the exploitation of the Neban must not continue. We have then to decide what action we can take against Kezzan. A military operation would obviously strain the loyalty of the units supporting the Committee.'

This was a nice way of saying that we could not count on them obeying their orders.

'I do not think that warfare is appropriate,' said Salam, the father of the Committee. 'The Kezzanis have not attacked us; they have not even issued a statement of defiance. I suggest that we suspend Rustum from duty pending court martial. A charge of slaving can then be heard in court.'

'Of course that is the best thing!' said Aziz.

Jason showed patience, as a President must. 'You are forgetting that I have no means of enforcing these decisions. In effect, you are recommending that I do nothing. But a grave inhuman offence has been committed against the Neban. I must take some action against the culprits if the Military Government is to survive.' He turned to me. 'Colonel, you bear no responsibility for the decisions of the Committee, but you are privy to our affairs. What do you recommend in the present situation?'

I was surprised that he asked me and spoke without reflection. 'Make the reports to the international agencies. Hold a press conference. Put the Army on first alert and prepare charges against Brigadier Rustum. Otherwise wait for world opinion to harden against Kezzan. In a fortnight your position may be much strengthened.'

'That seems to me sensible,' said Aziz, with the satisfaction of the landed proprietor who could spend another fortnight hunting

191

the gazelle.

'I agree,' said Salam.

Ismael didn't speak. He had travelled far in the direction of nonconformity and I wondered what appointment he had been offered in the reorganized state.

'You are right, of course,' Jason said, with a most courteous obeisance in my direction. 'I will do as you suggest. But the action is incomplete because it ignores the principal author of our difficulties.'

Oh no, I thought, not that! Leave Solly in arrest until the Kezzanis are disarmed. Let the old fool diminish in captivity.

But the President had resumed the path that led along the face of the cliff, where the fall was greatest. He was tired, ill-omened, impelled by dangerous forces. He spoke quietly, almost painfully:

'I shall in addition announce the public trial of General Suleiman, charged with an assault on the President and with slaving in the Neban. It would be an intolerable weakness if I were to ignore this enemy of the state. The General must be punished, the penalty must be sharp and salutary. I have quite made up my mind about it.'

§

After the meeting Jason went to his office and told his aide not to admit me: he knew very well what my argument would be and plainly did not wish to hear it. None the less I brushed the aide aside and faced him. He looked sulky and, if I was not mistaken, a little guilty.

'I'm not free to see you, Colonel. I have work to do.'

'Mr President, you cannot intend to kill General Suleiman.'

'Certainly not! It will be a judicial execution following a verdict of guilty.'

'It will be murder.'

'That is a remark you must withdraw.'

'You have the means to emerge from this with clean hands—your enemies defeated and General Suleiman broken as a political figure.'

'He must die; there is no other course. The sentence will be carried out in the great market.'

192

'A public execution will show the Military Government to be as barbarous as its opponents.'

'Beheaded! Kaput! His body left to the fury of the crowd.'

I was driving him more deeply into the absurd. For the first time I wondered if Jason was entirely sane. When I paused, he continued his line of thought with fresh vigour.

'He will be dragged through the dust, while the soldiers form a square. He will be abused by his brother officers. Then his head will be struck off and offered as a plaything to the crowd, who will toss it from hand to hand in anger and scorn.'

I could not take him seriously. I said, 'I'll come back when you feel inclined to discuss things rationally.' And I left the office without first bringing myself to attention, which had been my habit.

He shouted some words after me. 'When you go home, Colonel, you will tell them at Eastleigh what a barbarian I was. They will count it a failure in training.'

I didn't answer that. I went to my office and spent the next hour drafting signals to the international agencies concerned with human rights which I hoped Jason could be persuaded to release. I kept to the facts, suggesting that the trade route be picked up north of Amiri and traced to its destination, which was probably in Arabia. The government of the Saharan Republic would of course take vigorous action to suppress the traffic inside its frontiers. Next I prepared a signal to Brigadier Rustum ben Yusoff suspending him from duty until a board of enquiry had looked into the activities of units under his command.

I returned to the President, who was gazing at his finger-nails. He said then, from a great way off, 'Tell me, Peter—I have forgotten—what was the name of the game we played at Eastleigh, when we were blindfolded and tried to hit each other with rolled newspaper? I recall that I broke the Commandant's spectacles.'

' "Kill Moriarty",' I said. 'It's rather childish.'

'It is a game filled with amusement. We have never played it in our mess.'

'These signals are for you to consider, sir.'

'Signals, Peter? You are kind. In our army we are too serious.

193

We do not play enough funny games.'

That being so, I was tempted to suggest that he refrain from the murder of a brother officer, but instead I let the spirit of Eastleigh work upon him in silence.

'I suggest you hold a press conference tomorrow morning,' I said. 'Tell them the story. Let the facts speak for themselves.'

'Of course, dear friend. Whatever you say.'

He drew the signals towards him and authorized their release with his initials, but I don't think he read them. 'You have done well, Peter. The discovery of the slave trade was a master-stroke of initiative. You will have the highest decoration that we can bestow, for which I have already composed the citation.'

Clearly he had done nothing of the sort and I was content to let that remain a flight of his imagination. But Jason was never satisfied with one invention; he had to pursue an idea to the limit of development. 'Furthermore, I have telegraphed to the Commandant at Eastleigh telling him of your achievement. They will hang your picture in the hall, next to that of Colonel 'Toggs' Drummond-Aiken who crossed the Tasman Sea in a balloon.'

'Sir, I would advise you not to mention your plans for General Suleiman to the international press.'

He was silent. I did not know where his mind had gone.

'You understand me, sir — we cannot anticipate what a military court will decide. A mention of punishment would not be appropriate at this stage.'

He had lapsed into stupor. I tried to draw his gaze in my direction, to break the spell in which he was held, but he was too deeply detached to hear me.

Well, I had given him my advice as my duty required; that it had fallen on ears stopped against the smallest influence was hardly my fault. I recovered the signals and returned to leave.

The President said now, without the complete use of his voice, 'What did you say, Peter? Was it a matter of importance? You must realize that in the case of General Suleiman I have no choice. He has offended the President, therefore he must die.'

'There are alternatives, sir.'

'Alternatives? I do not understand you. What other penalties are there?'

'Cashiering, imprisonment, exile.'

'No, Peter, there are no alternatives. If I do not kill Solly, he will kill me. . . . You are going now? Is it so late?'

§

I took myself home bearing a sense of impending disaster. I might talk him out of it, but I was now fairly certain that Jason meant to kill Solly. I wanted Carol. If I didn't see her I would probably get drunk and that would help no one. I called her at the hotel and she came within the hour. She didn't ask me what was wrong; she had an instinct to comfort without words for which I was grateful. We walked together for half an hour in the tiny courtyard, making our own small space in a demented world. I had a question to ask but I left it as long as I could.

At last I said, 'When are you leaving?'

'In three days.'

'It's better that way. There will be trouble here. Later you will come back.'

The telephone was ringing, but I paid no attention because Ravi would answer it. The ringing stopped and I waited for Ravi to tell me who it was. He didn't come and I forgot it.

But not for long. Within a few minutes I remembered that someone had tried to reach me. I went into the house dragging Carol behind me and called for Ravi. He didn't answer. I called again and knew in the same instant that he wasn't there. Of course, I had not seen him that evening; I had only supposed him in the house — I had supposed that like all soft-footed Asian servants he was somewhere in the background waiting to come forward when I needed him.

I called his wife Tansha but she did not reply.

Then, as a shaft of fear struck somewhere in my body's core, I went out to the servants' quarters at the rear of the bungalow and hammered on the door. There was no light, no footstep; the sound of my knocking fell into a void. I opened the door and found the rooms empty. Ravi and Tansha and all their family had gone, taking their possessions with them.

'Damn,' I said.

'What has happened?' Carol asked.

195

'Oldest trick in the world. You attack your enemy through his servants.'

We were standing in the dark with only vague moon shadows for company. The house seemed very empty then.

'What sent them away?'

'Fear.'

'Of what?'

'Death, mutilation, the murder of their children. Who can say?'

'Who would do such a thing?'

I didn't answer; my mind was filled with the possibilities of violence. We went back into the lighted part of the house, where I gave us both a drink. Now I was houseboy, sweeper, peon, as I doubted if I could get servants to stay in a house marked with disfavour. Soldiers, perhaps; no one else.

I said, keeping the alarm from my voice, 'You may have to leave the country earlier than you plan. It may not be safe for you to stay here.'

She did not speak. She had been acquainted with the cruelty of politics.

The shutters were open on to the courtyard where the moonlight gave a soft illumination. There was nothing outside but the empty chairs. I took my glass and looked into it as if the future were written there, but it didn't help me. Then my eyes were drawn by a figure in the courtyard which I could swear had not been there a moment ago. A figure clothed in white. I supposed it to be Ravi, who would have come back for his money. I was angry with him for his desertion of me, and I went out to tell him he would get no money out of me. My sight was hampered by the darkness after the brilliance of the living-room and I could see only that the figure was tall, taller than Ravi, and motionless.

'Who is it?' I asked.

Osmani said, 'I called you on the telephone but you did not answer. Even your servants did not answer.'

'My servants have run away. Perhaps you knew that, Miss Mason.'

'I needed to speak to you. You see, I was in El Desmara.'

'I think you were on your way back from Kezzan.'

'My engagements take me to many places. Yesterday I had the

196

pleasure of singing for the Sultan and his entourage. They were very appreciative.'

'Your message will have been helpful to them, Miss Mason.'

She took a pace to one side, and I took a corresponding pace to keep her directly ahead of me.

'I have needed to keep busy since Mahmet died,' the singer said. 'At that time a light went out of my life. Mahmet was born to affect the lives of others.'

'He did, Miss Mason. Don't grieve.'

'His influence continues, of course.'

'I'm very much afraid that it does.' I had nothing to lose now, neither had the Langleys; I was not going to continue a game of insinuation when Osmani had played her most damaging stroke. 'As far as I am concerned, Mahmet's influence was one of unrelieved darkness. He was a man born wicked; he destroyed the one noble spirit in the country.'

She took a deep breath and I heard it rasp between her teeth. She moved more deeply into the shadows. 'The wickedness lies with the Junta, Colonel Warfield. Soldiers are created to destroy things. They must never be allowed to govern, to suppress the aspirations of the best among us.'

I let that one spend itself in silence. Then I said, 'Miss Mason, I think you came here to tell me something in particular. I think you wanted me to know that the secret of Miss Langley's friendship with the former ruler is now shared by the Kezzanis. In other words, you have told them, despite my asking you not to, in order to do as much damage as you can to the Military Government. That you acted in a spirit of revenge is too obvious to need emphasis.'

Osmani had a certain proud disdain for argument. She raised her head, as if lifting herself above the level of vulgar dispute. 'So much enlightenment has spread from Kezzan over the centuries. I am certain they have the means to save the country. A new spirit will spring from the holy city at the moment it is most needed.'

I laughed; I couldn't help it. 'You have made a serious mistake, Miss Mason.'

From the corner of my eye I could see that Carol had come out of the house and was now standing under the eaves. I did not want

197

Osmani to see her, but the singer was too acute to miss a third person in the courtyard.

She spoke softly, with the vibrancy of anger. 'Ah, Miss Langley, the lady at the heart of it all! She is lovely, is she not, Colonel Warfield? It does not surprise me that she has overthrown one head of state and may now overthrow another!'

Carol could not have heard that; it was spoken for my ear alone, to remind me that Carol had trodden the international pleasure circuit only a short time ago.

'Poor Khalid, he did not deserve his terrible end,' Osmani continued. 'I remember him so well. An overweight, balding man, showing all the marks of dissipation, but with an engaging smile. I do not think he was wicked, just weak and dissolute and given to a way of life that had to destroy him. The fatal friendship, Colonel Warfield! They put his head in a trash can, I believe.'

'His life resembled that of many Arab rulers, good and bad,' I said. 'Even his end was conventional.'

'The present dictator has no chance of staying in office, of course. His opponents are uniting against his brutalities. I suspect that only the infamous Colonel Nathan will support him when the re-alignment takes place.'

I was angry now. I said with helpless fury, 'You know very well that the country's on the brink of civil war and that power cannot be transferred without bloodshed. You have played an aggressive part in an explosive situation to satisfy your need for violence. Your motive was not charity, Miss Mason, but vindictiveness.'

Osmani had not come here to argue, but for the sweet pleasure of denouement, and she did not take up my challenge. Carol came forward and took my arm, I think perceiving only that I was angry.

'Why, Miss Langley, it surprises me to find you still here! You may find it necessary to recast your plans.'

'I see no reason to change anything,' Carol said, accepting the mood of antagonism without seeking its origin.

'Colonel Warfield can explain everything to you.'

'Is that necessary?'

'My dear, I think it is.'

'There is nothing more for us to say, Miss Mason,' I said. I was in a mood to propel her through the gate and I restrained myself with difficulty.

Osmani turned to go, gracefully, in her own time. She said, 'It was my intention only to give you warning.' Then she was gone, leaving a ripple of hauteur in the region of the gate.

'I didn't get all that,' Carol said; but I was too far gone in anger and dismay to explain to her now. I was trying to see the days ahead.

I said, 'Your father is a man with a lot behind him. How quickly could he get an aircraft to Sidi-bel-Said?'

'I don't know. It would depend on the schedules. Perhaps forty-eight hours.'

'Could he do it in less?'

'He might if he thought it necessary. There is usually a reserve One-Eleven at Luton.'

'Would he interrupt his schedules, strand his passengers and lose a large sum of money if he thought your life was in danger?'

The question was brutal but Carol stayed calm. 'I think he would.'

Of course he would. She was his precious emblem, for whom he wanted countries.

'We must speak to him. I will get the car.'

In a minute we were driving through the crowded streets towards the hotel at the top of the city. Donkey carts blocked our way where the road narrowed and I used the horn.

'Thank God for Langley's Tours,' I said.

§

Langley received us in emerald pyjamas; he was vastly out of sorts.

'Shall I tell you something? Do you want to hear?' These were not questions, just his prelude to grievance. 'This hotel is built to international standards at a cost of two point five millions on one of the best sites in North Africa and it runs like a tenth-rate boarding house. I ring the bell and nothing happens. I go down to the bar and they can't see me. Now the water doesn't come out of the taps and they're breaking up an ocean liner in the suite next door.'

199

'Sir, we must talk, we have little time.'

'Furthermore the manager has sent me a bill at twice the agreed figure three days before I'm due out. When I go to see him he just giggles. Christ, what goes on?'

'He's been intimidated. He's trying to get what he can out of you before you leave.'

'All he'll get out of me is one up the hairy division.'

This was defiance I understood; Langley was of my race. We sat on the snow-white chairs in the drawing room. A soft warm wind fanned through the open windows.

'Mr Langley, I must advise you and Carol to leave the country as quickly as you can,' I said. 'Get one of your aircraft to the airport and fly home. Suspend your business here. It may be possible for you to introduce tourists at a later time, but just now it's out of the question.'

'Listen, Colonel! No one's giving me the bum's rush out of this camel halt. I've invested six figures in rebuilding the holiday industry and I'm not going to be scared off by the Wogs.'

I took a deep breath, as if this would bring order to my tired mind, and gave him the story as I saw it. The Kezzanis had plainly decided to fight it out with the President. Three days ago Carol and I had discovered something so much to their discredit they were obliged to take action before their criminal behaviour was made public. They would fight with every means available to them, which included the intimidation of servants and officials and no doubt acts of terrorism. By chance a sharp weapon had been put into their hands and clearly they intended to use it.

I took Carol's hand; I was going to hurt her now. 'They must blacken the President because he has the means to blacken them. The President will charge Kezzan with slaving; the Kezzanis will charge him with irreligion. I'm afraid to say that Carol's friendship with the former Head of State, whose name is reviled by the whole country, was known to an American resident here, and she has informed the Kezzanis for reasons of her own. They of course will turn the President's dealings with you into a murderous conspiracy. They will present tourism as a vulgar affront to Islam that carries with it the very breath of Khalidism. Within a few days the Iman will have every young Arab on the streets yelling slogans against the President and his European connections.'

Langley had listened to this with his head bowed and I thought he might contradict me. In fact he said nothing; he simply looked at Carol, not in reproach but in some sort of apology.

'It doesn't matter, Dad,' she said.

He spoke to me then, while keeping his eyes on Carol. 'I thought the soldiers had everything in order. I thought there was discipline here.'

'Soldiers are not always as strong as they seem.'

'That's so? They're not strong?'

'There is a rift in the Army. It has always been there, but now it will be exploited for political reasons.'

'There will be fighting? There will be dead in the streets?'

'I expect so.'

I did not know how much of this Langley had taken in. Carol seemed to consume the whole of his attention. She got up from beside me and went to him; she sat on the edge of his chair with her arm along his shoulder.

'You did everything you could,' she said. 'It just wasn't possible.'

'They don't like corpses, girl. They won't go to a place where there are corpses.'

'I understand.'

'I wanted the bloody place. I wanted it for you.'

'I know.'

'You could have had it — lock, stock and barrel. It was all I could do.'

'Another time you may succeed,' I said. 'As it is, she won't be safe here.'

He nodded. Langley's empire had grown to its present size because he could recognize the strength or the weakness of the hand dealt him. He was big enough to admit failure. I had seen generals with smaller hearts.

'I'm sorry, girl,' he said.

His distraction lasted only a minute. Then he was on his feet examining the schedules he carried in his case.

He said, 'Tomorrow there's a One-Eleven returning from Madeira with the mid-week tourists. It's unlikely to be fully booked. It can divert to Sidi-bel-Said and take us from there.

ETA fourteen-thirty. If what you say is true, Colonel, you'd better come with us.'

'I'll hang on for the moment,' I said.

'Man, they'll kill you too!'

'I'll be safe as long as the President lasts.'

I wanted to speak to Carol but I didn't know what I would say. Not quite. We went together on to the roof where the lights and fires of the old town were thick beneath us.

I said, seeking my way, 'It's a mess, but it isn't your fault. Men turn women into something they are not and then fight over it. A woman takes the place of an idea. When the fight begins it will be because two generals dislike each other, because the people they come from have always been at odds, not because you came to the country. Please try to understand me.'

'It isn't easy to see it like that.'

'They'll use your name. They'll make you an excuse for their own violence.'

'I don't know why. I'm nothing, really.'

I took her hand and pressed it in both of mine. 'You'll wait for me somewhere? My job here won't last much longer and then I'll try to do something sensible.'

'I'll come wherever you are. What will you do?'

'I've always wanted to be a writer. In all this muddle there must be something to say.'

She turned away from me and her face was lighted by the fires below. Her next words did not come easily. 'I want you to be safe. I don't think I could stand it if you were killed, not after Khalid. That would mean that two friends had been killed because of me.'

'I'll get out as soon as I can give the President no further help.'

She was angry now, not greatly, but enough for me to see it inscribed in her cheek. 'You don't owe him anything. You don't have to stay here.'

I didn't deny it. Perhaps my commitment to Jason was no more than an absurd loyalty. But I knew I couldn't drop it because it had gone wrong, and that I would have to stay until Jason was either dead or victorious. I said, 'I should not have come here. Military Government usually goes wrong. But I can't leave when things are in a mess.'

'Why not? This isn't your country. Because you and the President once served together doesn't mean that you have to stay here.'

'A soldier needs a loyalty of some sort. Without it he falls to pieces. I still think that Jason's a better man than Solly and that he can rule generously given the chance.'

She faced me then. She had grown older and her eyes were marked by experience. She had been close to men of power—Khalid, Langley—and I had to take her seriously. 'That's silly, Peter. Jason will go the same way as Khalid. It's what happens. And whatever you do or say won't make the smallest difference.'

I had no answer to that. I knew that I still had things to do, words to say, no matter that they served no purpose. It was just my way. I said good-bye to Carol and her father and told them I would take them to the airport tomorrow. Then I drove home. The streets were crowded still, and these eager people showed no concern at the splitting of the Junta that might bring the country to war.

§

A note had been fixed to my door, written in fair Arabic. It said, more or less: *Stranger, where are your servants? Where is your bedfellow? What are you thinking now? Go home, abominable Khalidist. We do not want you here.*

I searched every corner of the bungalow but no one was there. Not a sound but for my own footsteps, not a sensation but for my lonely heartbeat. The house I had loved now had an ugly face. I put a chain on the gate and kept my pistol close to my hand, and in so doing I knew that I had taken up the instruments used by every illiberal tyrant when he sees the end in sight. I took a chair under the eaves and from a deep shadow watched the darkness. The last of the military advisers. A champion with buckler and mace.

Later I did what I had always done when times were bad. I took pencil and paper and tried to write it down. I didn't know the truth of it but at least I could record the facts. Others might judge—they might apportion praise or blame, or fit these events

203

to whatever scheme of history they preferred; I could only tell them what happened in the last days of Jason's Presidency.

# 16

The Iman had to strike quickly if he was not to be out-manoeuvred. His instinct would not let him wait. I remembered the hard intelligence that had shown in his eyes and in the fierce compression of his lips. Accordingly I went to the palace next morning expecting some sort of Kezzani defiance, and I did not have to wait for news: Jason met me in the hall looking more cheerful than for days past.

'Where have you been, dear boy? You're missing all the fun. Here I am fighting a war and my principal aide is having butter and honey for breakfast.'

'Tell me what has happened, sir.'

'In a minute. Now I am busy. What sport!'

He dived into the signals office and I followed at his heels. Here I had to wait several minutes while Jason read the messages that hung from the teleprinters. He looked confident, almost gleeful. He spoke to me without lifting his eyes from the messages. 'If Rustum wants to bat first, we'll let him. Like every amateur he'll establish a position too soon and lose the advantage.' He ripped off the messages and marched back to his office, myself in pursuit.

'Are you telling me the Iman has declared war?'

'My friend, no one declares war in Africa. An insult, an attitude, a stiffening of the spine — those are the declarations we understand. Last night the Iman issued a communiqué. He called me an enemy of Allah whom it was his purpose to disembowel. He has accused me of Khalidism, which is to say I am a political leper, an evil djinoon. He has called attention to my negotiations with Langley, the well-known Khalidist, whose daughter would have presided over a country given to all the habits condemned by

Allah. Like abandoning the veil, like gin and tonic. The message ends with a condemnation of military dictatorship and a eulogy of Prince Suleiman as an Islamic champion. Rustum has put his force astride the Kezzan road and is erecting wire.'

'It was predictable,' I said.

'And so were these,' said Jason, handing me the messages.

They were summaries from the world's press and broadcasting. As I had supposed, they were mostly hostile to Jason. He was described as a brutal dictator and the Iman's defiance was generally applauded. The scourging of Solly was recalled as an example of Jason's cruelty and Solly himself was presented as a hero of the resistance and political prisoner. In particular the Left had taken Solly to its heart and I judged he would be a martyr of the Revolution by nightfall.

'I am afraid the Kezzanis have gained the first point,' I said. 'We should have held your press conference yesterday. Coming on top of this, the slaving story is going to look like a clumsy invention.'

'Quite so, Peter! You are very bright this morning. None the less I shall entertain the press as planned. I shall tell them the Kezzanis have been forced to act to forestall my announcement. I shall use my most engaging manner. I shall leave my weapons of oppression in the desk drawer.'

'You must bring Nathan forward, sir.'

'He has already crossed the Skar with two companies. Goodness me, what a careless soldier you must think me! I too have read Clausewitz and McMahon. While you were taking your ample breakfast I was talking to Nathan on the telephone.'

'And the other brigades must mobilize, of course.'

'Done, Colonel, done! Those in El Desmara are jumping on their toes and banging side drums. Even Ben Talun has promised a platoon if he can find their overshoes.'

'I see you have attended to everything, sir.'

'I had the best instructors. But, dear friend, doesn't it make you laugh? Don't you want to hoot? Old Solly, whose politics are neolithic in origin, is now a deity in the Marxist pantheon. Solly, a bright star glowing red! In fact, I am the Socialist—I, tyrant that I am. The policies of the Officers' Committee were lifted from a Fabian pamphlet. Beatrice Webb and I are as alike as two peas.'

He slapped me on the shoulder in exuberant good humour and guided me to the map table, where Rustum's position had been marked with pins. 'I shan't attack him, of course. He would like me to, but it would be unwise before the loyalty of my troops has hardened. I shall place the Arab battalions in defensive positions outside El Desmara. I will use Nathan as a mobile force to inspire terror in Kezzani hearts. The Eastleigh solution! Firmness matched by restraint with a touch of menace thrown in. What do you think, my learned teacher?'

'Ten out of ten,' I said. Indeed he could not have judged it better. When Jason applied his mind he was a brilliant tactical soldier and he would be more than a match for Rustum. The Kezzanis would adopt an inflexible posture, digging themselves in a mile from the holy city, or so I judged the stiff aristocratic mind of the commander.

Jason then called Colonel Aziz, the acting Chief of Staff, and together we devised a logistic plan to meet a thirty-day period of operations. Poor Aziz, he found logistics a desert without landmarks, but fortunately he had some good junior officers.

'That's it,' said Jason, when we had completed our business. 'The threat from the lunatic Left is something I cannot guard against; we will simply have to devise measures if the need arises.' He gathered his papers into a neat pile and secured them with a pin.

I excused myself then. I had to take the Langleys to Sidi-bel-Said as I couldn't trust their safety to anyone else. I had gone no further than the forecourt, where the heat was already climbing towards the midday level, when Jason came running after me.

'You must not send them away without a message from the President. Tell them they can return when our affairs have stabilized. Tell the girl it was none of her fault. Don't look so glum, dear Peter. Our aims have never been so clear.'

I left him on the palace step and he waved as I drove out of the gate. I pressed the car through the crowded streets towards the depot where I would pick up Hatim and an escort of four soldiers. I understood the change in Jason. He was a soldier, not a man of politics, and now he was freed from the ambiguities of political rivalry and faced with a clear military problem. Pretence was abandoned; each side had disclosed its purpose. He had simply to fight an enemy who had dug in across the Kezzan road, plain to see, in a world boldly simplified.

§

The airfield at Sidi-bel-Said lay under a hard sun which distorted the distance with a thin mirage and made a fierce impact on the concrete apron outside the transit building. Hatim had disposed the four soldiers as an unobtrusive guard at the entrances and I felt reasonably safe in the lounge. Langley was sunk in bitter lethargy, as he had been when I first saw him in this same place. Now and then he shifted angrily in his chair as if the acid of frustration had poisoned his stomach. Carol was silent, her smile kept in place, I thought, with difficulty. I suppose we waited an hour, saying little.

The aircraft was already overdue when Hatim came to tell me a crowd had gathered in the main hall. He did not know who they were but they had asked for Langley. I went out to see them. I found about thirty people, polite, frightened, carrying suitcases. They told me they were Langley's associates — hotel proprietors, agents, men of business, together with their families; they had heard that he was leaving by one of his aircraft and they desired to accompany him out of the country.

'To where?' I asked.

They didn't know; they wanted only to leave.

I went back to Langley, cursing every thug and manipulator in the service of the Iman who used intimidation with such effect.

Langley did not pause for reflection. 'I'll take them. They will have to dump their baggage if the all-up weight is exceeded. Hell, what a country!'

'I doubt if they have papers.'

'Man, do you expect me to leave them? If I can't get them into Britain, my aircraft will take them elsewhere.'

I secured their right of exit with a telephone call to Jason and their gratitude was great. I watched them file into the departure hall, a new movement of refugees and the first in this country

208

since the exit of the Khalidists after the assassination: they moved into the oblivion of poverty and statelessness, thanking me for making it possible. I went back to Langley and told him he had gained a retinue of indigent businessmen. He simply shrugged his shoulders.

The aircraft landed a little before three o'clock and taxied on to the apron. It wore the flamboyant livery of Langley's Tours, a magenta fuselage and fin and the name of the proprietor featured in three-foot gold letters along the cabin roof. The engines stopped. There was a further delay while the aircraft took on additional fuel for the leg to Gibraltar. Then Langley led his column of fallen businessmen out of the terminal building and across the tarmac. I accompanied them, holding Carol's hand, wondering when I would see her again. We paused at the foot of the steps while the fugitives went on board. I don't remember what words I used. I expect they were ordinary. At any rate Carol just pressed my fingers and turned to the stair.

But Langley blocked the way, reluctant to leave the country. 'Don't think I'm through, Colonel Warfield. I won't let any shower of half-arsed Wogs stand in my road. You can tell that to the President.'

With that, he went up the stair wrapped in indignation, to be welcomed by the cabin staff in a manner appropriate for the head of the line. Carol followed him, turning to wave from the door. Then she disappeared into the aircraft, the door was shut and the stair taken away.

I could not stand on the tarmac gaping at the closed door, so I walked smartly back into the terminal building and looked for Hatim. The lounge was empty. I heard the aircraft engines start and, driven by what need of punishment I could not say, I went to the window and watched the brightly painted aircraft as it swung on the apron, raising a cloud of pink dust, and taxied towards the runway. It ran to the down-wind end of the airfield, a patch of colour behind the heat haze, turned into the lazy wind and arrested while the pilot opened the engines against the brakes. It moved forward, gathering flying speed, and tilted steeply into the air. Then it was gone and I watched two sparrows that flew down from the roof on to the apron.

Hatim came then. I did not hear him at first.

'We are ready to return, Colonel. I have recovered three of the four soldiers. One is in prayer.'

'Very well, Hatim. I'll join you at the car.'

Carol, at least, was safe; I had to be content with that. After a minute I followed Hatim out of the building and crossed the concrete towards flying control, where the cars were parked. I suppose we waited five minutes while the soldier completed his obligation, during which I restrained Hatim from setting him in movement with the toe of his shoe. Then we resumed our places in the car for the journey back to El Desmara.

§

As the car swung under the control tower I saw a man step on to the balcony above me. He stood quite still looking across the airfield towards the north. I don't know why he drew the attention of my empty mind but I told the driver to stop. I got out of the car and approached the foot of the tower.

'What is it?' I called to the man on the balcony.

'I'm not sure.'

He was one of the English controllers employed by the airport authority. He did not look in my direction.

'Is the aircraft in trouble?'

'I cannot say. The pilot is returning.'

My heart collapsed within me as I wondered what cliché of the present world could have overtaken Langley's aircraft within minutes of take-off.

'Will he be able to land?'

'In an hour, perhaps. First he must burn off some fuel. If you're the President's leg man, you'd better come up.'

My better mind raced through the possibilities of mishap that could have turned the aircraft back as I climbed the stair to the tower.

The duty controller was a young man with an aggressive manner that I expected to conceal some ineffectiveness. After all, what would a better man be doing in Sidi-bel-Said, which had perhaps fifty movements a week? He looked at me now as if I had personally interrupted the flight of Langley's aircraft out of his airspace. 'Don't ask me what's happened,' he said.

The aircraft was now within sight, making a left-handed orbit at about two thousand feet. The captain was silent despite the calling of the tower.

I asked, 'Is there some interference with the working of the aircraft?'

'I don't think it's mechanical. He would have said so.'

He alerted the airfield services and I saw the tenders moving towards the runway.

I freed myself from the spell that bound me. I wanted troops at the airfield; I had to be able to respond if violence were to break out at Sidi-bel-Said. From the tower I called Ben Talun at Mogalor and asked him to send an armed company to the airfield. Poor Ben Talun, he didn't like surprises; I could hear the dismay in his voice as he undertook to do what I asked.

I said, 'You had better come too, sir. I have no right to be making decisions.'

'There is a need for action?'

'There may be. I cannot say.'

'It is a matter on which I must reflect. Action sometimes takes an irreversible course.'

'Sir, our job will be to contain violence, not to add to it. The decisions will be obvious and necessary. You have one hour to get here.'

I rang off. We were not a strong team. The controller, who told me his name was Howells, had come to the end of his resources. The only other people in the tower were the plotter and a maintenance engineer. I went on to the balcony and shouted to Hatim, who was seated on the fender of the staff car in some paralysis of the spirit. I asked him to find the airport manager and make certain he came to the tower.

Still no voice came from the aircraft. It had made two complete orbits before the manager arrived. He was a small Tangieri of explosive demeanour. His temper was not improved by the fact that Hatim, in obedience to his instructions, had brought him in a policeman's grip. I asked him what contingency plans he had for the closure of the airfield and was barely surprised that he had none.

211

'That is inexcusable,' I said.

The gall in his stomach was released in savage repartee. 'So, he brings in soldiers! He turns the place into a battlefield, with sandbags and entrenchments! He makes a bloodbath in the restaurant!'

'That may not happen, sir. The moves are only precautionary. Hatim, it's not necessary for you to hold the gentleman's collar.'

'He was in dalliance, Colonel. His attention was imperfect.'

'Nevertheless you must release him.'

When Hatim relaxed his hold, the manager sank into a chair in angry disdain for me and my endeavours. 'Take charge, monsieur. Make a big war. Put dynamite in the closets. I do not understand why you must bring the Army here. Nothing has happened but that an aircraft has turned back.'

'I insist only that we close the airfield,' I said.

My tiny force of soldiers would have to secure the entrances until Ben Talun arrived. I went down to give the orders. The soldiers were to close the gates and let no one in or out until I instructed otherwise. I obeyed an old instinct that told me to fortify the perimeter.

Perhaps I was ten minutes placing the guard, during which time the aircraft continued to orbit the airfield. When I climbed back into the tower I could hear a voice on the loudspeaker — a voice calm enough but speaking a little above natural pitch. I did not hear what words were said, but when Howells had finished recording the message he tore the leaf from the pad and passed it to me. His face wore a look of sour accomplishment as if he had foretold this exact problem.

I read the message, trying to hold my hand steady. Howells had used the captain's own words.

> *Armed intrusion of flight deck reported. Aircraft move-*
> *ments now dictated by gunmen, suspect two only. Terms for*
> *release of the passengers will be made known by agent at*
> *airport. Failure to comply will result in destruction of*
> *aircraft. Will continue in vicinity of Sidi-bel-Said pending*
> *developments. Gunmen determined and fearless.*

I suppose I had expected this; at any rate I felt no sharpening of my anger. I looked at the manager but he simply waved a hand in

212

dismissal of the incident.

'Do not ask me what to do, brave soldier. I am under arrest. I am capable only of fatigue duties.'

'I will persuade him to help you if you wish,' Hatim offered.

'Let him be,' I said.

I asked Howells to open a line to the President's office while I went down to meet the gunmen's agent, who would no doubt present himself at the main gate. I felt no more than the need to keep going. I knew I must not collapse into frustration and tears.

The soldiers had closed the gate and, because the hour was quiet, no build-up of traffic had taken place — only small traders with their baskets sat on the poor grass outside waiting with an absence of interest unremarkable in the Maghreb for the gate to reopen. A man with a donkey came, and a beggar with a crutch. No one else was there. No one but a girl of striking beauty and a face robbed of all expression who stood at the pedestrian gate knowing she would be admitted. I did not have to search for her name; we had passed by one another once before.

I told the soldier to admit her and we walked in silence to the terminal building, stopping on the terrace under a pergola. We stopped in the broken shadow of the vines. The gardener had been here only a minute ago and his tools lay unminded on the pavings. The girl was calm, untroubled, living in a remote world that nowhere touched the world that I knew.

I said in French, 'Leisha, you must tell me what you want.'

'Our demands are written on this paper.'

'And you will destroy the aircraft and the lives of seventy people if they are not met?'

'Of course.'

I did not doubt it: there was a disengagement in this girl's eyes which compelled me to believe her. A bitter air blew upon us, like wind across the snows, having its origin somewhere in the cold heart of the twentieth century. I took the paper and opened it. The words were typewritten and in good French.

*The demands of the Revolutionary Movement for the Liberation of the Republic from Fascist Tyranny are as follows:*

*1. That the political prisoner Suleiman ben Yusoff be*

213

*released and accorded safe conduct to the Free City of Kezzan.*

*2. That the Fascist war-lord Samuel Nathan be punished for the murder of the Revolutionary Socialist Mahmet ben Daud.*

*3. That a million dinars be paid in cash.*

*4. That the members of the Commando be granted safe passage, with a hostage of their own choosing, to an airport in the Socialist World.*

The subscription at the foot of the page, as I had already guessed, was *Le Ciel Rouge*.

I said, 'No doubt the gunmen are Haida and Aissa, the sons of Daud?'

'Their antecedents are unimportant. They are the brothers of Mahmet.'

'And they are armed with pistols and grenades?'

'They are armed.'

They must have gained admission to the aircraft with the refugees, none of whom had been examined for identity. I had not recognised them in the hall. After all, they were just well-bred young Arabs with the anonymity of good looks.

'You know the aircraft is full of holiday-makers from Madeira who have no connection with this country?'

'The aircraft contains the Capitalist Langley and his Khalidist daughter, and many of their associates. The others are innocent and it is their misfortune to be overtaken by the movement of progress. You have six hours.'

I could not waste time arguing with Leisha. I returned to the tower, taking her with me, and there I placed her in the duty officer's bunk at the rear of the control room.

The magenta aircraft was still within view from the tower.

Howells had meanwhile cleared a line to the President. I prayed my practical mind would not desert me while there was business to do. I did not know what attitude Jason would take on political blackmail but I suspected it would be uncompromising. A moment later I heard Jason on the line, mercifully still in the mood of happy soldier. 'Well, Colonel, for which group of the oppressed are you acting this time?'

214

'Sir, we are in serious trouble.'

Perhaps he heard the chill in my voice, for he spoke next without gaiety. 'What is it, Peter?'

I told him then of the hi-jack and the demands of Le Ciel Rouge. 'There are more than seventy people on board, including the Langleys. I think the terrorists will carry out their threat if frustrated.'

'I see. It's a mess.' Jason thought about it for no more than ten seconds. As a man of action he was at the peak of his form. 'You may open negotiations on all the demands except the first. I am prepared to concede the money and the escape of the terrorists. The punishment of Nathan is not a serious condition as it could not be carried out within the time limit. The release of General Suleiman you have no authority to discuss.'

I said with difficulty, 'We'll have to discuss it ultimately, sir.'

'Of course, old boy. It's the meat in the pudding. I will come down myself and see this thing through. It wouldn't be fair to leave it to you.'

He meant, of course, that I was too deeply involved to take a firm line.

'It will be best if you come,' was all I said.

'Don't worry, Peter. I can be there in two hours.'

'Thank you. I appreciate the difficulty over General Suleiman.'

He spoke cheerfully then, like a general who must maintain the morale of his troops. 'I doubt if you do, Peter, my lad. For the last three hours there has been rioting in El Desmara. The Iman has brought every delinquent son of Mohammed on to the streets which needless to say has postponed my press conference. Nathan is up to his neck in it.'

'And they are calling for the release of General Suleiman?'

'With every breath. They are howling his name through the streets; they have written it on every wall. All at once Solly has become the most important person in the state and the alternative ruler.'

215

# 17

I do not remember what thoughts were in my mind in the next
ninety minutes. I remember only that I would willingly have
exchanged my consciousness for oblivion. The aircraft kept in a
wide orbit, the pilot remaining silent for the most part. Exceeding
my expectation, Ben Talun and a company at full strength
reached the airport in forty minutes and in fair order of
accoutrement. We placed detachments where they could
command the apron and the up-wind end of the runway with
small arms; we also sealed the remaining points of access, not
because I thought the airfield would be infiltrated but because, in
my helplessness, I could think of nothing better to do. We made
our headquarters in the tower.

Ben Talun had a kindly heart; his old face showed the greatest
concern. 'Good sir, you are distressed. I wish it were in my power
to comfort you.'

I replied in Arabic, as I did not trust my voice in English, telling
him I had friends in the aircraft. 'There is one whose life is more
important than my own.'

'It is so? I will pray for the safety of that person.' Then he said
timidly, 'It may help you to recall that the determinism of Allah is
absolute. There is nothing you or I can do to alter that powerful
will.'

'I know, my friend. None the less, we will keep the soldiers
alert.'

He had not heard me; the charity in his heart obscured the
commonplace. 'I am persuaded that God will show you mercy.
After all, your life has been one of service and dedication.'

'I deserve nothing,' I said; 'but there are many in the aircraft with a claim to divine lenience. Keep them in your prayers, master!'

The airport manager, still smarting from my interference in the working of the airfield, raised himself an inch in his chair and spoke to Ben Talun. His Arabic was that of the Rif. 'Place your hands upon your belly, O Believer! The Christian has stolen thy undergarment.'

Ben Talun ignored this interruption with quiet dignity.

We had now to bring the aircraft down and open negotiations with Haida and Aissa, and for this mundane purpose English was the proper language. The aircraft had been below a safe landing weight for some minutes. Howells informed the captain that an envoy of the President had been appointed with the power to discuss terms, for which purpose the aircraft was invited to land and park on the up-wind turning circle. Electrical and ventilation services would be connected there. The speed with which the reply came told me the gunmen had planned their next moves. The aircraft would park as directed but no ground services were to be brought out and only the envoy was to approach. He was first to be searched by the Revolutionary Socialist Leisha, who would then accompany him to the aircraft. Explosive charges had been placed in the aircraft and they would be detonated if an attempt was made to release the passengers. To these terms I agreed. I was going down from the tower with Leisha when Howells received a call from El Desmara telling him the President's aircraft was in the air with a flight time of twenty-six minutes.

Ben Talun came with me to the foot of the stair. Here he laid a gentle hand on my arm. His gift for friendship was of the kind that had drawn me to the Arab nation twenty years ago. 'My son, if a life is needed, let it be mine and not yours.'

'You are kind, old friend, but this job is laid upon me.'

'I am deficient as a soldier, but I am not afraid. I do not wish to see you lose your life in a country not your own.'

I said, 'It is written this way. I will not forget your friendship.'

He embraced me then, and let me go. I had still to give him his instructions. I took him to one side, where Leisha could not hear us, and said quickly, 'There are only two gunmen on the aircraft. If your soldiers can get a clear shot at them, they are not to

217

hesitate, even if I am in the line of sight. But it has to be a single volley giving them no chance to detonate the charges.'

'It is a terrible thing you are asking me to do.'

'We have no choice, sir. Finally we can only protect the greatest number.'

Leisha and I travelled in a Land Rover to the end of the runway where we got out into the sunlight. She made a thorough search of my clothing. She did not speak. The hard sun beat upon us as we waited.

The aircraft made a long approach and landed through a belt of mirage. The pilot taxied on to the turning circle, stopped against the brakes and cut the engines. The internal ladder was extended from the forward entrance and this I mounted, followed by Leisha. Inside the door, in the space used by the steward, I came face to face with one of the gunmen. The other I assumed to be on the flight deck covering the crew.

He told me his name was Haida. He was a handsome youth with a pale skin and dark, sensitive eyes; I had met many like him in the courts and seminaries of the Middle East. He spoke French and his manner was wholly courteous. 'I regret troubling you, monsieur, but you must accept that we will destroy the aircraft and the passengers if our demands are not met. We do not seek violent solutions; we respond only to the violence of the state. You understand me, yes? If these poor people lose their lives it will be an act of cruelty perpetrated by the Fascist Junta. We ourselves look forward to a future of unparalleled beauty and kindliness.'

His eyes carried some part of that future: I could believe that in different circumstances Haida might be kind. He held the gun at my chest almost with apology, like a tiresome expedient that had somehow come between us. I wondered if there was any point in working on his sympathy.

'Haida, in the matter of brutality, I have always been prepared to do simple arithmetic. Killing ten people is ten times as bad as killing one. We have a duty to reduce violence, not to magnify it.'

'I have to correct you, monsieur. There is a difference between creative violence borne upon the revolutionary impulse and the oppressive violence of conservatism.' He laughed in embarrassment; plainly he did not like telling me I was wrong.

218

'I have seen many corpses, Haida. They all looked the same to me.'

'Ah, but the causes for which they died were very different. Mahmet was killed to perpetuate tyranny.'

'They are all equally dead.'

'Monsieur, I must draw your attention to our demands. We cannot discuss the ethics of revolution at the moment. At another time, when our affairs are less pressing . . .' He gave me the charming smile of the well-bred Arab who does not like to impose restraints upon the stranger.

I said, 'The President has empowered me to negotiate — —'

'There can be no negotiations. Only the acceptance of our conditions.'

'— with a view to saving the lives of innocent people. If I concede some of your demands, including your escape, will you release the passengers?'

He looked at me with the sorrow of youth for the feeble-mindedness of middle age. 'Monsieur, I have already said that our demands cannot be discussed separately.'

'An equivalent number of passengers, then.' (Still in my mind was the arithmetic of violence.)

'I have to tell you that our demands are part of a single design, that of building Socialism in the Maghreb. Each is integral to our purpose.'

I was treading a path leading nowhere, but none the less I said, 'Haida, Haida, you cannot believe that General Suleiman is a Socialist, or that the leaders of the Kezzan rebellion are in any way given to Marxist principles. These men are immovably conservative.'

I should have remembered better the logic of revolution. 'The road to Socialism takes many strange turnings,' Haida said. 'Suleiman ben Yusoff is an opponent of militarism; he struck the Dictator in a gesture of political defiance. He has served the purpose of world revolution.' He returned with apparent regret to his principal subject. 'There is so little time, monsieur, we must not waste it talking! Our ultimatum expires in four and a half hours. Please, if you wish to prevent much suffering, grant our terms and let the passengers go free.'

219

I said, 'I can show you proof that the Kezzanis are conducting a traffic in slaves . . .' But I should have saved my breath; in the Marxist world there were slaves in plenty and Haida was not disturbed.

For the next ten minutes, while the heat in the aircraft grew and the smell from the lavatories became more vile, I argued the toss with Haida, knowing well enough I would get nowhere. He had realized, of course, that I did not have the authority to discuss all his conditions, and it was only his inextinguishable good manners that prevented him from sending me packing. In the corner of my vision, behind a curtain, I could see Langley seated in the cabin. His shoulders—built like those of a fighter—were bent forward, and he looked as if he might rise and join in the dispute given a chance. Carol I could not see.

I said finally, 'Look, Haida: the passengers will suffocate in this heat. Let me have an air-conditioning unit connected. There are children to be considered.'

'It is so? Yes, it is so! But I cannot help them. They are trapped in the fulcrum of change.'

I heard Jason's aircraft in the circuit and I had now to defer to a higher authority, not without relief. I told Haida I would leave the aircraft and consult the President. He actually bowed, and as I climbed through the door he placed a hand on my arm so that I should not fall. In his face was all the excitement of doom.

'Take care,' he said.

Ben Talun's soldiers would have their sights bearing upon us, but I knew the old man would never give the order to fire. Leisha followed me down to the tarmac.

I met Jason outside the terminal building. He looked tired but his movements were crisp and his voice firm. 'Well, my lad, how does the revolution prosper in Sidi-bel-Said? Nathan is getting the upper hand in the capital.'

'We have a problem,' I said.

I conducted him to the tower, when Ben Talun joined us. From the windows we could see the aircraft standing in the cruel sunlight at the end of the runway. I told Jason of my failure to negotiate with the terrorists. I did not conceal my belief that the release of Solly was their primary objective and the one from which they would not withdraw.

'How do you rate their determination?' he asked me.

'High to absolute.'

'Can they destroy the aircraft on the ground?'

'I doubt if they have placed charges, as they claim. They would throw grenades into the cabin. That might be enough to ignite the fuel tanks.'

'How many passengers might be saved, assuming there was no fire?'

'Your judgment would be as good as mine. Perhaps thirty per cent. If the tanks exploded I don't think we would save any.'

'We have one terrorist in our hands. Would the others be responsive if her life was threatened?'

Ben Talun, who had remained silent, now raised startled eyes to the President. 'She is fifteen years old! You cannot consider taking such a young life.'

'Brigadier, I would consider any solution that denied political blackmail.' Jason spoke with swift impatience and my heart sank.

I said, 'They have already accepted the possibility that Leisha will lose her life. We have to assume they are all ready to die. Furthermore . . .'

'What?'

'I may be wrong, but I think one at least, the boy called Haida, has actually a will to die. He sees this as a creative tragedy in which he is determined to play a part. He is a very dangerous person.'

Jason walked smartly towards the window and looked towards the aircraft. I knew he was judging the difficulty of storming it from the nearest cover; but the level airfield offered not the smallest concealment; there was nothing in which even a Bushman could have lain hidden.

I approached his shoulder. 'It cannot be done, sir. The soldiers would have to cross at least two hundred yards of open ground. The terrorists would have time to destroy the aircraft.'

'Then what do you suggest, Colonel? The country is on the brink of civil war. To release General Suleiman would provide my enemies with a popular leader about whom they would consolidate and warfare would certainly follow. There are

221

perhaps seventy people in the aircraft; conflict in the country would cost many more lives than these. And the President would be showing weakness at a time when he needs to show strength. I think you understand me.'

I did, and I searched in my barren mind for something to set against his argument. 'General Suleiman has no gift for leadership. His incapacity will soon become obvious. Let him go, let him lose his way in Kezzani politics——'

'That is nonsense, as you are aware. There is already a powerful leader in Kezzan. The General is important only as a symbol. You are allowing sentiment to get the better of your judgment.'

I had nothing to gain from dispute, but none the less my voice kept to its desperate course. 'That may be so. But had you not let your hatred of Solly decide every issue he would not have achieved his present importance.'

'You are out of order, Colonel. I shall put it down to emotional distress. Later, you must apologise.'

'You cannot let these people die.'

'I can only choose between one sacrifice and another. That is the penalty of leadership. Now, if you will take hold of yourself, we will examine the nearer ground.'

§

Jason meant to storm the aircraft; of this I was now certain. We drove with Ben Talun to the place a quarter of a mile short of the aircraft, where the company had deployed. We were beyond pistol shot. Forward of this position there was some low cover, mostly grass and thorn, but the open space across which the troops would have to advance looked formidably wide from here. The sun was on my cheek, the taste of the air upon my lip, but I had no sensation but for the chill of despair I carried within me.

The company commander was a young Arab who looked effective. He had probed the ground with single riflemen but they had got no nearer to the aircraft than two hundred and fifty yards. 'The gunmen are alert,' he said. 'One keeps watch from the forward entrance. We might pick him off from the forward position, but the second man would remain inside the aircraft.'

And the second man would lob grenades into the crowded

cabin. The seats, perhaps, would absorb some of the blast, but the jagged fragments would tear through the closely-seated passengers and those who were not dismembered would have their eyes and ears destroyed by the concussion. Then, true to the spirit of creative violence, the gunman would fire an automatic carbine into the smoke. We would get him, of course; he would be the focus of every weapon as he plunged through the aircraft door; but that would be dull satisfaction.

Jason said, 'The gunmen must be nearly blind to the rear. Major, you are to get a platoon as near as you can by approaching the tail in single file. They are to keep in radio contact. Send your best officer.' He turned to me. 'Peter, you do not have to remain here. You may go back to the tower.'

'I prefer to stay, sir.'

'You may be a hindrance to me. This is not a moment for weakness.'

'I will keep silent if you wish. I beg you to let me stay.'

'Very well. But you are not to take part in the operation. This is a job for resolute young men with nothing to lose.'

I offered my last advice, knowing he would not take it. 'This is a British aircraft. The consulate in Mogalor must be asked to give their opinion before you take an irreversible decision.'

He silenced the dissenting voice with an economy of effort any soldier would admire. 'In a matter of violent conflict you cannot resort to the committee. Finally the responsibility is mine, and I elect to take it now.'

I sat in the dust, my head between my hands, sickened by the soldier's inevitable appointment with bloodshed. I heard the voices of Jason and his officers as they devised a plan for taking the aircraft by assault. They sounded confident, but their tradition did not allow them to sound otherwise. They may have believed the gunmen were bluffing or that they would falter at the moment of crisis, but I knew better. This was the group that had killed Kemel with a single thrust of the bayonet. They were presenting a drama with the dedication of the artist and they would not be robbed of the ending.

Ben Talun's shadow fell across me. He spoke softly, so that only I should hear. 'God willing, your friend will be saved. There are many mercies. I have said a prayer.'

Without knowing where the words came from, I said, 'I have no claim upon mercy, as I have put my hand to violence. But some are innocent.'

There was a delay—there always is—while words I did not catch were spoken on the radio. A car came up the perimeter road, the dust blowing over me, but I did not raise my head. A new voice spoke, one that I knew but had not the curiosity to identify until I heard, unmistakably, Jason giving the order to suspend the operation. I lifted my eyes from the ground.

Osmani made an arresting figure in the company of soldiers. She was taller than the President. I could see she was entirely unafraid; she carried herself with a sad composure that did not lack dignity and for the moment I forgot the part she had played in the present disaster. When my mind cleared I understood what had brought her to the airfield. She wanted to speak to Haida and Aissa.

For the first time, as I judged, Jason could not see his way ahead. This was unmapped country, for there are no women in a military dictatorship. 'So, Miss Iris Mason, a singer of songs, wishes to intercede with the gunmen! She will persuade them to lay down their arms. Perhaps she will sing to them.'

'It is possible I can persuade them to release the passengers,' Osmani said.

'Madame, they are assassins who desire only death, for themselves and for others. They will not listen to words. They will not listen to songs.'

'They were my friends. Once they were capable of laughter. I cannot believe they will take the lives of innocent people.'

'She cannot believe it! They are part of a violent uprising which aims to overthrow the government. Already the passengers are suffocating.'

'They have cause for bitterness as their brother was murdered by the soldiers. I ask only that you let me speak to them.'

Jason broke into Arabic, disclosing his excitement. 'If we are speaking of bitterness we must go back to the murder of Kemel. He was my master, a light in the darkness. He was struck down in blasphemy.'

'I do not understand you, Mr President.'

I got to my feet. 'Let her speak to them, sir. There is time enough. What can we lose?'

'Ah, Colonel Warfield has risen from the dust! Like Miss Iris Mason, he knows best what I should do. How do I know this lady is not allied with the gunmen?'

'I am sure she is not a party to murder.'

'She has kept house for Le Ciel Rouge in Sidi-bel-Said. She has taken information to Kezzan.'

'She has been used by them. They have taken advantage of her liberal opinions.'

'That is an unbiased view, Colonel?'

'I believe so.'

Osmani had not looked at me while I was speaking; she was too proud for that. She gazed instead at the aircraft in pained detachment and I could believe she was numbed by the violence of Haida and Aissa.

Jason came to attention, stiffened by a new resolve. 'Very well! Let it be so! Who cares about the President's opinion? Miss Iris Mason will disarm the gunmen with sweet words and blandishments. Tell the aircraft captain she will approach in ten minutes, alone and on foot.'

This message was passed from the tower by radio-telephone and Leisha came out under escort to search Osmani before she went forward. I do not think Osmani looked at the girl, and Leisha herself lay far beyond the point where she could be reached. Certainly they did not speak.

Before the time elapsed, I spoke to Osmani.

'Take care, Miss Mason. These are not the boys you knew. They are enraptured by death.'

'I do not think they will harm me.'

'You are very brave. I wish things had been different between us.'

She did not reply at once. Then she said, 'Thank you, Peter.'

I watched her walk forwards towards the aircraft, moving gracefully between the thorns.

Jason held his mouth tightly shut as if to arrest his own voice. He put his uniform into immaculate shape with swift movements of his hands: he was restoring the sensations of discipline, bringing his mind back into familiar channels. He fell in beside me as though on parade.

He said, 'What madness! The lady has no chance. You should not have interceded on her behalf.'

'It is just possible she may influence the gunmen.'

'That is what you need to think, not what you believe. There is only one way out of this. An assault, no matter how bloody.'

'I wish you would not speak like that.'

'A nation has only the strength of its leader.'

'That is a foolish catch-phrase.'

'She is beautiful — is she not — Miss Iris Mason?'

'I suppose so.'

He turned fully about, so that he was facing away from Osmani's now distant figure. 'We should not have let a woman go into danger. It is not seemly in an Islamic nation.'

'There are many women inside the aircraft.'

'She has reached the aircraft? She is speaking to the terrorists?'

'Not yet.'

'Tell me, Peter — tell me frankly — are you in love with Miss Carol Langley?'

I said, 'Yes.'

'She is as beautiful as Miss Iris Mason?'

'More, to me.'

'I have no eyes for such things. We did not distinguish beauty in the Neban, only hunger and thirst. But I would concede that you think she is beautiful. If Miss Langley and Miss Mason come to harm I will of course kill both terrorists and the girl Leisha.'

'That is no comfort to me, sir.'

'I have the strength, the will. Your love will be avenged even though it is the painting of your imagination.'

I did not answer that; speaking of Carol had destroyed my power to shape words. The tears were falling from my eyes more quickly than the sun could dry them. Jason was aware of my distress.

'Come, Peter, we are military men! We do not yield to emotion.' To endorse this opinion he turned smartly to face the aircraft, bringing his feet back together in the manner approved at Sandhurst. 'See, Miss Mason is negotiating with the terrorists. In a moment they will surrender.'

Osmani had stopped beneath the aircraft door. She made a stroke of white on the grey tarmac. The sun was so strong her figure was devoid of detail and I could not tell if she was speaking. I strained my ear across the sun-soaked airfield but not a sound reached me. She stood there a long time while nearer to us the haze played over the parched grass. Then, in a movement so small it might have been a trick of my vision, I saw Osmani retreat perhaps half a step. She placed a hand upon her shoulder in a gesture that seemed theatrical and started her long walk back to where we were standing. She moved with the same slow grace she had shown us previously. I wondered what news she brought, what message from the gunman. It was only when she approached within thirty yards that I saw the stains on her clothing and I ran forward to offer the support she had been denied until then.

'The fault was mine,' she said. 'I told him he was not serious.'

'It was Haida?'

She nodded. 'He is eighteen. He may be less. I did not want him shot like a dog.'

'Let me help you,' I said.

'Miss Mason, Miss Mason!' the President cried.

With greater presence of mind that I would have thought possible Ben Talun had called forward one of the ambulances that were now concentrated on the airfield. Osmani would not be assisted.

'My lady, you will have the finest medical treatment.' Jason said. 'We will send you to America if necessary.'

'You must concern yourself with the release of the passengers.'

'You have great courage. You shall have a medal!'

Before she mounted the ambulance Osmani turned again to the President. 'Le Ciel Rouge have repeated their demands, General. They require Suleiman ben Yusoff set free.'

'Of course. It is their obsession.'

She paused, breathing deeply. Her next words were spoken with difficulty and I turned away in my embarrassment.

'I think they will carry out their threat if the prisoner is not released.'

The President bowed, I think in recognition of her courage. Then the ambulance carried her away towards the gate.

§

'It is monstrous,' said Jason; 'a retreat from sanity, an insult to God!'

The light had weakened and some of the heat had gone out of the day. He had not yet given the order for the operation to resume. He paced back and forth in the little command tent the brigade had put up a hundred yards short of the forward position.

'I shall wait until dark; then I shall lead the assault myself. One, two, three—wallop! I shall personally take the life of the gunman who wounded Miss Iris Mason.'

'Sir, listen to me!'

I was very tired. I could not lift my spirit from the place where it had fallen.

'Oh ho! I am to listen to Colonel Warfield. I am to throw away my Presidency and take up the collection of butterflies.'

'What is left, at the end, but concern?'

It sounded silly in the tent crammed with weapons and communications equipment. I had made it easy for him to mock me.

'I do not understand the word. It does not belong in Africa. It is something that Colonel Warfield learnt in Wimbledon, where he spent his childhood.'

'But you can show friendship, you can show kindness.'

'Never! I am a soldier and celibate; I deal in practical things. I do not know the meaning of affection. I have no wife, no family . . .'

'Jason, I have met your wife. I thought her charming. You have two fine children.'

He stared at me in astonishment; then inwardly he collapsed a little. 'A long time ago I was married. We were very young. It is not a matter of importance.'

'Your wife is concerned for you still.'

'Yes?' He picked up an automatic weapon and looked at the bolt with fierce concentration. 'It is so?'

228

'I don't understand why you renounced your family. It wasn't necessary.'

'We were a government of soldiers. I had to make harsh decisions; I could show no weakness. I was the strong man! A woman does not understand such things. Why, what could a woman do against a gunman like Haida?'

I struggled to keep my mind open, to find what I really meant. I said, 'A leader is lost when he forgets that he is also a human being.'

'A leader is lost when his judgment is clouded by what you call love.'

That seemed to be his last pronouncement. He marched out of the tent and I heard him call for the company commander outside. I sat with my head in my hands while the light failed and the shadows grew in the recesses of the tent. My mind had cleared in my distress and I could see clearly what would happen to Jason if he assaulted the aircraft. I had not expected him to come back, but some part of our argument still disturbed him, and now he re-entered the tent and stood beside me, silently.

I spoke first, while I had a chance. 'Sir, there are leaders good and bad. A soldier isn't a bad ruler because he is a soldier. What finally makes a tyrant is a lack of sympathy.' He said nothing, and I kept to my point while my mind stayed clear. 'I have never seen you as a tyrant. I have seen you as a soldier trying to put things straight. Heaven knows there was a need for it, as there always is. Soldiers have a gift for good order. But if you sacrifice these people you will become a tyrant because you will have lost the best part of yourself.'

This was beyond the calling of a military adviser and he would not have been wrong to rebuke me. I looked up at him and our eyes met, but he had not the courage to hold my gaze. When he replied his voice was more African than I had known it.

'Peter—my dear Peter—a dictator must be without remorse or he is lost. It is the manner of the job. I told you that at Eastleigh.'

He left me then, going out into the gathering dusk, and I suspected that he would straightway set the operation in movement. I returned my head into my hands, my mind quite empty but for the ache that lay there. I did not hold back my tears; now that Jason had finally ignored my advice I had no further business in the country and no need to keep my discipline. I did not know what I would do with myself when this was over. I would simply go away, having failed in my mission, and try to forget that I had ever been a soldier. I had only one duty in these last minutes of my military life—to keep Carol in my mind, as though the strength of my love might put a shield around her. It was a small, hopeless task that did not arrest my tears and would not make the smallest difference to the unfolding of violence in the world outside. I suppose some part of my mind was waiting for the gunfire to begin, and when it did not, I looked up, startled by the silence.

There was more light outside than within. Through the tent door, where the canvas parted in a triangle, I could see Jason standing by himself. He was not looking at the aircraft: he was looking at me. The starch that usually supported him had gone out of his body. He did not exactly smile; rather he wore a look of quiet indulgence that did not leave his face as I watched him. Then, freed from the restraints of the drill book, he ducked under the canvas and knelt beside me. He took my hand in both of his. In his eyes was the wonderful sympathy of the African.

In the thick accent of the Neban, he said, 'Dear friend, I care nothing for the aircraft, but I cannot watch your tears.'

Not a word could I manage. I simply held his hands.

'I have given orders that Solly is to be released.'

I do not recall that I thanked him. I remember nothing but that the last of the light was vanishing inside the tent and that his face became veiled in shadow. Perhaps we stayed there a long time; perhaps not. At length we went out into the cool night air and prepared for the release of the passengers.

# 18

For me, the rest of that night has become overlaid by its final, violent image, and it is hard for me now to put the events into their proper order. There was a long delay while Solly was taken from confinement and conveyed under guard to the airfield at El Desmara. The terrorists would not free the passengers until Solly had been flown to Kezzan and had assured them by radio-telephone that he had reached the holy city. Then the first of the passengers were allowed to disembark. These were the women and children, with Carol among them. We met, shyly at first, as if the interval had been years and not hours, at the edge of the hardstanding; she was tired, quiet, sapped of life, but the moonlight drew her figure in firm, comforting lines, and I led her away from the aircraft murmuring thanks to the God I didn't quite believe in. Meanwhile, with a speed possible only in a dictatorship, a million dinars had been brought from a bank in Mogalor and offered to Leisha for verification. I do not know what promise Jason made about the punishment of Nathan, but some undertaking was given. I believed this condition to have been made for publicity reasons and that Jason would ignore whatever bargain he had struck.

We came finally to the appointment of hostages. Four were demanded from among the remaining passengers, and it did not surprise me that those chosen were three businessmen from Sidi-bel-Said, and Langley.

'Why must it be him?' Carol asked me. She had no tears left and her voice was small and bewildered.

Why? Because his was a big, expensive life—because there would be no point in the murder of a slave or scullion.

'I am sure they will release him when they get to their destination,' I said. Indeed, Haida would have that much regard for a bargain if I judged him correctly.

But for the hostages, the rest of the passengers were released soon afterwards; and then we spent the remaining hours of the long night waiting in the tower while the military headquarters in El Desmara found a country that would receive the aircraft and the errant warriors it contained. The tiny airfield at Kezzan would not accommodate an aircraft of this size. A welcome in the Socialist world was not at once apparent; these countries had troubles enough without taking in such champions of their cause. At last, an Arab country to the north, whose sympathy for revolutionaries of any hue was greater than its need for the world's good opinion, offered landing facilities and the aircraft was prepared for flight.

At the last moment there was a hitch: the gunmen could not resist a final affirmation of faith and a messenger was called for. I think their need was as much to speak to someone familiar because they named me as emissary. I did not hesitate in obeying that instruction. I went down into the darkness, which had now the chill of early morning, and walked the distance to the aircraft with Leisha following a pace behind me. A light burned in the entrance and I clambered up the ladder to where Haida waited for me.

He was pale, and the night's exertions had plainly tired him, but he treated me with the same courtesy as before. 'Monsieur, it is necessary for me to speak, to explain . . .'

'There is no point in explanation, Haida.'

'But there is! I want you to understand the reason for our actions; I want you to know why we had to use violence. You must tell others, you must tell Osmani.'

I got the point. He had expected to die, and now that he had not he needed someone to believe in him. I had already decided not to argue.

'You are lucky that Miss Mason is not seriously hurt,' I said.

'She is not? I am glad!'

I listened then to what Haida had to say, making no interruption; he told me the aim of Le Ciel Rouge was that of

232

universal justice; he told me that this could only be achieved through dynamic action against the forces of tyranny; he spoke with an engagement I had barely heard since my days in college. Meanwhile Leisha had climbed the steps and taken her place beside her brother. She did not speak; her conviction was more complete than his and did not need to be stated. And another figure, that of Aissa, had come rearward from the flight deck to join this meeting as if he too hoped I would not get the wrong impression. They might have been students bringing some radical opinion to a sympathetic tutor. I was conscious of their extreme good looks.

'You see how it is, monsieur? You understand me, yes?'

'I understand you, Haida, but I do not agree. Will you allow me a word with the hostages?'

'Of course! But Leisha must accompany you.'

I went into the passenger cabin where the hostages were grouped in the first-class seats immediately to the rear of the entrance. A panel light in the ceiling gave the only illumination, but the broad figure of Albert Langley was easy to see. He was very much awake and stirred by an indignation that frightened me.

'Sir, I want you to listen carefully,' I said. I did not think that Leisha could speak much English but none the less I kept my voice low. 'I know this is hard for you to bear, but for everyone's sake you must be patient. I am sure you will be released when you get to the other end.'

'One opportunity,' he said. 'Just one. I'm not used to treatment of this sort.'

'The safety of the aircraft will depend upon your restraint.'

'Brother, this is my aircraft and I'll smash it up if I like.'

'There are others aboard apart from the gunmen.'

'Look, son; I never duck out. It's not my way, see? I got where I am because I'm a fighter. I don't go along with patience and all that stuff, and I'll see this lot in hell before I admit they've got the better of me.'

The greatest danger lay here. I waited for his anger to subside, and then I said, 'Mr Langley, the crew are your employees, the other hostages are your business associates; for their safety you must keep your anger in check until you are released.'

'Do you want me to just sit here?'

'Yes, sir.'

'I tell you it's not my way.'

'Then make it so.'

'You're asking me to accept defeat, and that I've never done.'

'It takes courage of another sort.'

'Not in my world, Colonel Warfield.'

I said with anger of my own, 'You must swallow your pride, sir. Think of Carol. After all, you came here because of her.'

'Yes, I did that,' he said.

I left him with that thought. Perhaps he had softened a little, but his shoulders were still braced for action when I had my last sight of him.

Haida conducted me to the steps in a flutter of consideration. I could have liked Haida if things had been different. When I had climbed down to the tarmac I looked back through the open door at Le Ciel Rouge, all of them for the moment within my sight, and I was impressed by their beauty and supposed that Mahmet had been made in the same mould.

The light was spreading in the lower sky as I walked back to the tower; in the air were all the scents of dawn. It was the hour of prayer, but no prayer was on my lips; I felt nothing but a sick dismay at the madness that went hand in hand with reason; that, and tiredness. Jason and Ben Talun met me under the tower.

'What did they want?' the President asked.

'To talk, to wrap it up in words.'

'Their maturity begins to speak to them,' said Ben Talun, with the wisdom of a timid soul. 'They will live long enough to realize their error.'

'They may,' I said. 'I do not know.'

We went up the tower and out on to the balcony to watch the take-off. The sky was a brilliant white over the hills and feathers of mist, at a height no greater than the taller grasses, still lay over the airfield. There was light enough for us to see the aircraft in the vulgar colours chosen by the proprietor. Carol came from the rest room. Hatim, too, was there. We heard the captain start one engine, then the other. The aircraft turned on to the runway and

234

taxied slowly towards the southern end of the airfield, where it swung about and faced the direction of take-off. The tower gave clearance; the aircraft and its parcel of trouble rolled forward, gained pace to flying speed and went into a steep climb. Carol did not look. She had turned her face into my shirt. I watched the wheels fold; I watched the aircraft ascending into the dawn-flooded sky.

We had seen the last of the beautiful people who, in Ben Talun's mind, needed time to see the magnitude of their mistake.

It must have been in this minute that Langley made his move. I can't say what it was. I like to think he had strength enough to deal with the first of the terrorists, giving a good account of himself in the few seconds that remained of the aircraft's flight. We know nothing of this. We know simply that the fuselage was ruptured by a grenade aft of the flight deck and that the control and hydraulic lines were broken. I saw the aircraft stall, hang for a moment tail down, and then fall away in a slow cartwheel of gay colour that carried it forward perhaps another half-mile towards its destination. The impact was out of our sight, behind a fold in the rough ground to the north.

The President was the first to recover his voice. 'Well, somebody fought them,' he said.

# 19

Nathan had taken the capital firmly into his grip. He had secured the main thoroughfares and markets with units of armour and Nebanese soldiers were everywhere in the streets. He had enforced a soldier's solution, driving the rioters indoors, and he could sustain it for a while. Poor Sadek Ali: the police had once again been put into the shade by the Army, but the Commissioner had arrested some youths, guilty of probably no more than excitement, and these were now impounded at police headquarters. We drove into El Desmara at noon, having finished our business at Sidi-bel-Said. The streets were littered with the debris of riot which a company of engineers was now trying to remove. Every door and shutter was closed; only the dogs had still their liberty. I had not brought Carol back to this. Soon after daylight I had put her on a plane to Gibraltar, comforting her as well as I could with the promise that I would join her there in a few days' time.

A few days. It would not be more. The Iman had tried his strength and found it sufficient. That morning, General Suleiman had been greeted in Kezzan as a leader appointed by God. They had driven him through the streets in an open car. He had addressed the people in the Golden Mosque, the Iman at his side, and he had condemned the Military Government as an unholy and repressive tyranny supported only by the Nebanese. He announced the re-establishment of Sharifian government in Kezzan, which would be extended to the whole country notwithstanding the resistance of menials and the mixers of pig swill. (I knew my Solly: this was an unguarded reference to the black people of the south, whose advancement was not amongst his obsessions.) He made a feature of the President's sympathy with Khalidism and his intention to sell the country to the international financier Langley. His master-stroke was to reveal that Langley's daughter had been the handmaiden of the infamous Khalid. He had concluded by declaring Jihad, or holy war, against the Officers' Committee.

§

There was a curfew that night, but after it was dark and accompanied by a single soldier I went again to the house in the Medina where we had found, I think, a friend. The door opened to my repeated knock and I was taken through the labyrinth of passages to the dark chamber smelling of herbs and cedarwood I had visited before. The old man with the face of grave scholarship came almost at once, and he would not let me speak until I had taken a glass of *thé Maroccaine*.

Finally I said, 'Lord Pasha, you have watched over General Khymer since he was a young man. I believe that after Kemel al Marabout you have had the greatest influence upon his mind.'

The Pasha spoke in his faultless Arabic, a trace of amusement in his voice. 'I am an old man; he is a great general. What is it you would have me tell him, friend?'

'I believe him to be in danger. You will know that his enemies aim to take the headship of the state away from him. In particular, General Suleiman has a hatred for him that will not be satisfied by his own assumption of power. He will require, I am sure, his life.'

'Why should that be? They are fellow soldiers.'

'Lord, there are some conflicts that can be resolved only by death. I want you to speak to him. I want you to persuade him there is nothing more he can do in this country and that he must go away. I want you to tell him his friendship has value for many people. You see, I must save his life if I can.'

'I understand. I have been told.'

'Of what, master?'

For a moment he did not continue. Then he said, 'I believe the President released General Suleiman as a gesture of friendship, no matter that it would destroy his safety. Of course that leaves the friend with an unalterable duty to save him.'

'It is a duty I accept.'

'You are obedient to the laws of Islam, my friend.'

'I have found them apt since I was a young man. But, master, the laws of Christendom are no different in this matter.'

The ghost of a smile was upon his lips. 'I am not instructed in the rule of the Nazarene,' he said.

'Will you help me? Will you help me in my obligation?'

He was looking across my shoulder into the darkness behind me. I turned but could see nothing.

'There is one who can help you better than I,' the Pasha said.

'Who is it?' I asked. 'Is someone there?'

A third voice said in English, 'It is only me.'

A figure had entered the room from a doorway I could not see, or perhaps she had been there all the time. She seated herself beside me and took my hand. It was Helen, Jason's wife.

She looked at me with calm eyes that did not seem afraid. She said, 'Tell me, Peter—if Jason could be persuaded to leave, is there a way he could be taken out of the country?'

'I think so. There are tracks, footpaths, desert airstrips.'

'But he would need friends in Africa.'

'He has them.'

'I do not know of any.'

'Helen, Jason was at Eastleigh. There are graduates of the college all over Africa and the Middle East and many of them are in positions of great authority. They have a boyish sense of fellowship that is larger than politics. One of them, I am sure, will send Jason an aircraft.'

The Pasha had followed our English with close attention. Now he said in his own language, 'That is so? That is the way of the military?'

'It doesn't make much sense, but they are like that.'

Helen said, 'You will speak to them, Peter?'

'I will; but that isn't the real difficulty.'

'I know, I know,' she said, pressing my hand. 'The real difficulty will be getting Jason to leave.'

'In that I must depend upon you and my lord Pasha.'

Helen nodded, and I went away, back to my office at the

Tamran Palace where I took the chair and fell into a dream-filled sleep.

§

I was wakened by the guard changing below my window. It was an hour before dawn here on the Atlantic coast but morning in Africa and Asia. I went to the communications room, taking with me a copy of *The Pelican,* the journal of Eastleigh to which once a year the graduates of the college reported their whereabouts or sometimes (let it be admitted) their continued existence. Jason rose early, but not so early as this.

I started with a country close to the Saharan Republic where the Chief of the Air Staff was Air Marshal 'Trigger' Abdullah. I remembered him as a jovial giant who had played a ferocious game of squash. The telephonist was an age getting a line to his office and then I found myself speaking to an aide.

Was the Air Marshal available? I asked.

No, he was out.

When would he be back?

He did not know. A long time.

I scented political embarrassment but I had no time to lose.

Was Air Marshal Abdullah still in office? I asked firmly.

Well, no. He was on extended leave. The aide could not say quite where he was.

Nor could anyone, I thought, as I rang off; he was in disfavour and possibly taking his leave in the next world. I cast the net wider. At a greater distance and to the south was an equatorial country, wholly African in leadership and sympathy, where the Army Commander, General St George Noko Akomfi, was also the tribal chieftain. We had called him Niki. Only minutes later he came through loud and clear in the unmistakable accent of Eastleigh.

'Yes, old boy. What's the beef?'

I explained my problem: I wanted him to save the life of a fellow Pelican.

'Sorry, Peter. No can do. My master's talking to Kezzan.'

'But they're not a legal government!'

'Soon will be. We don't give Jason more than a couple of days.

239

Boy, I'd get shot. 'Bye now.'

I had no better luck with two other Pelicans, one a divisional commander, the other the head of his country. Then Niki rang back.

'Try Buster Mohamet,' he said. 'Got him on the blower a moment ago and mentioned your problem. He's very big stuff these days — bags of oil, bags of French weapons, no real worries. And he's much closer to you than I am. When are you coming down for the shooting?'

'Soon,' I said. 'Bless you, Niki.'

In my copy of *The Pelican*, not yet a year old, Buster Mohamet was shown as a lieutenant-colonel commanding a battalion of infantry in an Islamic kingdom to the east; plainly his star had risen. I could not picture him clearly, but when half an hour later I heard his diffident voice on the 'phone I recalled the spare, inoffensive young officer who had said not a word and once got stoned on a glass of sherry.

'Commander-in-Chief speaking.'

I repeated my request with little hope that General Mohamet would have the guts for this adventure; but I had forgotten the lion that may reside in a timid breast and he interrupted me before I had finished.

'Of course, dear boy. When you want an aircraft I'll get one to whichever strip you choose. Don't bother about the over-flying rights; there's nothing but desert between you and me and the radar's not effective below five thousand feet. Jason will have to lose himself when he gets here and I'll have to deny everything. No problem. See you.'

I felt a brief comfort in having secured Jason's line of retreat. I went back to the house in the Medina, where now I felt myself at home, and told the Pasha and Jason's wife what I had done. Helen had already brought her children from Sidi-bel-Said and would leave with the President — that is, if we could persuade him to go.

'We must find words to reach him,' the Pasha said. 'And you, dear Colonel, must look to your own safety. Even now your life will be in danger.'

'I'll get myself out somehow. If necessary, I will go through the Neban. I think the commander there will help me.'

240

'When it is time to act, you must tell me.'
It was not yet. The Presidency had still some hours of life.

# 20

I expected Rustum to attack down the main road with a screen of armoured vehicles in fan formation ahead of him. Small units would advance along parallel tracks. In other words he would do what it said in the handbook as he had not the imagination to devise methods of his own. Simultaneously the Iman would call out the rioters in El Desmara to absorb Jason's military strength. And this is what happened the following day, Rustum giving further proof of a conventional mind by mounting his attack at noon precisely.

The two brigades from El Desmara had been responsive to their orders so far. They were deployed twenty miles outside the city walls and a long way short of Rustum's forward positions. Nathan was in the city and still obedient. General Salam and Colonel Aziz had presented themselves for duty that morning, but Captain Ismael was nowhere to be found and was no doubt offering his services to the alternative government.

When news of the Kezzani advance reached us, the President and I left the Tamran Palace and drove up the road towards the brigades. Jason was of the opinion that as Commander-in-Chief he must show himself to the Army and remind them to whom their loyalty was pledged. It was probably too late, but I didn't argue. We had passed through the northern gate, preceded by an escort, and driven a mile through the orchards before Jason said anything. He was in a mood of whimsical detachment.

'How strange, Peter! How very strange! I will speak to the troops in the manner of every commander since Alexander, urging them to fight for their legitimate leader. But I am neither king nor prince. I am a Nebanese blanket boy whose destiny was servitude.'

I let that go; and I don't remember that he said anything else as we drove the remaining miles towards the defending army. It was a bright clear day and in the orchards they were shaking down the olives and burning the branches with the unconcern of peasants anywhere for what lay below the horizon.

We had left the olives behind and were in a region of poor grazing when I saw the first soldier. He was seated on a milestone, his tunic open, his cap gone; he carried no weapon. I didn't like the look of it but I kept myself quiet. A mile further on and there were soldiers in the fields moving rearward in no sort of order and, as far as I could see, under no authority. I counted twenty, thirty. Jason gave no sign that he had seen them.

A short distance further and we met transport and some field weapons coming back. It did not look like a rout; they were simply travelling to the rear under their NCOs. I stopped a vehicle in which there was a sergeant.

Why was the Army in retreat? I asked.

There was no retreat, he said. There was no enemy. He had seen only soldiers in his own uniform who had stopped for prayer at the same time he did.

Had the officers given him no instructions?

No, the officers had said nothing that he could understand.

We drove forward another half-mile and were stopped behind a column of vehicles facing Kezzan but whose crews were resting under the eucalyptus trees at the side of the road. It looked like the better part of a battalion's stores. I got out to speak to the men, but they were sullen and did not even lift their heads.

I reported to Jason. 'These men are lost. There is no direction.'

We had to find the officers, who were presumably somewhere forward. We took the car through the fields, avoiding the column, and then made another three miles up the road passing through the rear sections of the Army. There must have been a thousand men in the vicinity: some were asleep, but most just sat in the shade in gloomy introspection. This army had not even the resource to feed itself.

We came to a halt, finally it seemed, behind an armoured personnel carrier that must have belonged to the forward elements of the Army. I heard single shots from somewhere up the road, perhaps at a distance of four miles; there must have been someone with nerve enough to resist the enemy, but the firing was not prolonged. We got out of the car and, with the escort, went in search of the local battalion commander. We followed where the soldiers pointed, crossing a plantation of figs to a building of mud brick which might once have been a granary.

Here we found a lieutenant-colonel and the rudiments of a staff. It was Zarahid, the tough old professional whom I had consulted earlier about the soldiers' spirit.

Jason said, 'Well, Colonel, you have not engaged the enemy. Your soldiers have run away into the fields. Have you no courage?'

Zarahid was an older man than Jason and hardened by experience. A year ago he would have been senior to the President. 'I do not lack courage,' he said. 'The Army has no stomach for this thing.'

Jason spoke in the mincing voice he used when he disagreed with an opinion. 'You were ordered to prevent the Kezzani advance, but I find your battalion in disarray. For this I could have you shot.'

'Oh yes, you could have me shot!' Zarahid said, with the emphasis of mockery. 'That is, if you can find six soldiers still carrying their rifles. Six Nebanese, perhaps.'

'I am not joking, Colonel.'

'Neither am I. See here, my lord and master—the Army has disintegrated because you have placed it between its town of origin and its religious capital. You have placed it between yourself and General Suleiman. I don't give a rap what differences there are between yourself and the Chief of Staff, but give an army two loyalties and very soon it can't bury its excrement. So, shoot away, soldier! This defeat is of your own making.'

Had Jason been in better form he would have arrested Zarahid, but some reverie of his own still occupied his mind. He said without force, 'You have defied lawful orders. I will hold you to account.'

'Lawful? What is lawful?' Zarahid, old fighter that he was, had clearly decided he had nothing to lose. 'The only lawful orders are those you have the power to enforce. The strongest man in the country at the moment is Brigadier Rustum, who commands the largest body of obedient troops. Believe me, Rustum is giving the only lawful orders!'

In the seconds that followed—during which, I afterwards felt, Jason finally lost his authority—I watched not the angry sweat-stained colonel but the face of the man whose fortunes I had shared in the last months. He did not seem disturbed. His eyes showed a wistful amusement as if a comedy of his own devising had been brought to a conclusion. He did not abuse Zarahid; that would have been superfluous, like words spoken after the curtain. Finally he nodded to me and walked out of the building.

I caught up with him under the fig trees outside. No advice of mine would have counted for much just then. I remember that he laughed.

'How comic he looked, Peter! Did you see how his cheeks quivered? He must have supposed that I took myself seriously. Actually he is one of the best field commanders we have.'

Across an open space and beyond a thicket of tamarisk I could see the movement of troop-carrying vehicles. The dust drifted away into the afternoon sunlight. The direction they took, and their deliberate pace, held my attention. I could not be sure but I suspected them to be Rustum's infantry.

'Sir, we must hurry. It is not safe for you here.'

'Where are we going, Peter? Why must we hurry?'

'The Kezzanis would treat you roughly. We do not know where their forward positions are.'

'What sport, old son! Any minute Solly may jump out of a tree, like a jungle man.'

'Please be serious. You cannot be protected here.'

'As if it mattered! I was a man of straw from the beginning.'

I heard a step behind us. It was Zarahid, hatless and with his tunic undone. He said abruptly, 'Do as you please. Talk here all afternoon. But the Kezzanis will be south of this position in half an hour. No government units have put up more than a feeble resistance.' He turned to me, speaking more intimately now. 'Brother, I don't know what business you still have in the country, but I should hop it. The Kezzanis are drunk with the spirit of Islam. A Christian, particularly one close to the President, won't stand a chance. Get me?'

I nodded. 'What will you do?' I asked.

'Nothing that need concern you or the President.'

He left us then, and I guided Jason back to the car. The escort had remained impassive, and now they helped turn the car and clear the road of a litter of soldiers and equipment so that the President could drive back to the capital. Then for two whole hours, until it was dusk, we travelled at the speed of the retreating Army and at length came under the walls of El Desmara.

§

All day Nathan had kept the town subdued with baton and rubber bullet, but he would not be able to sustain this position when Rustum broke through the northern gate, probably a few minutes after dawn prayer tomorrow morning. My task was now to preserve what I could, including my own life, in the hours of defeat. I went to the house in the Medina and brought my two friends back to the palace. I asked them to wait in an ante-room while I approached the President.

I attacked Jason squarely. 'Mr President, the military situation is hopeless. If Nathan stays on the streets he will be caught between the Kezzanis and the mob, and he'll need all his strength to defend himself. The city would fall in a few hours. Ben Talun might try to relieve you, but he has not the capacity for this sort of warfare. If you want to continue the struggle by military means, you'll have to go into the Neban and let Nathan hold the Skar crossings.'

He looked at me from under his eyelids in some secret cunning and I feared the worst. 'You wish me to retreat, Colonel Warfield? That is your advice?'

'We have lost. There is nothing more you can do as President. You should leave the country.'

'Very good. The Eastleigh solution, written on pink paper to remind the directing staff not to show it to the students—the military answer that ignores every consideration other than tactics.'

'At the end there is only the military issue.'

'These matters are not decided by armies, Colonel.'

My hopes, never great, were vanishing fast; we'd get nowhere if

246

Jason retreated into mysticism.

'General Suleiman will be ruthless towards you.'

'No doubt. It is a matter of no consequence.'

'Your life is of consequence, sir. It matters a great deal to some people.'

'It matters to no one! I am alone. I was born in a ditch of no one in particular and my only duty was to a slave-master long dead. I may seek whatever fulfilment I please.'

I could not tell if he was joking, but I feared not. I would get no further on my own. I said, but I don't know if he heard me, 'Your Eastleigh friends will save you if you wish. An aircraft will be sent overnight and you may continue your life in another country. It's not as if your Presidency was other than accidental.'

I left him sitting at his desk and went to the ante-room, from where I conducted Helen and the Pasha to his office. They perhaps might persuade him. He had left his desk and gone on to the terrace and I could see his white uniform beyond the pergola. We followed him into the garden where it was dark but for the light of the fires outside the wall. The voice of the professional adviser would be of little use in this last appeal; I therefore spoke in Arabic.

'Jason, here are the two people who love you best. I too count myself your friend, as you have saved the life of the person I most care for and offered your own instead. To keep you from harm is the duty laid upon us. We therefore beg you to leave the country tonight.'

He stared at us across the grass, his eyes resting at last upon the Pasha. 'Master,' was his only word.

The Pasha said, 'You have done all you can, my son. You did not seek the Presidency, therefore you cannot be held to it now. Had you been born to it, or had you fought to attain it, I would have told you to stay until death—indeed, that would have been my command as your elder and guardian. But you were chosen by others for a task you did not want and now you may lay it down.'

'It is so,' Helen said. 'My lord Pasha releases you from any obligations to the state.'

'What is more, it is my wish that you go to another country and there develop the virtue I know to be in you, together with your

247

wife and children.'

Jason dropped his head; he had to admit the power of his spiritual guardian. I stepped into the shadows, knowing I could play no part in these Islamic disciplines.

Jason said weakly, 'Lord, I am Commander-in-Chief of an army still engaged.'

'Shame, that you cannot accept the truth!' Now the Pasha spoke with the anger of love, in a manner beyond the range of the present-day Christian. 'Have you forgotten your tutor? Have you forgotten Kemel? You were instructed by the most luminous mind in the Maghreb and yet you fall into the sin of pride. Where are your armies? How can you fight without weapons? The Marabout would have beaten you with his own hands for such a failure of the spirit.'

More simply, Helen said, 'It's better for you to go, Jason. Peter has arranged everything.'

Jason had listened to the Pasha in respectful silence, and now he turned towards a dark corner of the garden. He could not contradict his patron directly. 'I cherish the memory of Kemel, master. I revere your wisdom, respect your authority. But I am the President.'

'A contrivance of the soldiers. Nothing more.'

'I accepted their decision. The duty is not discharged.'

The Pasha looked at me, as this was my territory. Now I spoke in English. 'That's stupid, and you know it. Your command of the Army is beyond saving. If you remain in El Desmara it will mean bloodshed, as Nathan will be obliged to defend you.'

His voice, directed away from me, was so indistinct I could barely hear it. 'I shall tell Nathan to withdraw. His soldiers will leave the city before first light.'

'Then there will be not the slightest point in your staying here.'

He looked at me across his shoulder; his English, spoken softly, was meant for me alone. 'Dear, honest Peter, you see things so simply. Go now, save your life; Nathan will take you across the Skar. The end of this thing is nothing to do with you.'

'If you won't listen to me, then listen to the Pasha and to Helen.'

'I cannot, though I love them.'

'You must be out of your mind.'

His next words were firmly said, with the force of the highest office in the country. He addressed himself to the Pasha. 'Master, my decision is made. I cannot run away. It is true I have not taken my office seriously. I have used it to make a mockery of my enemies because they were pompous fools who really believed that power can be exercised. I could not believe it. It was all so funny, so absurd. But I am, after all, the President, and I cannot make a mockery of the end.'

The Pasha had followed him closely and did not argue. He approached Jason and laid a hand on his shoulder in some sort of blessing. Helen remained calm and did not renew her appeal. Then Jason conducted us back to the terrace with the authority of a man who has made up his mind.

In the hall, Helen turned to me. 'It was hopeless from the start. He did not intend to live. Peter, for my sake, don't wait any longer. You cannot help him now. Go; please go.'

# 21

I did not intend to let Solly catch me, but I did not leave at once. With an escort of infantry I paid a last visit to my house and recovered the few books and possessions I cared for. The product of my life filled no more than one valise. I had come to the Saharan Republic travelling light and I would certainly leave in the same manner. I moved my gear into the Tamran Palace and left the straps fastened.

Then I saw Nathan in the operations room and discussed the timing of his withdrawal. His forces would have to evacuate before morning if it was not to be a fighting retreat, but it seemed unlikely that Rustum would pursue him along the Dharat road; there was nothing in the south of much interest to the Kezzanis. One company would remain to protect the palace.

'Leave me a vehicle and a weapon of some sort,' I asked him. 'I won't be far behind you.'

'Why should I save your skin, brother? You're nothing to me.'

Nevertheless, having got that off his chest, he gave me a Land Rover and my old friend the Lee Enfield with sixty rounds. I put my valise in the back of the vehicle, secured the rifle in the locker and immobilized the engine. This gave me a line of retreat: in my lifetime I had asked for nothing more.

With Nathan, I went on to the roof from where we had a sight of the Medina. It was after midnight. There was no moon but the streets were lighted by fires and I could see the line of the old wall beyond the roofs. The riots were over for a time but I could hear voices, angry, plaintive, from every part of the city. Dogs were barking outside the wall.

'It wasn't much of a war,' Nathan said.

'What will you do?'

'The boy asks me what I will do! Why, retreat in good order, re-polish the brasses. Leave this rotten place to fester.'

'That was not what I meant.'

He laughed. 'The best decisions don't have to be made, son. You should have shot me in the desert when you had a gun in your hand and I had nothing.'

'I suppose you had guessed about the slaving.'

'There was no other explanation. Villages destroyed, old people murdered. But I couldn't prove it. You did well to trap them.'

'I wouldn't blame you if you went your own way.'

He turned to go down; he hadn't time to waste in gossip. 'Leave by the south gate; don't stop on the road. I'll look for you at the Skar. If my boys shoot you, that's just too bad.'

§

The last hours of the night I spent in improving the defences of the palace; I didn't know for what purpose, but it gave me something to do. Jason stayed in his office and I believed him to be in prayer or some other state of arrest. Sometime before dawn he came into the hall, which now resembled a dugout, and looked at these preparations as if he did not understand their meaning.

I gave him my opinion, knowing that it made no difference. 'If the palace comes under mortar fire, you will find the greatest safety in the hall. The other rooms on the ground floor have flat roofs which offer no protection. The soldiers will fall back to this point.'

Whatever prayers he had said were still in the centre of his mind. 'You are thorough, as always, Peter. It doesn't matter greatly.'

I agreed with that, but said nothing.

'Dear friend, I have been in thought. I have sought clarity. You see, I wish to understand my situation.'

It seemed plain enough to me. And now there was a freshness in the air, warning us of first light, the moment when Rustum would press through the northern gate and direct his soldiers to the palace. I said, 'You have done your best, sir. The military government was run fairly.'

251

'Oh, my Presidency was nothing! A sham, a pretence! The Kezzanis never intended me to rule for long. But I might have sustained my authority. I should have ranted at the microphone. I should have cast my statue in gold and put it in the market where the morning sun would have caught the helmet.'

I found it difficult to adapt to these ideas while the soldiers were still erecting sandbags.

'A dictator must act flamboyantly, cruelly,' Jason continued. 'He must accept flattery as truth. In each of his mistakes he must see the conspiracy of others. Khalid had some of these things; he was a better dictator than I.'

The light was growing behind the windows. A signals clerk had pushed a message into my hand, one originated some hours earlier, and from which I read of the only resistance to Rustum's army.

'Sir, Zarahid is dead, together with three soldiers. He held up the Kezzani advance for ninety minutes.'

'He should not have died. My dictatorship was not worth defending.'

'Come, it was as good as you could make it!'

'I should have displayed my picture on every wall. I should have become a majestic tyrant.'

I wondered if he knew what time it was, or how near was Rustum's infantry.

'Dear instructor, you taught me too well,' he said. 'I loved the fellowship of Eastleigh and the suggestion we take nothing quite seriously. You did not let us speak politics; it was not done. We accepted that all politicians were vulgar apes it was our duty to serve but not to believe in. You made me into a soldier like yourself. You made me into an Englishman.'

'We taught you what we knew, sir. We may have been wrong.'

'You taught me restraint. You should have instructed me in the politics of excess. You had no experience of dictatorship.'

'Mr President, it is nearly first light. We must deploy the remaining soldiers. If your training was faulty, I am sorry.'

'It was dearer to me than life. I *was* such a soldier.'

I wondered if Rustum had yet ordered his infantry through the gate. The townspeople would side with the Kezzanis once they had

252

passed the wall and Rustum would use them as a second arm in his assault on the palace.

'You are armed?' I asked him.

'I am not.'

'Take a pistol, at least.'

'There is no point. The matter is decided. My English training will at least help me in the next hour.'

There was still no sound outside the palace walls; there was just a white light in the windows. At this moment I could not give my mind to the defects in Jason's instruction that had brought him to this end, though the subject was later to obsess me. As we stood between the sandbags, waiting for the firing to begin, his fall from power seemed no more than a mishap of history, an agony without point.

§

I mounted the gunstep on the palace wall. The dawn was brighter now. From here I could overlook the broad road lined with palms which led up to the palace from the northern gateway; I could also command the tumbled roofs on either side. If Rustum brought the palace under fire I meant to have a crack at him. Hatim had brought me a self-loading rifle of British origin which was just the weapon for probing this space. I watched the light grow. I heard the wail of prayer that not even an approaching army could interrupt. The keen air excited me no matter that our cause was hopeless and that by now I should have been far to the south with Nathan's forces.

Ten minutes later, when a misty sunlight was colouring the trees, the sound of prayer was overtaken by cheering in the northern quarter of the city. I could not have said when the one ended and the other began; in any case, both were founded in a fierce love of Allah. I was frightened but I could not run away. Such a sound of exalted menace had rocked the walls of Medina when the Prophet entered there thirteen hundred years ago. I knew what Rustum would do: he would drive the townspeople in front of his armour, screening his forces from the palace guard, the solution of an aristocratic soldier who did not bother his mind with civilian casualties. I saw shutters closing down the length of

253

the road. Soldiers of the palace company came up to the wall.

The sunlight grew in strength, beating in the empty road.

The first movement was a long way off. Men in the white and brown robes of city folk were swelling into the street, pressed from behind. I could see no soldiers at whom I might chance a shot.

Damn Rustum! I thought, feeling the frustration of a rifleman who cannot bring his weapon to bear.

The knots of people grew and joined together and came nearer to the wall. The soldiers left and right of me had not used their weapons; they just looked at the thickening crowd, recognizing where the greater strength lay. Swallows were in demented flight above the palm trees, rising higher and higher.

The townspeople halted twenty yards from the wall in a hard line behind which their density increased. Now there must have been five thousand people facing the palace but still I could not see Rustum's men. The crowd had been sobered by the sight of the guards and their sound had fallen to a low pitch; but soon their anger would be greater than their fear.

A strong voice — I could not tell from where it came — called out the name of Prince Suleiman, that champion of Allah; and it was taken up with terrible emphasis by the crowd below the wall.

They shouted his name until they lost their breath.

Then, in the pause that followed, the inevitable shot. Was it ours, theirs? Which way had it gone? I could not be sure, but the distance from me suggested a rifleman in the roofs opposite, where the differing levels threw shadows deep enough to hide a hundred marksmen.

The troops manning the wall had been well controlled until then, but their nerves were at breaking point, and I heard the discharge of perhaps six rifles and saw the blue smoke rising above the gunstep. The platoon commander called sharply for a cessation of firing and struck the soldier nearest to him; but both sides had found relief in action; and now an answering fire was opened from the roofs — a fire well directed, the work of soldiers — and the bullets cracked in the air above our heads and struck the edge of the wall where the mud brick was torn apart.

I searched the roofs, moving my eyes from level to level, until I saw what might have been a uniformed sniper behind a screen of matting. I brought the sight to bear, dropped it a fraction to allow for the upward recoil, and fired three rounds into the place.

I could not see what damage I had done: one seldom can. Meanwhile the soldiers beside me, at a word from their officer, had opened a random fire upon the houses opposite which did not look effective. In the street below, startled by the noise, the crowd swung back and forth behind a curtain of dust.

In the next minutes I emptied the magazine into the roofs, firing wherever I saw movement. I may have done something to reduce the accuracy of Rustum's marksmen. Even so, two of our soldiers were now lying, their bodies strangely angled, between the step and the inner wall.

A calm voice spoke behind me, with the inflection of Eastleigh. 'Good shooting, Peter! You should gain at least the silver medal.'

It was Jason. He wore full service dress and his braided cap. He carried a cane and gloves. He was making not the slightest effort to protect himself though that part of the garden would have been commanded from the higher roofs.

I jumped down from the gunstep and guided him into the shelter of the wall.

'You should go inside, sir. It is not safe for you here.'

'With respect, the same applies to you, Colonel Warfield.' He was at his most courteous, using the manner that had charmed us in England.

'I wanted to have a go. That was my business.'

'I think it was mine.'

'Very well; I owed you that much.'

He took my hand and stroked the back of it with his thumb. 'Whatever you owed me, Peter, you have more than repaid. Now you must go. It is still possible to leave by the rear exits.'

Outside the anger of the crowd was mounting. In a little while they would have enough mindless courage to storm the wall.

'If you wish, I will stay.'

I really meant it then.

'I want you to go,' he said in his softest voice. 'I want you to rejoin Miss Carol Langley. Dear friend, do not have me make it an order.'

'It would help me if you did.'

'It is not fitting between friends.'

'I would prefer it so.'

'As you wish, Peter.' He spoke in the same whisper, barely audible above the noise of the crowd. 'We are both soldiers and I am your superior by several ranks. You are to leave the palace and join Nathan in the Neban. Then you are to leave the country by the quickest route.'

I did not argue with that: it was, after all, a legal order, because in these last minutes Jason was incontestably still the President.

I said, 'Very well, sir. Thank you.'

I do not remember how we said good-bye. Probably we shook hands. And then I ran, bent double, across the garden and back into the palace, catching sight of Jason as I passed the sandbagged entrance—Jason at his most soldierly, walking the length of the gunstep with his hands behind his back and his cane under his arm.

§

I ran through one hall after another, making my way to the rear of the palace where I had left the Land Rover. A step behind me kept the same pace: it was Hatim, still in attendance upon me and plainly of the opinion that he had better leave the palace as well. He wore a robe instead of his uniform and he had brought a jellaba for me. I dumped my khaki jacket, pulled the robe over my head and raised the hood. I was too tall for an Arab of this region but I was burned enough to deceive anyone who did not look closely.

I drove to a gate behind the kitchens which I knew to open into a narrow street where they traded in vegetables and dried herbs. In the kitchen yard there was no one about; the servants had left during the night and the soldiers had all gone to the quarter most threatened. From the front of the palace I could hear the roar of the crowd as they beat against the wall, no doubt driven forward by Rustum's bayonets. In minutes they would mount the parapet and come tumbling into the garden. The gate was fastened by a beam resting in wooden brackets. Using all his strength, Hatim lifted the beam clear of the brackets and laid it to one side. My nerves tautened as he pulled the heavy gates open; he might admit a parcel of maddened townspeople; but in fact I saw only a quiet alley with the sun lying aslant the walls, a beggar asleep under a heap of rags and, further away, the stall keepers doing no less than their usual business in mint and cinnamon.

As I took the vehicle outside the gate, I heard the shouts of savage achievement as the first of the mob straddled the wall and fought with the soldiers on the inside. I waited while Hatim drew the gate closed, and then I drove as fast as the road allowed away from the palace.

I suppose we went half a mile before we could go no further. The street, and those adjoining, was stopped by a congestion of people and animals and I could not force the vehicle forward. I judged we were about two streets short of the great market, over which we had to pass to reach the southern gate and the Dharat road. I did not use the horn; I did not wish to draw attention to two Arabs in a Land Rover, one of whom was less than authentic; and so we waited.

Twenty minutes later we moved forward, gaining the next corner, but only to see a press of people reaching out of sight in the street beyond. And then, as the minutes passed, we were carried inch by inch towards the destination of the crowd, dragged by a current we could not resist. We were going to a spectacle; that much was clear to me. We were responding to a plan not our own that required the people of the town to come together.

After an hour we had gained the edge of the great market, where the Land Rover finally came to a halt between a donkey cart and a buttress of the old city wall which here flanked the vast dusty square. Usually the square was occupied by traders, scribes, jugglers and the tellers of tales, but you could not have found space enough to spin a plate this morning. Stretching away from me towards a central space cleared by the soldiers was an expanse of heads packed as tightly as cobblestones.

Hatim said, barely getting through to me,. 'It was different with Khalid. Of course, there was no conflict that time. We acted in secrecy.'

I did not understand him at once; I had lost the power of reason. I could only think of the friend I had known. 'What did you say?' I asked.

But my aide did not repeat himself. He was bored by the whole business.

'Hatim, are you telling me you played some part in the assassination of Khalid?'

'He died without dignity. He tried to run away.'

I lost the thread of it then. On the far side of the market, a great distance off, Rustum's soldiers were entering the square in column. Their discipline was good; they kept their step. After all, they were once the Royal Guard. Of the officers who came next I recognized at first only one, the tall unbending figure of Prince Suleiman ben Yusoff, shortly to be Head of State. The soldiers halted in the centre of the market where the cordon had kept an open rectangle; but something was wrong, something did not please the Sharifian prince. I saw the soldiers pressing back the crowd on the opposite side of the market and could not guess what they were doing. Only later, when it was over, did I get the point of it: Solly was seeking the place of his own humiliation, where the soldiers had thrown him into the dust and the townspeople had kicked him and rubbed his face with unclean things. How like Solly to think it mattered! When he had found the right ground, the soldiers formed a square about it, facing inward, and Solly and the other officers stood in a group at one end. Now I could recognize another figure—the spare frame of Captain Ismael, the inevitable survivor, who must exploit any agony for the sake of a creed.

I had no word to say, neither to Hatim nor in the privacy of my mind. I could not even contrive a prayer.

I heard voices raised in anger and contempt, and I saw the soldiers who lined the path of entrance leaning against the thrust of the crowd: another group of soldiers was entering the market. The dust rose about them, yellow in the morning sun. I could not see the President; he was shorter than the Kezzani guards who flanked him on either side. He was taken into the hollow square and I do not think he stumbled. The guards came to a halt in front of General Suleiman, and then fell back left and right, revealing the President to the crowd in the market. He was hatless, his uniform had been ripped and dirtied, but he stood with something like his accustomed bearing. The people swayed forward with loathing, and I saw the soldiers fighting them back, using their rifle butts.

Solly had not come to attention, neither had the other officers. In Solly's demeanour I saw his contempt for the Nebanese slave who had been his Commander-in-Chief and indeed was still as they stood face to face in the early sunlight. I don't know what he said to Jason, but savage words were spoken; perhaps he pointed to the ground on which they stood and recalled what happened there. Solly was stupid enough for that.

'It is taking a long time,' Hatim said, and collapsed into his seat with the air of a man who had seen it all before. 'The appointment of a menial was of course mistaken.'

With the vision my pain had given me, I said, 'It was you, was it not, who killed Khalid.'

'There was a need for change.'

'And it was done on the orders of your kinsman, the Iman.'

'With two strokes of the sword.'

'I suppose the Sharifian family had always intended to recover the leadership.'

'Of course; it is theirs. A Nebanese was only appointed because they were frightened of Nathan.'

The rest of the brief ceremony I compelled myself to watch from a loyalty I could not escape. Someone in the vast crowd had to be for the President. Better me than no one. I was a President's man! I watched the guards take hold of Jason's arms and compel him to kneel in the dust two yards short of General Suleiman. The noise in the market stilled to a terrible silence. A soldier whose face I could not see, but who carried a broadsword such as the Berbers use, came forward and performed his duty with a single downward stroke of the blade. The crowd shuddered with a thrill of excitement and horror. I saw the soldiers drop the thing they held, which now had lost its usefulness, and kick it towards those who were nearest and straining to lay their hands upon it.

I did not watch the rest, which was a scene the old market had known before. I heard cries of madness as the body was taken into the crowd and pulled this way and that in the oldest of sports. The throng of people who had trapped the vehicle now loosened as the

259

game swung to the other side of the market. I started the engine and edged along the wall towards the southern gate, aware that the President had done me a last service, for no one in the demented crowd had an interest in stopping me. What did it matter if a stranger escaped? When I came to the gate I drove violently through and, putting the vehicle in top gear, made the best pace I could towards the Skar.

§

Nathan had waited for me at the river. He actually took my arm when I stepped down from the Land Rover.

'You don't have to tell me about it, old boy,' he said. 'I've had it on the telegraph.'

He said nothing of his intentions, but he told me that Jason's wife had reached Dharat the night before with an escort of Berbers provided by the Pasha. She would return soon: a Moslem leadership would not think it worthwhile to pursue a woman. Nathan took the vehicle and the weapon from me and sent me on to his headquarters in a staff car.

I waited there a day. Then, in the aircraft that General Buster Mohamet had intended for the President's escape, I flew to Marrakesh and from there continued by civil airline to Gibraltar.

I could bring no sense to my mind. An account of Jason's Presidency would have to wait. I carried in my valise the only photographs of Kezzani slavers in the Red Desert and these I would use as best I could. Later would come the book; but not now, not yet. I had to wait until the violence had gone away from me. I just wanted Carol. She met me on the airfield under the Rock and shared the following days.

Two letters reached me in Gibraltar. The first was a short note from Helen, written with greater composure than I could have managed. She thanked me for what I had done (God, it was not much, and it had failed!) and ended with a sweetly phrased blessing for Carol and me. The second was in a firm hand and written in a tone of voice I recognized.

*You asked me what I would do. I see no reason why I should tell you but you might as well know as not. Why should I care? I shall hold the Skar if they attack me (but I don't suppose they will as*

260

*they haven't the courage) and I shall set up some sort of administration in Dharat. Call it a military dictatorship if you like but there's nothing else in the territory that can hold things together. Call me a Fascist. It doesn't matter to me. I may even—old son, don't tell the press, they'd be so disappointed!—allow some civil management and set up a civil judiciary. I may even retire. At any rate I'm faced with the problem and have to do something. A soldier's lot. You should have shot me through the head when you had the chance.*

*Don't come back. There's nothing for you here. Boy, didn't we have fun!*

*SAMUEL NATHAN*
*Colonel*

So that was it. There was a new country in Africa. Whether it was a dictatorship or not I could not have said, but the Mamelukes would have been at home in the Neban. I didn't fancy going there. For one thing, I couldn't stand bread and water, and for another the company of soldiers gets boring in the end. But though I did not write I wished him well for as long as his Presidency lasted. It would not be for long.